PAROUSIA

...and man made God

m. jerista lampman

PAROUSIA

...and man made God

DaHood Publishing, Inc.   Kutztown, PA

PAROUSIA

...and man made God

Printed in the U.S. of America
DaHood Publishing, Inc. Edition/May 1999

www.Parousianovel.com

THIS BOOK IS DEDICATED TO DAVE,
MY "IDEA MAN AND BELOVED."
TO MY CHILDREN, REBEKAH AND DAVID.
TO ERIC AND JIM
AND A SPECIAL THANKS TO MY PARENTS,
MICHAEL AND EMILY JERISTA
WITH ALL MY LOVE AND GRATITUDE.

COVER CREATION AND DESIGN BY:
ERIC ARMUSIK

PAROUSIA
...and man made God.

THE LIFE OF EVERY MAN IS A DIARY IN
WHICH HE MEANS TO WRITE ONE STORY
AND WRITES ANOTHER: AND HIS HUMBLEST
HOUR IS WHEN HE COMPARES THE VOLUME
AS IT IS WITH WHAT HE VOWED TO MAKE.

J.M. Barrie

THE MORE FAITHFULLY YOU LISTEN TO
THE VOICE WITHIN YOU, THE BETTER YOU
WILL HEAR WHAT IS SOUNDING OUTSIDE.
AND ONLY HE WHO LISTENS CAN SPEAK.
                                    Dag Hammarskjold

CHAPTER I

FEBRUARY 13, 1945 - THE SISTINE CHAPEL IN THE VATICAN

There was a stillness. The early dawn light was
pale and the sun's rays were spotted with tiny particles
of floating dust. The silence permeated throughout the
sanctified place and he was aware of the quiet and
happy for its peace. He pulled his black cardigan
around his midsection against the dampness that
prevailed within this holy sanctum. He finished
reciting the Divine Office and knew that he could no
longer kneel on the hard altar steps.

Slowly, he got to his feet and was relieved to feel
the blood rush back to his knees. He stood still for a
few seconds while he searched his cassock pocket for
the familiar touch of his rosary. He fingered the
wooden beads rendered smooth from daily use, made
the sign of the cross and whispered the Creed as he
began to walk around the Sistine Chapel.

With each repetition of the Ave Maria, he
meditated on the magnificent reminders of his faith. He
contemplated the nine scenes depicting Genesis created
more than four hundred years ago by Michelangelo. As

he ambled around the chapel, a quote from Matthew 6:27 interrupted his prayer, "Which of you by worrying can add a moment to his life-span?" His mood became dark and somber and a feeling of utter despair enveloped him until he felt as though he would choke from it.

He was aptly aware, as a man of God, that despair is a serious sin. He took a deep breath and tried hard to concentrate on his rosary. He just finished the first decade when his eyes were drawn to the *Creation of Adam* in which God imparts life into the image made in His own likeness with a simple touch of His hand. Cardinal DeGroot shivered not from the dampness that emitted from the chapel, but from his very soul. He was overcome with fear and guilt because of his part in the plan and he worried that the conclave had overstepped the boundary line between humanity and divinity.

When he turned to face the altar, his eyes wandered to the figures depicting Christ's ancestors and again his prayers were cast aside. Finally, his worried blue eyes rested on the magnificence of the *Final Judgment* that graced the area behind the mother-of-pearl altar used exclusively by the Holy Father. Michelangelo's rendering of Christ separating the saved from the damned only reinforced the Cardinal's uneasiness and he tried to rationalize his fear by attributing it to Cardinal Brazini's pressing command to meet this afternoon.

Paul DeGroot thought of his native land and longed for the childhood security of Holland, but he knew that his country had been in constant danger during Hitler's mad campaign for world control. Antonio Brazini's insistence on meeting stemmed from his mania to put their plan in motion and now, a sense of urgency persisted especially with the rumors that the war was in its final days. Within a short time, Germany would be in a state of chaos and it would become impossible to attain their goal. Before walking to the side exit of the Chapel, Cardinal DeGroot whispered a fervent prayer in hopes of quelling his feelings of impending doom. He begged God to give him and the others the strength to carry out their plan and his prayer did not fail to include the innocent who was about to become involved in the treacherous mission.

Paul DeGroot opened the door to leave and was suddenly face to face with Cardinal LeBlanc. Rene LeBlanc, of France, almost jumped when he was confronted by his fellow cardinal.

"Rene, I am so happy to see you here," said Cardinal DeGroot as he greeted his old friend. "I was just about to go to your chambers. Antonio said that it is imperative for our group to meet as soon as possible. Can you do me a favor and contact the others? Have them gather in the library at 2:00 this afternoon and please, stress the urgency of this meeting. I must attend to some pressing details this morning."

"Certainly, Paul, I will be happy to do as you ask. I will notify everyone when I finish my prayers," answered the small built man who appeared to be in constant motion. His friends always teased LeBlanc that if Catholics believed in reincarnation, LeBlanc would come back as a hummingbird.

"Thank you, Rene, I will see you at 2:00," answered Cardinal DeGroot as he left to begin his daily duties and his preparations for the meeting.

FEBRUARY 13, 1945 - 2:00 PM

The men gathered in a secluded reading room located in the Vatican Library where priceless artwork done by impressive Italian masters adorned the ceilings and walls. The elaborate Library and the scarlet-robed Cardinals indicated a Church rich in style, pomp and tradition. Each man chose a place at the large mahogany table and settled into one of the heavy, dark throne-like chairs. The Cardinals originated from various areas of the globe, but came together for a common purpose. The diverse group compiled an interesting melting pot because of their physical, intellectual and temperamental differences.

Cardinal Paul DeGroot stood and thanked his brothers in Christ for setting aside their duties in order to attend the conclave. Due to his compassion and his reputation for being even-tempered and dependable, DeGroot would prove to be an asset to their mission. DeGroot nodded to Cardinal Antonio Brazini and when Brazini stood and began to speak, a silence settled upon the room. He began the meeting with a prayer and traces of his Italian accent flowed through the traditional Latin. Brazini, a large stocky built man from a wealthy family, enjoyed his position in the Church hierarchy. Years before, his father was a high ranking official in the Italian government and because of this, Brazini also envisioned himself as a powerful leader. His one flaw was his quick and violent temper which often instilled fear, rather than respect, in his colleagues. When the prayer ended, Brazini addressed the men.

"My brothers in Christ, we must act swiftly as time is running out. My informants have told me that there are plans to assassinate Hitler. If that happens, it will become more difficult to carry out our mission because once the allies get into Germany, we will never be able to bring Rupert Bertram into Rome. We must send our envoy into Berlin by the end of the week."

When Brazini finished speaking, excited whispers in native accents intermingled at the table and when Cardinal Milos Kowalsky stood and nervously spoke aloud, silence once again prevailed.

"Are you sure that you have chosen the right man for this job? I know how dangerous Europe is now. I have heard horrible stories of what Hitler has done in my native Poland and what he has done to the gypsies, to the Jews, and to anyone he considers to be of an impure race." Kowalsky's face is lined by a perpetual look of anxiety and his fellow clergy often remarked that he looked like he carried the weight of the world on his shoulders like St. Christopher.

Cardinal DeGroot quickly put Cardinal Kowalsky's mind at ease by reminding him that they have been preparing the envoy for the past few years.

"Milos, we agreed to form our group because the six of us firmly believe in protecting the world and Our Holy Mother Church from the atrocities of Hitler and any others like him. For the last several years, we have met in secret and have honed our plans well. We cannot and will not fail because what we are about to do, we do in the name of Christ.

Ironically, it was the high-strung, Cardinal LeBlanc who tried to put Cardinal Kowalsky at ease, "Milos, relax, Father Raymond Pascal from the Untied States is an excellent choice for this mission because he spent his childhood in Berlin and he speaks German like a native. Besides, his passport is in perfect order and all the documents carry the papal seal including Bertram's new passport."

Cardinal Acietuno chuckled at the "hummingbird's" attempt to calm Kowalsky as he turned to Cardinal Brazini and asked, "What have you told Father Pascal about this mission?"

Brazini looked over at Cardinal Jorge Acietuno of Cuba and answered the question with a sly look on his face, "I have told him the truth, my brothers, I told him that he is helping to save a man's life and his soul. He knows that Rupert Bertram wants to finish his studies for the priesthood and that we are his only salvation to escape from Germany. Bertram is aware that the end of the war is near and that his fate will be sealed if he remains with Hitler."

Cardinal Acietuno seemed satisfied by his answer as his large frame once again relaxed. His green eyes twinkled and his sense of humor and quick wit usually helped to keep disagreements within perspective. When he chuckled and quickly added in the universal tongue of Latin, laced with his native Spanish accent: "And the truth shall set you free!" Laughter sounded throughout the room, easing the tension. When the laughter finally diminished, Cardinal LeBlanc announced that Father Pascal would leave for Germany on Friday.

"He will meet Monsignor Arnold Wenniger at St.. Boniface Church in Bonn. The good Monsignor will take Father Pascal to Berlin to meet Rupert Bertram under his new identity, Michael Bachman. From there, with the help of God, Father Pascal and Bachman should have no trouble getting out. Arnold is a good and trustworthy friend and he has assured me that everything will go smoothly. The papal seal should guarantee Pascal and Bachman's safety and it will also act as diplomatic immunity if the allies stop them. They should be back in Rome within a few weeks."

Cardinal Chinua Belawa's deep baritone voice echoed throughout the room, "What did you tell Pius about all of this, Antonio?"

Cardinal Acietuno quickly glanced at Brazini. When he saw his nod of assent, Jorge Acietuno responded to the question, "Chinua, the Holy Father is only aware that Father Pascal and Bachman will be bringing back some sacred relics and works of art that were taken by the Nazi's during their invasion of France, Czechoslovakia, and Poland. Unfortunately, many of the treasures were ruined or destroyed, but many were saved thanks to the greed of the Nazis officers. Pius XII is overjoyed that we have made plans to save them. So don't worry my brother, our plan is solid.

He continued, "We are indeed fortunate that Pius has done all he could to keep the line of communication open with Germany. The Church has had to compromise to get Bertram and the Church treasures safely back into the Vatican. We promised to provide safe passage to freedom for a few Nazis officers who have known for some time that Hitler is mad and now, we must uphold our end of the bargain. These officials have indicated that they are aware that Hitler's diabolical plan to rule the world is completely insane and they fear for their lives and have told us they would like to make amends for the atrocities that were done by their people.

When Jorge Acietuno saw the reactions of his fellow Cardinals, he added, "As members of the Body of Christ, we would be remiss in our Christian duty not to comply. We cannot turn a deaf ear to their requests nor can we allow Bertram to remain in Germany, especially now. In return, these officers have promised to return the Church's property and keep Bertram safe."

"I realize that this may seem like a difficult bargain to many of us, but I agree that it is the only means we have in order to initiate our plan," added Cardinal Belawa, a tall, slender stately looking Black man. Chinua Belawa's voice and outgoing disposition had a naturally soothing affect on the group and the rest of the Cardinals agreed with him.

As the meeting concluded, the six men knelt in prayer and asked God to bless their plan. Not only did they pray for the mission's success, but the men included prayers for his own country as each one had something to win or lose from the success or failure of the mission. The group believed that they were working toward a common goal, but in truth, each Cardinal had a personal reason for taking part in the dangerous scheme. When they finished praying, Cardinal Brazini announced that they would meet again when Father Pascal and Michael Bachman were safely in Rome. As they filed out of the conference room, the uneasiness that Cardinal DeGroot felt earlier in the chapel returned and nearly suffocated him again. Although he was hesitant about what he and the others were going to do, he was afraid to go against the others, especially Brazini. He was also fully aware the plan had already been set in motion.

A LITTLE TRUTH HELPS THE LIE GO DOWN.
Italian Proverb

CHAPTER II

THE VATICAN - 1945

After the meeting, Cardinal Antonio Brazini went back into his private study and began to reflect on what had just taken place. His thoughts wandered back eight years ago to 1937 when Pius XI was pope. He remembered that a nun and Jewish convert pleaded with Pius to speak out against the horrors of Nazism. Pius agreed and his encyclical, *Mit brennender Sorge*, was the first official public document to denounce Nazism. It was smuggled into Germany and read from the pulpits on Palm Sunday in March, 1937.

The men who smuggled the documents reported the results back to the Curia, and Brazini remembered that this was the first time he had heard about Hitler's diabolical schemes. Even though Milos Kowalsky had told them about the atrocities that were reported to him by his personal informants, none of the other cardinals were fully aware of the horrible experiments being performed by Hitler's doctors, especially in the genetic field. In spite of these reports, it was his father's deathbed confession that was the primary reason for forming the conclave of six cardinals.

That fateful day was seared into his memory, for it was not only the beginning of the secret cartel, but the beginning of his secret plan to save the Church and the world. He smiled to himself as he thought of the power, prestige and fame he would acquire for being the master planner. As he sat in the darkened room, once again, Brazini was back in 1937. He could almost feel the chill of that cold February day when, as a young Bishop, he was called to his father's bedside.

"My son, I am so happy that you are here with me. Please clear the room of everyone, there is something I must tell you and you alone," begged his father, Dr. Giovanni Brazini, one of Italy's most prominent government officials and Mussolini's personal physician.

"Do you wish to confess to me, Papa?" asked Bishop Brazini.

"It is not so much a confession but it is something that is very important and may be helpful to your career in the Church. Do as I say, Antonio, and tell the others to wait outside the room."

"Si, Papa," responded Bishop Brazini as he quietly whispered to his sobbing mother, sister, and brothers that his dying father wished to make his last confession. As he led his aging mother to the warm kitchen area, Bishop Brazini looked around his childhood home and saw that it had changed considerably since he had left to study for the priesthood. His younger sister and brothers had many more advantages than he did and he knew that many of the conveniences were gifts from Mussolini. When the others were out of the room, Giovanni told his son to get some paper to take notes. Bishop Brazini did as his father requested and pulled his chair next to the bed so that the old man did not have to strain to be heard.

"Antonio, what I am about to tell you will shock you. You must promise not to reveal it to anyone until you find others that you can fully trust. I have learned from Il Duce that Hitler's scientists have discovered the secret to immortality."

"What?" interrupted Antonio thinking that he did not hear his father correctly. "What are you saying, Papa, how could Mussolini know this?"

"Be quiet and listen to me, Antonio," hissed the old man in a scolding tone. "Do not interrupt me again until I am finished. I know that I am quickly running out of time and strength and I must tell you this before it is too late. Last year, Mussolini and I were having an important meeting about the campaign and we talked about what Hitler was doing in Germany. Mussolini confided that he had just met with Adolf and the meeting was very productive. Hitler was boasting as usual and Mussolini knew that Hitler loved to be complimented, so he lavishly praised him for his ability to unite Germany."

The old man stopped to catch his breath before going on, "Mussolini told Hitler that he admired him for trying to purify his race. Il Duce related that he would like to do the same with the Italian people and rid the race of impure blood. Hitler became intoxicated by the compliments and boastfully revealed that there was one sure way to accomplish this. He insisted that he had the most brilliant scientists in the world working on a plan. These men were working under the leadership of one young genius. This young doctor had figured out the way to make Hitler and others of his choosing immortal."

The old man paused to sip the water that his son offered him, "When Mussolini mentioned this to me, of course, I thought it was nonsense and I wondered if he had too much wine to drink during dinner. However, when he continued to explain what Hitler had told him, I realized that Il Duce was very sober and very serious. Naturally, I was afraid at first, but then I became curious when I heard the word immortal. As I heard more about this plan, I knew immediately that Hitler was going too far and I did not believe that he was totally sane. Hitler did not just want to eliminate those he didn't like, he also wanted to play God! Mussolini wanted me to do the same by learning the techniques that Hitler's doctors had discovered, but I became ill and could not continue my research"

"Papa, please, I do not quite understand why you are telling me this. It does not make any sense, besides what you are telling me is only the boastful rambling of an egotistical lunatic. I am surprised that Mussolini even repeated this absurd story to you and I am even more shocked that you believed it when you, yourself, are a doctor and a man of science."

"Antonio, that is precisely why I do believe it! I know that you do not agree with Mussolini and what he is doing in Italy, but you must listen to what I am telling you. The way that Mussolini explained the process to me makes me believe that this procedure can work. If this geneticist that Hitler has working for him is the genius that they claim he is, I have no doubts that what Hitler told Mussolini is entirely possible."

His father's voice took on an urgent tone, "You must do whatever is in your power to get this young scientist out of Germany before he has time to use his knowledge. The young man's name is Rupert Bertram and Hitler told Mussolini that before Bertram became a doctor, he was studying for the priesthood. When Hitler came into power, he closed the seminaries in order to eliminate religion and make Nazism the only philosophy for Germany. Later, when Hitler met this young man and was informed of his great ability and potential in the field of science, Bertram was immediately sent to medical school. Because of his intellect, Bertram quickly completed his training and began to specialize in genetics as commanded by Hitler. Within a short time, he made amazing advances that resulted in successful experiments that were never attempted before."

Brazini tried to calm the old man, but he waved him away, "What Bertram has accomplished is something that will change the world. It is for this reason, my son, that he must be bought back to the Vatican and hidden from that lunatic, Hitler. Hitler knows that he is powerful, but he also knows that he is not immortal and has enemies even in his own ranks. As a man of God, you must do all that you can to save the world from Hitler's plan. You must use this young scientist and his knowledge for the good of Holy Mother Church and for the good of mankind. Promise me that you will do this, Antonio, so that I can die in peace and be absolved from my sins."

"I will do whatever I can, Papa, but I do not have the power nor the authority to do this. How do you propose that I get Bertram out of Germany alone?"

"You will have more power and authority. As a favor for my loyal services, Il Duce is planning on having you named a Cardinal during the next investiture service. He has already spoken to the Holy Father and Pius XI has already agreed to the appointment."

Giovanni smiled at his son and his pride was evident in his face, "As the Guardian of the Shroud of Turin, you have done a magnificent job for the Church and Pius is very pleased with you so you do not have to feel that the new title is undeserved. As for accomplishing this feat alone, my son, do not worry, I know that there are other men in the Curia who feel as we do. You must know many of these men yourself. Try to talk to a few others without revealing everything you know to them and I am sure that you will find support to bring this young man, Bertram, to our side. It is important that whatever work he does, he does in the name of Christ and for the glory of the Church. I feel that I must do something to vindicate myself for the things I have done in my past," explained the old man as he gave his son the details to locate Dr. Rupert Bertram.

"I will do what you say, Papa, and now I see that you are tired. I will give you my blessing and then you must rest. I will tell the others to let you sleep for awhile before they come in to see you again." promised Bishop Brazini as he prayed over his dying father and gave him his blessing. He waited until the old man was asleep before leaving the room.

Three days later, Dr. Giovanni Brazini passed away and the young Bishop stayed with his family until his father was buried. As he reflected on the burial services, Brazini remembered that Mussolini was very attentive to him. He could sense the evil force of Mussolini's power and was determined to do as his father requested in order to spare the world form any more horror. When he had a chance to be alone, he read over his notes with names and places that his father had given him and seared them into his memory before he burned the papers.

As Antonio sat in his study and relived those fateful days, he thought of his investiture as Cardinal Brazini. He knew how proud his family was to see him grow in power within the Church hierarchy. He also remembered how easy it was to find five other cardinals who felt the same way he did about trying to stop Hitler's madness in Germany and Mussolini's in Italy. It was not difficult to convince the others that Rupert Bertram, a young twenty-year old genius and Hitler's leading geneticist, was desperate to leave Germany and return to the seminary. Brazini told them that they must do everything in their power to help save this young man's life and soul by bringing him to the Vatican so that he could safely return to his priestly studies. He also mentioned to the others that Bertram's background in genetics may be helpful in proving that the Shroud of Turin, the presumed burial cloth of Christ, is indeed authentic.

Brazini's pleasant reverie was abruptly interrupted and he was brought back into the present by his valet's knock on the study door and the announcement that it was time for evening prayer. As Brazini left for chapel, he felt assured that as the master planner, he was in total control of the events that were about to begin.

THE MOST MELANCHOLY OF HUMAN REFLECTIONS, PERHAPS, IS THAT, ON THE WHOLE, IT IS A QUESTION WHETHER THE BENEVOLENCE OF MANKIND DOES MORE HARM THAN GOOD.   Walter Bagehot

CHAPTER III

THE PAPAL CHAMBER IN THE VATICAN - April 16, 1997

Cardinal DeGroot entered the papal chambers, briefly took into account Raphael's paintings that adorned the walls and admired the grandeur of the room. When he reached the gilded papal throne, the Cardinal knelt down, took the Pope's hand and kissed the Ring of the Fisherman before he addressed the Pontiff.

"Holy Father, I am here on behalf of the faithful, it is time that you meet with him"

The Pope answered him with kindness, "My brother, you of all people should know that our time to meet has not yet arrived. When the time is right, I shall know it."

Cardinal DeGroot was visibly confused, "Your Holiness, I am afraid that I do not understand you. What do you mean that you will know when the time is

right? Is there something that you are not telling me?
Why do you refuse to confide in me when we have
been close friends since our early days in the Vatican?
You do not have to hide from me. You know that you
can tell me the truth."

"My brother, it is you who are afraid to speak the
truth. Tell me what is troubling you, Paul. Perhaps you
should clear your conscience and bare your soul. We
are now in the beginning of the Holy Triduum of the
Church, our greatest and most solemn Holy Days. As
Easter Sunday approaches, my friend, it would do you
well to make a good confession. Tomorrow is Good
Friday, the day that our Lord gave up his life so that we
can have eternal life. Think of Him, my brother, and all
that He suffered for mankind. Now, Paul, tell me who
or what it is that you fear,"
pleaded the Pope.

"It is not man that I fear."

"Then, Paul, if it is God that you fear, you must
confess and put your soul at rest."

"Holy Father, you are correct as always. But,
please promise me that you will not think too badly of
me. I want to remain your trusted friend. Do you have
time to hear my confession now?" begged Cardinal
DeGroot.

The Pope put his hand on Cardinal DeGroot's
shoulder and looked deeply into his eyes, "Paul, I have
loved you like a brother and we have been through
many turbulent times together. Please do not worry that
I will judge you, for only God can do that. Feel free to
confess everything to me so that you can unburden your
conscience and your soul and, perhaps, find some
peace."

"I hope that God does not judge me too harshly,"
answered DeGroot in a low worried tone of voice.

"Much of what I am about to relate to you, I, have either witnessed or issued the orders to have the plans carried out," whispered DeGroot as he made the sign of the cross and began his confession.

"Bless me, Holy Father, for I have sinned....

"Our plans became organized in 1940 as a means to help Our Holy Mother Church and mankind. We hoped that we could do something positive to end the misery and destruction that was taking place all over the world. One evening as we listened to the latest reports on the war, Milos Kowalsky began to inform us of the horrors that were taking place in Germany and Poland. Since his family was still in Poland, Milos was afraid for them and kept in close contact with his underground connections. Milos told us what he had heard about the scientific experiments that were being performed in the concentration camps. As the rest of us sat and listened to his shocking revelations of these despicable crimes, we decided that we could no longer be idle. At Antonio Brazini's suggestion, six of us formed a secret cartel that would work together to help stop Hitler and others like him throughout the world. You must believe me, Holy Father, I don't know how our plans became as twisted as they did because we honestly believed that what we were about to do was for the good of Holy Mother Church and for the good of all mankind. I do recall that we moved quickly and within the next few years, as the war was coming to an end in 1945, we sent a young priest into Germany on a very dangerous mission. It was like sending an innocent lamb to the slaughter yet, we had to take the risk in order to initiate our plans. We chose and prepared Father Raymond Pascal, a young priest, as our emissary because of his German background and his excellent language abilities. As you know, Holy

Father, he was raised in Berlin until he was fifteen and speaks fluent German. Father Pascal, being a young and naive priest, was awed by the fact that six very powerful Cardinals from different parts of the world would choose him to rescue Michael Bachman from Hitler's evil clutch."

The Holy Father interrupted the confession, "Did Pius XII know about this and, if so, what reason did you give him for this mission to Germany?"

"Yes, Holy Father, he knew of the mission, however we lied to him although it was not truly a lie, we simply withheld part of the truth. We told Pope Pius that we were sending an envoy into Germany in order to retrieve many of the stolen Church treasures and relics that were in the possession of the Nazis."

"And what did Father Pascal know of his mission," questioned the Holy Father.

"He only knew that he was to meet another young man named Michael Bachman, who was a former seminarian before he was forced into Hitler's movement. Pascal was told that Bachman would assist him in gathering the sacred treasures. In turn, Pascal was to bring Michael back to Rome so that he could complete his studies for the priesthood. Ray Pascal has never been told the truth nor was he ever aware of Bachman's true identity."

"What is the truth, my friend?" asked the Pope.

"My confession will reveal the plans of the cartel, Holy Father, it is a long and complex story. I hope that you have the patience to listen to it all."

"Paul, your confession is most important because I can see how upset you are. Your inner turmoil has taken its toll. You must confess it all in order to free yourself from anymore guilt. I have the time to listen and if we must continue later, so be it. Now, please go on," encouraged the Holy Father.

"Thank you, Holy Father, you are truly a wonderful friend. I am not sure that I can recall all of the events, but I will try. It was in the beginning of March 1945, when Father Pascal arrived in Rome with Michael Bachman. They also had many of the Church's greatest treasures with them and Pius was very pleased with their success. When the other cardinals met Bachman, they were speechless."

The Cardinal continued to recount his initial meeting with the young man, "Michael was only about twenty-four years old, but his carriage and demeanor indicated to us that he was a true prodigy. Bachman was fluent in several languages and taught himself to hide obvious traces of his German accent when he spoke other languages."

DeGroot paused for a moment, then continued with his story, "It was easy to understand Hitler's fascination with Michael, not only because of his intellect but because of his physical appearance. Michael was the epitome of the perfect Aryan that Hitler extolled and the first time I saw him, I was reminded of the Viking warriors and I immediately knew that he must have been a part of Hitler's youth movement. He was tall and muscular and his hair was white blond. However, I was most fascinated by his eyes. Michael's eyes were such a light shade of blue that they appeared almost colorless. When he looked at me, I could see that they were the eyes of an intelligent leader, yet those eyes also instilled a sense of fear and foreboding in me."

DeGroot shuddered as he remembered the plan to cover-up Michael's identity, "The Cardinals and I suggested that Michael dye his hair dark brown and wear tinted glasses in order to hide his most identifiable traits. We also discussed the possibility of Michael having some minor plastic surgery to further conceal his identity and he complied. He soon re-entered the seminary under his new identity and resumed his studies for the priesthood. This was a double protection from the chance that Hitler's henchmen would find him."

"Did the young man re-enter the seminary just for protection?" inquired the Pope.

"No, Holy Father, when Michael arrived in Rome, he was visibly shaken and upset with the things that he had done in Germany and Poland. He told us that he was afraid for his life, but more importantly, he was adamant about devoting his life to the Church in atonement for his sins against God and man," answered Cardinal DeGroot.

"What sins did he commit, Paul?"

"Unspeakable sins, Holy Father. History has revealed the atrocities that have taken place within the death camps of Poland and Germany and although Michael has never openly admitted to or revealed what he actually did there, but we learned much later of his capabilities in genetic research. As Hitler's top scientist in this field, there's no doubt that he was involved in the worst of the inhumane experiments that were taking place on the innocent victims of the camps, but Michael never spoke to us about them. We thought that he was afraid of being caught or perhaps that he was filled with guilt for what he had done."

"Paul, I must know the entire story along with the names of those you have involved. What you are implying can have severe repercussions." answered the Pope with sadness in his voice.

"Holy Father, when Michael Bachman arrived in Rome with Father Pascal, the other Cardinals and I met with him and agreed to protect his identity and his well being by keeping him safe within the walls of the seminary. In return, we asked him to meet with Dr. Alex Stewart, who was working on an archaeology project for Pius XII. We asked Michael to help Dr. Stewart with this project at Qumran and also help Stewart trace the genealogy of the House of David to the present time."

Cardinal DeGroot's voice became raspy as he continued to confess, " It is somewhat ironic that the most vivid memory I have of that day is the child-like excitement of Father Pascal. He was thrilled that we allowed him to be a part of the ceremony inducting Michael into the seminary. We felt we owed Pascal this honor since he was the one who had risked his life to bring Michael to Rome. During the ceremony Pascal asked to have a photograph taken and, of course, we agreed. This act of gratitude nearly damned us and that one simple photograph has come to haunt us and condemn us for what we have done."

Calm down, Paul, would you like to stop and rest for a while?" asked the Holy Father with concern in his voice. "No, no, your Excellency, I'm alright, it's just that reliving the past can sometimes be upsetting, but I would rather continue. I recall that the next few years passed quickly and Father Bachman finished his studies and was ordained a priest. His genius, his easy-going personality and his commitment to hard work allowed him to gain the confidence of the other Cardinals and within a short time, he was named a Monsignor."

About this time, Pius XII began to ask questions about the amount of money and time that was being spent on tracing the genealogy of the House of David.

Pius also questioned Monsignor Bachman's involvement with the research in Masada and that is when I first feared that our plans would be discovered. It was then, Holy Father, that my sleepless nights began."

The Pope interrupted Cardinal DeGroot's confession, "Now it is I who do not understand. Why did you fear Pius XII? What could he have uncovered? Was it Father Bachman's true identity? You must tell me everything with every name and detail if you intend to clear your conscience and your soul by making a good confession, Paul."

Cardinal DeGroot continued in a monotone voice, "Yes, Holy Father, I will finally unburden myself to you." He seemed to enter a trance-like state as he began revealing the past and reliving his worst nightmares...

HYPOCRISY IS A SORT OF HOMAGE, THAT VICE PAYS TO VIRTUE.   La Rochefoucauld

CHAPTER IV

THE VATICAN - 1997

Cardinal DeGroot droned on..."It was November, 1956 when Pope Pius XII began to question the Cardinals about the money being spent on the search for the Scrolls and he wanted to know more about the rumors that Monsignor Bachman was soon to be named Bishop. Pius XII knew that he was still a very young man and that he had been a priest for only a short period of time. From those he questioned, the Pope learned of Bachman's intellect and his dedication to scientific research. He also heard about his devotion to God, the Church and his almost obsessive devotion to Our Blessed Mother. As you well remember, Holy Father, Pius XII, was very devoted to Our Lady so he believed that Bachman would be perfect for the difficult task that needed to be done."

"Cardinal Acietuno prepared Michael for his meeting with the Pope. He went over the usual formalities of etiquette and prompted Michael on subjects that Pius found interesting. When Bachman returned from the papal throne room, we realized that he needed no help from any of us. The meeting was overheard by Cardinal Brazini who, trusting no one, was in the next room and was able to hear everything that was being said."

"Pius called Monsignor Bachman into the throne room and as he entered, the young Monsignor knelt before him and kissed his Fisherman's ring."

"Pius XII spoke to him in a weak voice, "Rise, my son, I have heard many wonderful things about you from your fellow priests and from some of the most powerful Cardinals in the Vatican. It seems that everyone is very impressed with your genius and with your dedication to Our Holy Mother Church. I am particularly impressed with what I hear about your dedicated devotion to Our Blessed Mother."

"Bachman rose from his knees and looked at Pius, "What you say about my genius is flattering Holy Father but it embarrasses me to hear such things. I do admit that I enjoy working on scientific projects for the Church. It is also true that I have a complete devotion to Our Lady. As you already know, Your Holiness, I am still working on the genealogy of the House of David."

"Pius interrupted him, "Ah, yes, my son, and how is that proceeding?"

"Very well, Holy Father, I am making progress even though it is a very slow and complex process. I owe a great deal to Dr. Stewart. His Middle Eastern background and knowledge of ancient Aramaic, Arabic and Hebrew has been a great help to me."

"I do not want to overburden you, my son, but I have another very important project that I would like you to work on for me. It seems that of all the people in the Vatican, you are the most learned and qualified to work on the project. It is even more appropriate since you are so dedicated to Mary."

"What is it, Holy Father?" You know that no matter what you ask of me, I am more than willing to do it if it is within my power," answered Michael.

"I know that my son, and God will bless you for your sacrifices. I would like you to read and verify the letters of Fatima, the letters of verification of the apparitions of Our Blessed Mother that were written by Lucia. I would also like you to authenticate the miracles of Fatima. Remember, my son, this is no easy task and it is not without sacrifice. You must keep this a secret from everyone as the last letter contains the prophecies made by Mary during her final appearance to the children. I am not to open the letter and make its contents public until I can be sure that the apparitions are authentic."

"I will be honored to do this research, Holy Father, not just for you but in honor of our blessed Mother. Thank you for giving me this opportunity and I promise to do my best," answered Monsignor Bachman smiling at the Pope.

"May God be with you Michael," answered the Holy Father after he gave the young man his blessing.

"Within a few weeks after the meeting, the Monsignor had gained the confidence of the Pope and was a frequent visitor to the Papal Chambers. They would meet almost every evening to discuss the progress of Lucia's letters over a glass of wine. We all began to believe that the hand of God was with us since Bachman had gained the respect and admiration of Pius XII. The Pope was very taken with Michael and within two months he sent his approval to have him named a Bishop of the Church. Since Pius was old and in a weakened state, he was very happy to have the company the young intelligent man who shared his complete devotion to God's mother."

"Bachman reported that he told the Holy Father that he dedicates all of his work to the Blessed Mother because as a child, he was very ill with a fever and his mother prayed to Our Lady for his recovery. Since his recovery, he has a great devotion to Her. Bachman told us that the Holy Father listened intently and was emotionally touched by his story," revealed DeGroot.

"I still tremble with fear, when I recalled a slight sneer and cold look in Bachman's eyes after he related that story to us. No one else appeared to notice his facial expressions and if they did, no one mentioned it aloud. This, of course, was not the first time that I did not feel comfortable about Michael or our plan but, I was afraid to disappoint the others, by objecting to them," explained Cardinal DeGroot as he continued his confession...

"Stay calm, my friend, take your time and continue with your intriguing story," responded the Holy Father.

"Thank you, Holy Father. I remember that in the following weeks everything progressed smoothly, especially when Bishop Bachman came to us to tell us his good news. I will never forget the joyful expression on his face on that particular day. I can honestly say that it was the very first time that I heard him laugh. He was full of excitement and he almost stuttered as he told us the news. It was odd to see him so happy and emotional." As Cardinal DeGroot rambled on, his mind wandered back in the time period.

"My brothers in Christ, you will not believe what our Holy Father has asked me to do!" Michael Bachman shouted aloud as he entered the conference room, "Pius had told me that he desperately needs my expertise. The team of scientists that are working in Turin, are in need of a geneticist and Pius is sending me to help them. I will be working on the Shroud of Our Lord, Jesus Christ!" shouted Bishop Bachman. "This is the opportunity of a life-time. I cannot wait to leave for Turin."

"When do you leave?'" asked Cardinal Acietuno.

"Sometime soon," answered the young Bishop. "The Holy Father is anxious for me to do some testing of the samples that the other scientists are working on. Apparently they are not sure how to test the specimens that they believe to be the body and blood fluids on the Shroud. So, I am the one that will do that part of the research!" answered Bachman in an excited tone.

Cardinal Brazini looked at him and smiled, "What we have been waiting for has finally happened. You will do well, Michael. You will also report your findings to us before you even tell our Holy Father. Do you understand?"

The smile faded from Bishop Bachman's face as he realized that it was not a request that Cardinal Brazini was making but a command. We believed that the young man was intimidated by Brazini's large stocky frame, piercing dark eyes and powerful presence as much as the rest of us were when Brazini made his authority known.

Michael hesitated only for a second before he answered, "Of course, your Eminence, whatever you wish me to do, I will do it. You know that I am eternally grateful for what you have done for me and I can never do enough to repay you for saving my life and my sanity."

After a few seconds, Cardinal Brazini finally patted the young Bishop on the back and smiled at him, "You are indeed a wise man, Michael, and I know that you will do well and succeed with this project. May God be with you and remember that all you do, you do in the name of Christ. Report to me tomorrow morning and I will instruct you on how we want you to handle the reports."

"Yes, Cardinal, whatever you say. I'll come to your private quarters shortly after Mass," answered Michael as he walked toward the door.

We waited until Bishop Bachman left the room and we continued to sit around the conference table for several hours sipping wine, discussing our instructions that would be given to Michael, and wondering where our plans would take us. The six of us were overjoyed at our blessings and were filled with hope that our mission would finally become a reality. We had no sense of impending doom, not even myself or Milos who always seemed to look at the bleak side of everything," confessed Cardinal DeGroot.

**HONESTY IS THE BEST POLICY; BUT HE
WHO IS GOVERNED BY THAT MAXIM IS NOT
AN HONEST MAN.   Richard Whately**

CHAPTER V

THE VATICAN, 1997

As Cardinal DeGroot continued to confess the events that happened so many years ago, he felt as though he were reliving the entire episode as he spoke.

"In January of 1957, Bishop Bachman was preparing for his trip to Turin with the help of Cardinal Acietuno and myself. While he was gathering his research equipment together, Cardinal Brazini stepped into the room. He looked at Bishop Bachman and asked him if he was almost ready to leave. The Bishop was so involved in checking his equipment, that he gave Brazini a short answer."

"Brazini grabbed his hand and as he stared at Michael, his dark eyes flashed with anger and he warned him again in a threatening voice.

"My friend, do not forget with whom you are speaking. I am well aware of your superior intellect however, you lack the level of power that I have. Do not become distracted by your success or by your friendship with Pope Pius. He is an old man and will not last forever. Anyone of us may be the next pope.

Please remember what I told you earlier this week. Whatever experiments you do and whatever you find out about the authenticity of the Shroud, you will report to us before you tell the Holy Father. Again, I am asking you if you fully understand these instructions, Michael?"

"I recall that Michael stared at him with a blank expression, but he smiled at Brazini and was very docile in his reply," related DeGroot.

"Yes, Cardinal Brazini, I fully understand what you have requested and I will not fail you. You will learn everything you wish to know as soon as possible."

"We were interrupted by a loud knock on Michael's door and heard the papal valet's frantic cries for help, 'Bishop Bachman, you must hurry, The Holy Father needs you immediately. Please come, it is urgent!'"

"Bachman dropped his bag and ran out the door before we could even comprehend what was happening. Michael entered Pius XII's private chambers first and found the Holy Father on the floor unconscious. This was just the beginning of the events that were to change history," continued Cardinal DeGroot.

"I discovered later that the events that occurred before we entered the room were crucial and would eventually benefit Michael as it gave him the power that he needed against Brazini. Michael relayed that as soon as he entered the Papal chambers, he knelt down, he quickly began to feel for a pulse and realized that the Pope was still alive. He told us that he noticed a letter bearing a wax seal clutched in Pius's hand. Michael said that he quickly looked around to make sure that no one else was in the room and that he pried the letter from the Pope's hand and read it. He had not quite finished reading when he heard our running footsteps approach the Papal chamber. He hid the letter inside of his cassock and began to administer first aid to the Pontiff. The Pope's doctor was with us when we entered the chamber and when Brazini saw Michael taking care of the Pope, he pushed him aside and began barking orders to the doctor."

"Michael's trip to Turin was postponed until the following day when it was reported that the Holy Father had suffered a mild stroke which affected his speech and short term memory. The Pontiff's personal physician and the specialist were hopeful that the Pius would recover. But because of his age and weakened state, they could not give us a guarantee for a full recovery. Michael seemed genuinely concerned about the Pope's condition and he requested a meeting with the six of us for later that evening."

THE VATICAN CONFERENCE ROOM
JANUARY, 1957 - 8:00 PM

"Cardinals Brazini, Acietuno, Belawa, LeBlanc, and Kowalsky and myself were already comfortably seated at the conference room table when Michael entered the room." recalled DeGroot.

"Good evening, Michael, I hope that you are much more relaxed now after that harrowing experience you had this afternoon," remarked Cardinal Belawa.

"Yes, it was quite an ordeal and I was shaken, but I am feeling much better now. However, I am worried about something and I need to speak to all of you immediately. I could not leave here tomorrow without telling you what I found when I ran into help His

Holiness," answered the Bishop looking haggard from his ordeal with the Pontiff.

"And what is that?" questioned Brazini.

"Your Eminence," said Michael as he sat down at the large table, "when I entered the Papal chambers, I saw Pius lying on the floor and in his hand was an opened letter. After reading a portion of the document, I realized that it was the prophetic letter from Our Lady when she appeared for the final time to the children at Fatima. I was so nervous that I hid the letter inside my cassock and then took it back to my room to read it thoroughly. I blame myself for the Holy Father's condition since I had recently verified the authenticity of the Fatima apparitions. This prompted Pius to read the final letter. Because of his age and health, he should not have been alone. May God grant him the strength he needs to recover. However, I knew that all of you would be interested in the contents of this final prophecy."

"Well," said Cardinal Brazini impatiently, "of course we are interested. Show us the letter."

"That is the problem, I can't. I was so nervous and feeling guilty about what had happened to Pius that I didn't realize that I had taken it. Later, I was unsure of how to return the letter to the Pope's chambers, so I destroyed it. I burned it soon after I reread it," Michael answered sheepishly as he looked directly at Cardinal Brazini.

"Cardinal Brazini coldly stared at Michael, but remained silent for a few moments. Then, as he spoke, the anger bubbled beneath his words, 'You destroyed the final letter of Fatima? How could you be such an irresponsible fool? I warned you this morning about becoming too sure of yourself. You surely must have realized what you were doing, Michael,' Cardinal

Brazini's anger had now surfaced as he rose from his chair and approached the Bishop with an ugly look of wrath on his face."

"Cardinal LeBlanc stepped between the two men and put his hand on Brazini's arm, 'Antonio, my friend, think of what you are doing! What is done is done. There is no way to bring the letter back. The young man was afraid for our Holy Father and for himself. He did not destroy the letter on purpose. Calm yourself and let us listen to what Michael has to tell us. Besides, the Holy Father may not even realize what had transpired before he was stricken ill and he may not remember reading the letter.'"

"Michael continued to stare at Cardinal Brazini, but his face no longer had a look of terror or shock. Now, his face became calm, but his eyes turned like ice. He thanked Cardinal LeBlanc for his efforts and waited until Brazini was seated again before revealing the contents of the letter," continued Cardinal DeGroot as he recalled that fateful night.

"Once again, my brothers, forgive me for my impertinence and for my hasty actions. But, please believe me, I did not do it on purpose. I acted out of fear and I am also convinced that my reaction of destroying the letter stems from working under the scrutiny of the Nazi regime. All is not lost, however, since God has blessed me with a photographic memory. I can relate to you word for word, the exact contents of the letter," answered Michael, "but the part of the letter that will interest you the most states something that is unbelievable. You are all aware that I have been working closely with Dr. Stewart on the genealogy of the House of David. This letter is a miracle in itself for it reveals the name and location of the young girl who is the most recent descendent of Christ's family!"

"Oh, good Lord," gasped Cardinal Kowalsky. "We thought that we were doing the right thing when we began our plans and now it looks as though God has chosen the six of us to do His work. Now, we can prove to the world that Christ truly is the Messiah!"

"Be quiet, Milos, you're rambling," growled Cardinal Brazini. "I want to know what else is in the letter." Brazini turned to Michael and began to raise his voice, "You mentioned something before that leads me to believe that there is much more that you have not told us. I refuse to be controlled by a mere sniffling Bishop. Remember, Michael, I am the master-mind of the plan that gave you sanctuary. Don't trifle with me and never forget my power and position in the Vatican. Now, tell me what was in the letter!"

"Michael's expression turned as hard as steel as he looked towards Brazini and said in a strong threatening voice, 'Brazini, today I have seen your dark side, but let me remind you that I have worked for an ambitious man before coming here, a man who was more ambitious and more powerful than you will ever be. During that time, I learned a valuable lesson. If nothing else, I learned that knowledge is power and I believe that what I have discovered today has placed me on the same level in the Church hierarchy as you. There is nothing else that you need to know at this time. I, again, am telling you, that I will no longer fear you or anyone else and that the knowledge I have gained from the letter will seal my power and protect me from you and the world.'"

"We were in the state of shock after hearing the words that came from Michael's mouth. We did not know what to think of his anger and his threatening outburst. But, we were quickly brought back to the reality of the situation when we looked at Antonio. His face turned red with anger and a look of absolute hatred emitted from his dark eyes as he stared at Michael. He abruptly turned and left the room without uttering a word," explained Cardinal DeGroot as he explained the twisted plan that he and the others had implemented.

"Can you continue with your story, Paul? You seem shaken. I am now beginning to understand some of the tension that I've always felt whenever Antonio and Michael were together in the same room. Did they ever get a chance to resolve their differences?" questioned the Pontiff.

"No, Holy Father, they never resolved their differences mainly because of their stubborn pride and that pride turned out to be terribly destructive. Shall I continue with my confession?"

"Yes, continue Paul, I am interested in what happened next."

WE HAVE JUST ENOUGH RELIGION TO MAKE US HATE, BUT NOT ENOUGH TO MAKE US LOVE ONE ANOTHER.   Jonathan Swift

CHAPTER VI

THE VATICAN - 1997

"When Brazini stomped out of the conference room, we were not sure what to do and of course, Milos was very worried," resumed Cardinal DeGroot.

"Oh, no!" lamented Milos Kowalsky, "Now what are we going to do? Antonio is very upset! Someone must go after him and calm him."

"I'll go, he'll listen to me," offered Cardinal LeBlanc.

"About ten minutes later, LeBlanc returned to the conference room with Cardinal Brazini. As they approached the conference room table, Brazini apologized."

"I am sorry that I lost my temper, my brothers. I suppose that I am just too set in my ways. I did not mean to sound so accusatory or insensitive to Michael, however, I guess that my nerves are on edge and I am worried that our plans will be put in jeopardy. Please forgive me, Michael."

"Michael did not answer him. He looked directly at Brazini, gave him a cold smile and nodded his head."

"Please continue, Michael, you started to tell us the name and location of the young girl who is the direct descendant of Our Lord," asked Brazini in a subdued voice.

"Yes," answered Michael, "the prophecy states that her family surname is Sharone and the girl's first name is Miriam. According to the dates given in the letter, she was born in 1948 which would make her about eight or nine years old now."

"This information is incredible, but how are we going to locate her and what do we tell her when we do find her?" questioned Cardinal Belawa.

"The letter states that the girl can be found somewhere in the northeastern section of North America," answered Michael.

"Oh, well, it narrows down the area in which we have to search. Now, at least we have a starting point," chuckled Cardinal Acietuno. "We know that Bishop Pascal is always willing to help in anyway. Perhaps we can have him re-assigned to a diocese in the general northeastern area of the United States and let it proceed from there."

"Of course! That's an excellent idea, Jorge," said Rene LeBlanc.

"Michael interrupted, 'Wait, there was something else about the family that I did not quite understand. Hopefully, one of you may be able to shed some light on this part of the prophecy.'"

"What is it, Michael?" asked Chinua Belawa eager to help.

"The prophecy states that Miriam is a Jewish girl but that she will belong to some type of new movement, one that is not accepted by all Jews. I am really perplexed as to the meaning of this part of the letter," admitted Bachman.

"I'm sorry, Michael, but I am not aware of this movement," responded Cardinal Belawa with regret.

"I've heard of them!" exclaimed Cardinal LeBlanc. "They are called the Messianic Jewish movement because the followers are really Jewish but they believe that Christ is truly the Messiah that was prophesized in the Old Testament. However, instead of becoming Christian, the members still practice the Jewish ways by attending a synagogue and by practicing the holidays and traditions of the Jewish religion. There is a large group in Montreal, Canada, and since that is in the general vicinity, it seems logical to search around that area first."

"What an interesting concept. I don't suppose the majority of the Jewish community is agreeable with the beliefs of this group," remarked Cardinal Kowalsky.

"No, you're right, Milos, many of the traditional Jews do not acknowledge the Messianic Jews as real Jews," explained LeBlanc.

"Since the girl's family should be in the northeastern section of North America, why not have Bishop Pascal transferred to the Diocese of Scranton in Pennsylvania? It's in the northeastern part of the United States and is close enough to the Canadian border. Scranton is a fairly large diocese and the majority of the faithful are very religious and hard-working. I know because I have been there to celebrate several happy occasions and the people are very friendly. I think that Raymond will be very content with the Scranton Diocese because it is larger than the one he has now, so it will be a promotion for him. Besides, Raymond will not argue because he is an avid trout fisherman and fishing is a popular sport in that area. For this reason alone, I know that he will be pleased with the transfer," laughed Cardinal Kowalsky.

"I think that you have an excellent idea, Milos," remarked Brazini to the older man. "If the girl is about eight years old now, we must keep a close watch on her and her family for the next ten years or so. We want no harm to come to her. Hopefully, if we move him to the Scranton Diocese, Bishop Pascal will be close enough to the area where the Sharone family lives. It will certainly help to keep our plans less complicated especially since we know that we can trust Bishop Pascal. In the past, he was so eager to help us that I am sure he'll be agreeable to the change."

"I'm not finished. There's more good news. Do you remember Dr. Alex Stewart? He has been working with me on this project and I know that he is currently teaching an archaeology course in a college that is only about three hours outside of Scranton. This stroke of good luck may also be an asset in formulating our plans. Don't you agree, my brothers?" asked Michael.

"Milos Kowalsky's face brightened, 'Not luck, Michael, a miracle! My brothers in Christ, it is too wonderful to be a mere coincidence. It must be the workings of Our Lord. I cannot believe how smoothly everything is progressing. Now, let us kneel and thank God for all of His help and for all of His many blessings that He has bestowed on us.'"

"We all knelt down as Milos requested and thanked almighty God for his help and blessings with our plan. As soon as our prayer was finished, Michael rose to his feet, looked at his watch and said, 'I hate to break up this meeting, but I must hurry. My train for Turin leaves within the next hour and I want to go to the Holy Father and bid him farewell before I leave. I hear that he is feeling much better, but that he is still having a difficult time remembering what happened that day. His doctor also told me that his speech is still slurred and it is difficult to understand him, but that his speech may improve with time."

"Don't worry about the Pope, he'll be fine. I must agree with Milos, the hand of God seems to be moving everything along just fine. And, by the way, Michael, we will be expecting your phone call as soon as you discover anything worthwhile concerning your research on the Shroud," remarked Cardinal Brazini with an authoritative tone.

"Michael gave him a cold look and smiled slightly as he said,
'You've made your point, Cardinal.'"

THE NEARER THE CHURCH, THE
FURTHER FROM GOD.   John Ray

CHAPTER VII

"Bishop Bachman spent several months in Turin working with other scientists on the Holy Shroud. He reported any findings to Brazini who, in turn, informed us. The research progressed slowly and we all became very anxious, especially Brazini. He became more short-tempered than usual and the rest of us tried hard to avoid him except when necessary," continued the Cardinal. "Once again during that October, our plans were in jeopardy which caused another confrontation between Bachman and Brazini."
OCTOBER 9, 1958 - TURIN, ITALY - 4:00 AM
Bishop Bachman reached for the telephone and answered in a sleepy voice.

"Yes, Bishop Bachman here. Oh, no! When did this happen? Yes, Your Excellency, I can catch the 6:00 AM train and be in Rome by 8:00 this morning. May God rest his soul."

Michael knew that after hearing the sad news he would not be able to sleep. He considered Pius XII to be his friend and protector and now that he was dead, Michael wondered about the future of his plans. He got out of bed, filled the coffeepot and stepped into the shower. By 5:30 AM, he was nearing the train station. At 8:30 AM, Bishop Bachman arrived at the Vatican and was quickly ushered into the conference room where the six Cardinals greeted him in hushed tones.

"By the time Michael arrived, the entire Vatican was draped in black as a sign of mourning for the late Pope Pius XII. The Curia was busy making preparations for the public viewing and funeral arrangements for the Pontiff. I was named Chamberlain to head the Sacred College of Cardinals and our group knew that soon after the burial, we would have to enter the voting room and remain in seclusion until a new Pope could be elected. But as a member of the Sacred College, you already know all of this, Holy Father, I hope that I am not being too long winded," apologized Cardinal DeGroot.

"Not at all, Paul, I want you to relax and relay all of the events as you remember them. Please continue," encouraged the Pope.

As we sat around the conference table to discuss some of the protocol for the up-coming funeral service, Cardinal Antonio Brazini, who was seated across from Michael, leaned over and asked him if there was any news to report about the experiments on the Shroud. Bishop Bachman told him that he had just begun testing some of the dried body fluid samples. He explained that he was delayed because other scientists were testing the cloth for age and pollen samples.

"Last week," he explained with pride, "I was asked to give a seminar about my part of the research and testing procedures. Many of the other scientists seemed fascinated at what we geneticists can do."

"Don't you realize that we are playing against the clock here, Michael?" questioned Brazini impatiently. "We've been waiting for months now and we don't have time for you to show off your talents and your intellect to the others. The newly elected Pope may question the work being done on the Shroud and ruin our plans. You don't have time to flaunt your ego! You must work quickly and secretly! You should know better than to reveal too much to anyone outside our cartel about what you are doing!"

"By this time, Antonio's harsh voice was getting louder, Holy Father, and we were afraid of another confrontation between these two head-strong men. Bachman stared at Antonio and curtly responded,

'You do what you must to get a pope elected who will allow this experiment to continue and I will do my part with the Shroud. Do not threaten me Brazini and do not ever again accuse me of showing off my intellect. Just remember, knowledge is power and I hold the key to the rest of the prophecy!'"

"Cardinal Brazini's face reddened with anger and he gave Michael a hateful look but said nothing. The rest of us were relieved that Antonio had controlled his temper and we assured Michael that we would do everything within our power to elect a pope that would not interfere with our plans."

"Several days later, as you recall, the Sacred College of Cardinals secluded themselves from the rest of the world and we set about the task of electing a new pontiff. I remember what a difficult struggle it was. For three days we cast our ballots trying to elect a pope that would continue to keep our Holy Mother Church as great and powerful as it was during the days of Pius XII, especially against those who wanted to break with Pius's triumphalist Church. I will never forget the many debates and recasting of ballots before the world saw white instead of black smoke rising from the stack. Our cartel was desperate to elect a passive man who would not interfere with our business and we were happy when Cardinal Roncalli was elected as our new Church leader."

"We were surprised when he took the name of Pope John XXIII the exact name as the Anti-Pope of the Middle Ages who was later forced to abdicate the papal throne. Our group believed it to be an omen and ironically, like the Anti-Pope, Roncalli also called a council together to try to unite and reform the Church. As Pope John XXIII, Cardinal Angelo Roncalli began some of the most controversial events in the history of the Church. We all knew that Cardinal Brazini did his job well in pushing for this lovable old Cardinal to be elected and thankfully, John XXIII's interest in reforming the Church helped to keep our plans alive."

"The new pontiff was so busy calling the Ecumenical Council in January 1959 that he was too distracted to bother with our investigations into the Shroud. Brazini, knowing that Roncalli was already 76 years old, was very sure that even if he did find out about the cartel's plan, he would not hinder us too long because of his age. So this election assured us that Michael would be able to continue his secret investigations on the Shroud of Turin."

The Holy Father stopped Cardinal DeGroot before he could continue his fascinating account of the past, "What type of secret investigations was Bishop Bachman making on the Shroud, Paul? You keep alluding to these secret experiments, but so far you have not satisfied my curiosity nor have you actually told me the reason for the investigations. When will you finally get to the truth?" the Holy Father demanded.

"I guess I am to ashamed and afraid to actually say the words, Holy Father. I know that you are becoming anxious, but please be patient with me and I promise that I will reveal everything to you," answered Cardinal DeGroot.

"I do not mean to rush you or confuse you Paul, but I am becoming curious and I just want to make sure that you make a thorough confession for your sake and for mine. I must know everything. But, please forgive me for interrupting your confession. Continue where you left off," the Pontiff said apologetically.

"Do not apologize, Holy Father, I will try to get to the heart of the matter as quickly as possible. It is just that it has been so long ago and there were many people involved in the complex scheme. I'll try hard to include all the details so that you can get a clear picture of what occurred," sighed Cardinal DeGroot as he continued his confession.

"Michael did exactly as Cardinal Brazini instructed him to do and he continued to come to us before reporting his findings to the Pope. We told him to withhold some of the information from John XXIII because he was too busy with the current Vatican Council to be bothered with the Shroud investigations. Michael was told to simply tell the Pontiff that the Shroud of Turin could not be officially authenticated at this time due to the margin of error with his test results."

"Antonio Brazini's prophetic notion that John XXIII would not rule for too long became a reality. In less than five years, Pope John XXIII was dead. We were fortunate that Cardinal Montini was elected as Pope Paul VI because he was kept very busy as he continued John's work with the Church's reforms."

"You know, Holiness, that we were all from the old conservative school. Not one of the six of us agreed with the radical changes that were taking place within the Church and we were especially concerned about the effect these changes had on the Church hierarchy. Most of us were afraid of losing the power we held in the Vatican. But, we were nearing the time that our plan was to take effect so none of our conclave had time to spend fighting with Paul VI and his changes."

"Many church officials as well as the laity felt the same way, Paul, in fact, many Catholics still long for the old Church. It was truly a difficult time for many people. I am sure that if some of the changes had come about in a more gradual fashion, the Church would have had an easier time of it," conceded the Pontiff.

FE QUE NO DUDA ES FE MUERTA
FAITH WHICH DOES NOT DOUBT IS A DEAD
FAITH.   **Miquel de Unamuno**

CHAPTER VIII

THE VATICAN - 1997

"I agree with you, Holy Father, by 1967 the American Church was in the state of total chaos and upheaval as you well remember. Priests and nuns were leaving the Church in droves and the laity was no longer under the control of the religious. It was like the world went crazy. Everyone was doing his own thing and the people were no longer faithful to the Church rules. Many had stopped attending Mass even on Sundays and young people were in a state of absolute rebellion and revolution not only against their parents, but against the government and the Church. They marched along side ex-priests and ex-nuns against the injustices of the war in Vietnam and in protest of other social problems in American culture."

The Cardinal stopped to take a breath, "Along with the war and social protests, they refused to be a part of the antiquated Church. I remember being appalled when I heard that masses were being held on hillsides and that radical priests were using pizza as communion. As the young people protested, their parents and Church hierarchy were in the state of shocked confusion."

"It was during this chaotic time, Holy Father, that we made our connection with the young girl we called the Chosen One. Ironically, she was one of the many arrested in demonstrations that continually made the local news coverage in the United States. It was really amazing how all of the pieces of the puzzle fit together and how easy it was to find her," continued DeGroot.

"Dr. Alex Stewart, a young archaeologist, was teaching in a university only two hours away from the Scranton diocese. A close friend of his, Mr. John Karnovsky, often went to hear his lectures about Stewart's most recent research. Since Dr. Stewart was working on a research assignment for Pius XII, Mr. Karnovsky, a high school history and archaeology teacher, was particularly interested in what he had to say. After the lecture on King's University campus, Mr. Karnovsky waited for Dr. Stewart, who related the startling events to me when he returned to Rome..."

WILKES-BARRE, PA - 1967

"Alex, what a great lecture! I hope that I can join the dig this summer. If all goes well on the home front, I may be able to get away for a few weeks." smiled Karnovsky shaking Alex's hand.

"Johnny K.! It's great to see you again. I was hoping to run into you again at one of these lectures. Are you still teaching at the high school?" asked Alex as he grabbed John and gave him a bear hug. His tall muscular built almost smothered the shorter high school teacher.

"Yeah, and you seem to be in great shape from all your work outdoors," replied Karnovsky smiling when he heard his nickname. Everyone, including his students, called him Johnny K. "How about getting some lunch and it will give us a chance to catch up on a few things. There's a great place near here and I know you'll enjoy it. You'll feel like you're back in the 1940's. It's the perfect place for guys like us who love living in the past! The food is home-cooked and the prices are from the forties too! Lunch is on me!"

"In that case," laughed Alex his dark blue eyes twinkling with joy at seeing his old friend, "let's go!"

When they arrived at The Duchess Bar and Grill, Alex told Johnny K. that the place looked exactly as he described it. The decor had not changed for the past twenty years and the service and prices were great. Johnny told Alex that the biggest brewery in Northeastern Pennsylvania was right next door and according to the bar keep, the beer was piped in fresh from the vats.

" You really fit right in here Johnny, your outfit looks like you bought it about twenty-five years ago," joked Alex as he gave Karnovsky's bow-tie and straight-leg slacks a once over.

"Hey, Alex, Catholic high school teachers don't get the funding that you guys do. Besides, I don't have any interest in the fashion world. And, for your information, you look like one of the local hippies with your bell-bottomed jeans and wild tie-dyed shirt. Aren't you ever going to grow up?" asked Johnny K. laughing.

"Hell no. At least not until I really have to!" retorted Alex as he sipped his beer. "It's really great to see you again, Johnny, even if you insulted my stylish outfit!"

"Well, I know how to make you feel better, I'll take you to another historic site on the way back to my place. Remember when I told you about Father Murgas, the pastor of Sacred Heart Church in Wilkes-Barre - the priest responsible for the transmission of the first radio message across land?"

"Of course I do, why?" asked Alex.

"Well, the church has a few of his paintings on the altars and some of his butterfly collections on display and it's right around the corner. The site where the first radio message was transmitted is just across the street from the church. In fact, there are photographs of Teddy Roosevelt visiting the site when the transmission was sent. Unfortunately, not many people give the old priest credit for his inventions and for his work with the radio signals," answered Johnny K. "Anyway, since we're so close, I thought you'd be interested in seeing it."

"I certainly am. Let's finish our lunch, have a few beers and be off," said Alex as he lifted the beer glass to his mouth and was startled by Johnny's exclamation.

"Oh my God! I know her!" exclaimed Karnovsky looking up at the bar T.V. that was suspended from the ceiling.

"What? Who is she?" asked Alex wiping up his spilled beer.

"One of my former students. Her name is Miriam Sharone."

"Are you joking?" asked Alex with a shocked expression on his face.

"What's wrong with you? You look as if you've seen a ghost," asked Johnny K., "Do you know her, too?"

"No, not personally, but Miriam Sharone is the person that I have been tracing for more than seventeen years!" answered Alex. "This is unbelievable! How well do you know her, Johnny?"

"Fairly well, she and her parents moved from Montreal when she was a freshman. Her family is part of the Messianic Jewish movement but they attend the same synagogue as I do. We have a lot in common and we've become good friends in the last four or five years. We often attend lectures on the movement together," answered Johnny as he continued, "I feel sorry for the girl though. Why have you been looking for her?"

"Why, is there something wrong with her? And, what the hell is a Messianic Jew? I've lived and worked in the Middle East for most of my life and never heard of this sect of Jews," remarked Alex in a surprised tone.

"Well, to answer your first question, it's hard to say what's wrong with her. Her parents are convinced that like most of the teenagers today, she's on drugs because she has been having strange dreams or hallucinations. Recently, she has been having seizures but so far, the doctors don't know why," answered Johnny.

"Is she an epileptic?" inquired Alex.

"Not according to the medical test results. The doctors seem baffled, but her parents are convinced that it's drug induced and they have her blood tested periodically for traces of drugs."

"You knew her in high school, Johnny, what do you think? Would you say she's a typical druggie?" asked Alex.

"That's the strange thing," said Johnny K. thoughtfully, "that's the last thing that I'd think of. Of course, she's out of high school now, but when she was in my class, she was very mature and very bright, in fact, she skipped a grade and graduated early. Miriam is not only a very religious young woman, she is very sympathetic toward the poor and suffering in the world. As you just saw, she is also very anti-war."

"You still didn't explain the Messianic Jews to me. What do you know about it and where does the girl live?" asked Alex.

"She lives in Kingston, right over the bridge from the college where you gave your lecture. I've been to their house to dinner several times. Why are you so curious? And, why the hell do you always ask two and three questions at a time? You drive me crazy with that! Now, to answer your question about the Messianic Jews - they're Jews who believe that Christ is the Messiah but still practice most of the traditional Jewish ways. I have become very interested in them, but I'm surprised that you've never heard of them" remarked Johnny.

"Well, Johnny, I've got the superior intellect, but you've got one on me. I guess teaching in a Catholic high school for so long is finally rubbing off on you!" quipped Alex.

"Yeah, well, just don't tell my wife. Her father is an orthodox Rabbi! So, tell me why you're so interested in Miriam Sharone? And, please don't tell me it's because you're ready to join the peace movement!" joked Karnovsky.

"Maybe I will join the peace movement! I agree with most of what they believe. I wish I could tell you why I'm looking for Miriam, Johnny, but it's a research project that I've been working on for the Vatican. It started years ago and it's funny that my hunt has led me here and you're part of it. I promise that I'll let you in on the whole thing as soon as I'm given permission from my bosses," Alex told him.

Johnny looked at him and smiled, "You always wanted to work for a secret organization, but the Vatican? Why not the CIA?"

"Ah, very funny, Johnny! Let's get on with the guided tour you promised me," said Alex as they got up to leave the bar.

Cardinal DeGroot continued with his confession, "That evening according to Bishop Pascal, Alex Stewart phoned him from his hotel room..."

"Raymie, you're not going to believe this. Guess who I saw on the news this afternoon?"

Pascal laughed as he answered him, "The same person I saw, Miriam Sharone!"

"Yeah, did you know that she's living in Kingston, just about thirty minutes away from the Chancellory?" asked Alex.

"No," answered the Bishop, "but the hand of God moves in mysterious ways."

"Well, I don't know about the hand of God, but I do know that I had lunch with an old friend today and as it turns out he was her former high school history teacher and is a close friend of her parents! Do you think it's fate, or God?" quipped Alex.

"Don't be a smart aleck, Alex, you already know what I believe and if I were you, I would have more faith in the workings of God!" answered the Bishop.

"You know me Bishop, I am just testing you," answered Alex.

"You are too much, my friend. When will I get to see you? Since you're in town, how about stopping at the Chancellory for lunch or dinner before you leave for Philadelphia?'

"I'd love to see you and I'd like to talk to you, too. I have a few things to do but I can be there for dinner tonight. I'm hoping to get a chance to meet the Sharone family through Johnny K. tomorrow afternoon," said Alex.

"Johnny K.? Another one of your silly nicknames, Alex?" asked the Bishop whom Alex always referred to as Raymie.

"Yeah, but I didn't invent this one. One of his students did many years ago. His real name is John Karnovsky, he teaches at one of the local Catholic high schools. But here's the kicker, Raymie, he's Jewish. But he told me today that he is learning quite a bit about the Messianic Jewish movement from the Sharone family."

"That is very interesting," answered the Bishop, "You can tell me more when you get here for dinner. Can you be here about 6:30?"

"Sure, Raymie, until dinnertime. Oh, by the way, make sure you serve something I like."

"I will and don't call me Raymie when you're in the Chancellory!" chuckled the Bishop as he hung up the phone.

**POWER IS THE GRIM IDOL THAT THE
WORLD ADORES.   William Hazlitt**

CHAPTER IX

**LATER THAT DAY - SCRANTON
CHANCELLORY**

"I'm here Raymie, what's for dinner?" laughed
Alex as a young priest, Father Sean Ryan, opened the
door to the main area of the Chancellory.

"You are incorrigible, Alex, and in the presence of
my aid and valet. Meet Father Sean Ryan," quipped
Pascal as he introduced the young priest to Alex.

Alex shook his hand and after Father Ryan
exchanged his greeting with Alex, he quickly left the
two friends alone.

"You guys in the church really crack me up!"
exclaimed Alex shaking his head and laughing as he
looked around the large room. A large crystal
chandelier hung from the middle of the ceiling, heavy
velvet drapes framed the windows and beautiful oil
paintings hung on the walls. The polished hardwood
floors were covered with oriental rugs in rich shades of
burgundy and green and the large room was tastefully
decorated with heavy mahogany antiques that were
gleaming from being recently waxed.

"Not only do you run around in long dresses, but
why do you have to have a valet to help you? Can't you

manage on your own Raymie? And, look at this place! Who pays for all of this?"

"If you keep up your accusatory attitude, my friend, I may begin the paperwork for you excommunication!" retorted the Bishop shaking his finger and smiling at Alex. " I realize that the Church hierarchy nonsense can get in the way of religion and I can easily understand why the young people are against many of the formalities within the Church," said Alex. The Bishop retorted, "But, my friend, you of all people should know our history! It's been this way for hundreds of years and change does not come easy! The laity has always put the clergy on a higher plane."

"Well said, Raymie, but I think it's time to land the plane! It's because of this kind of thing that I can fully sympathize with these demonstrators. A lot of these kids are fairly well educated and are questioning the many crazy rules imposed by our government and by the Church that don't seem to make any sense to anyone. You know, Raymie, just because something is a tradition, doesn't make it right!" retorted Alex.

"I agree and won't argue with you, but for now, dinner will be ready in about 15 minutes. Let's have a drink before we sit down and by the way, you still make lousy puns!" joked Ray.

"You have always been envious of my quick wit! That drink sounds good to me," answered Alex. Make mine a double. I have a feeling I'll need it before this evening is over."

"You're probably right, Alex. I called the Vatican shortly after you called me with the news. I spoke with Cardinal Brazini and he was very excited to hear that we located Miriam and he wants to know how soon we can get in touch with her. I told him that we were meeting for dinner and would try to make arrangements tonight. I told him that I would get back to him tomorrow. I'm sure you'll remember that Cardinal Brazini is a very impatient man."

"Oh, yes, I remember his quick temper, too. But, Raymie, do you realize what we've found? If this girl is truly a direct descendent of the House of David, that means she has the same genes that Jesus Christ had in his body. It seems absolutely unbelievable, but according to the genealogical tracing that Bishop Bachman and I have done, it's almost certain that Miriam is the one." explained Alex.

"You mean Cardinal Bachman. He was elevated to the rank of Cardinal within the last two years. He is a powerful guy in Rome now, almost as powerful as the rest of that group that we met many years ago." corrected the Bishop.

"I haven't seen him nor been in touch with him for a while. Once I'm involved in a dig site, I don't get time to stay in contact with too many people outside of my crew. I am given orders from the Vatican through an aide, but I'm really not surprised that he was made a Cardinal. Michael Bachman is probably the most intelligent person I know, next to myself, of course," quipped Alex.

"Oh brother, I think it's time to fill that mouth with some food. Let's eat!" laughed the Bishop, as he led Alex into the large ornately decorated dining room and sat down at the long table that was perfectly set with fine china and crystal.

"Later, according to what Bishop Pascal told me, the two men sat and discussed the instructions that were given to Bishop Pascal by Cardinal Brazini and Pascal outlined the plan for Dr. Stewart," explained Cardinal DeGroot.

"Alex, it is imperative that we get Miriam to Rome. The Cardinals and, of course, our Holy Father, are very anxious to meet with her. I'm not sure how we are to do this because Brazini was explicit when he told me that she was not to be told about her genealogy."

"Well, as I started to tell you over the phone, my good friend, Johnny K. is a close friend of her family and he may be able to help us. Oh, he also told me that the poor girl has been having some health problems. Although she has been tested for various things, the doctors cannot seem to pinpoint her problem. I hope this doesn't interfere with Brazini's instructions and his plan to get her to Rome," remarked Alex.

"What kind of problems, Alex? I hope it's nothing serious because I don't want to have to be the one to tell Brazini that there is something wrong with her!" responded the Bishop with a worried look.

"Chill out Raymie, it can't be that bad. She is an intelligent and mature girl from what Johnny K. has told me. It's just that she has either been plagued with hallucinations or wild dreams. Lately she's been experiencing seizures which have caused her to black out several times. Just because we are in the middle of a social revolution, her parents are convinced that the kid is on some kind of drug and they've had her tested several times. However, none of her blood tests have come back positive for any illegal drugs," Alex told him.

"Should I tell Cardinal Brazini about the seizures or should we keep this to ourselves?" inquired the Bishop.

"Knowing what I know about Cardinal Brazini, I would definitely tell him, but downplay it as much as possible. If he ever finds out that you have been holding out on him, you'll never become a pope!" laughed Alex.

"That's all I need, then I'd never be able to go fishing! Which reminds me, I forgot to show you the huge Palomino trout I caught with my good buddy Jim. We went to one of Jim's favorite spots in Muncy and I hooked him but it took me twenty minutes to reel him in. Jim was kind enough to have him mounted for me for my birthday. I know you're eyes will pop out when you see this beauty!" said Pascal as he led Alex to his den.

Alex just shook his head and laughed as he followed the bishop, " You fishermen are all alike! No pun intended!"

"Another lousy pun! Well if I'm supposed to be a fisher of men, like Christ intended, I guess I should get busy trying to snag your soul back into the church. I hope that you're still a practicing Catholic!" retorted the bishop.

"Did you ask me here so that I could go to confession? Stop worrying about my soul and show me the fish!" exclaimed Alex. "I have to check and see if it's bigger than the last one I caught, but more importantly, I have to make sure that you're not lying, Bishop!" Alex laughed as he patted his old friend's shoulder.

"You, my friend, really are incorrigible!" laughed the Bishop.

A WISE MAN WILL MAKE MORE OPPORTUNITIES THAN HE FINDS.
Francis Bacon

CHAPTER X

Cardinal DeGroot continued his confession..."According to the reports by Bishop Pascal and Dr. Stewart, they spent the next several hours talking and making plans to meet Miriam. Alex suggested that he call his friend, John Karnovsky, and have him set up a meeting with her parents. The Bishop agreed and told Alex to make the call immediately."

"O.K." answered Alex, "but what time is it? I don't want to wake the poor guy up."

"It's only 9:30, unless he's a farmer, he should still be awake, besides, the sooner we get our plans formulated, the better I'll feel," answered the Bishop.

"Well, I know he's not a farmer, you better hope that he's not a fisherman!" retorted Alex as he dialed the phone.

"Johnny K, how are you, it's Alex Stewart. I'm here with Bishop Pascal and he wants to know if it's possible for you to arrange a time for me to meet with the Sharones? I'd be very grateful if you could. Great! I'll see you at the school at 10:00 tomorrow morning. I owe you one Johnny even though you're making me do this. Lunch is on me next time! Good night and thanks, I'll see you tomorrow," said Alex as he hung up the phone.

"Well that was easy! How did you arrange that? asked the Bishop with a surprise look on his face.

"God is my co-pilot, what can I say?" laughed Alex. Actually, there is a special program at the school tomorrow about Judaism and Johnny said that he just talked to the Sharones and that they are planning to attend. There's a catch, though, I have to get up and say a few words to the kids about my latest research project. I thought I was finished lecturing for a while. I didn't teach this semester because I knew I would be leaving early in the year to get back to the dig."

"Well, you know what they say, Alex, one hand washes the other. Besides, you love hearing yourself talk!" laughed Ray. "Don't forget to call me as soon as you get back from your meeting, or better yet, stop here and let me know what's up. I have instructions to do whatever I can to help the cause."

"I promise to call, but it is getting late and I think it's time for me to head back to my hotel room and get some notes ready for my talk tomorrow,: answered Alex as he got up to leave his friend. "Thanks for the delicious meal, the steak was perfect. Give my compliments to the chef."

The following day, after the lecture at the school was finished, Johnny K. introduced Rebekah, David and Miriam Sharone to Alex and he was surprised to see the young girl and wondered about her recent arrest. Alex was immediately struck by Miriam's beauty and he thought that she was absolutely breathtaking with her dark, blue-eyes, pale skin and classical features. He had a hard time convincing himself that she was only nineteen years old and he suddenly felt very old at forty.

"Later that afternoon, Holy Father, Alex and his friend John Karnovsky, were invited to visit with the Sharones at their home. It was then that Alex learned of the parents' plans. Needless to say, they were both distraught about Miriam's dreams and seizures. They were convinced that she was being influenced by her "hippie" friends, the peace and civil rights marches, and the drugs even though they admitted that the test results were negative. Rebekah and David decided that the best thing to do was to send their only child to Israel so that she could spend the summer with David's parents. They believed it was the perfect solution to getting her away from her friends and from the turmoil that was occurring all over the country and Alex admitted that he couldn't believe his luck when he told me what had transpired," confessed Cardinal DeGroot.

"I will be returning to the Middle East very soon since I must get back to the dig site, maybe we can all fly over together," he suggested.

"That's our problem," replied David who was a handsome man with graying brown hair, warm brown eyes and a medium build, Rebekah and I cannot go. I am in the middle of designing a shopping center and Rebekah has begun the Executive Training program at Boscov's Department Store and neither of us can get away until August. We are hoping to try to find someone who could fly over with Miriam. We're afraid to let her fly alone because of her seizures although the doctors assured us that the medication they prescribed for her should prevent them from reoccurring."

"Well, she could fly over with me, if it's O.K. with you. I wouldn't mind, but there's a problem. I must report to Rome before I leave for the Middle East. The Pope is waiting to hear the report on the project I am working on." Alex answered as he looked at both of the young girl's parents. He could see the striking resemblance between Miriam and her mother and noticed that Rebekah and Miriam shared the same unusual violet-blue eyes.

"Alex reported to us that both Rebekah and David Sharone were thrilled with his offer and were happy that Miriam would get a chance to see Rome with an experienced tour guide. Dr. Stewart reported that the young girl seemed oddly distant and her eyes seemed vacant, but when she smiled and thanked Alex for his offer, Miriam seemed eager to go. The arrangements for the upcoming flight to Rome were partially settled before Alex left the Sharones that evening."

"The next morning he called Bishop Pascal to report his good fortune. Pascal was relieved to hear how smoothly the evening progressed. When he called the Vatican to relay the flight number and the arrival date, Antonio assured him that someone would meet the couple when they landed in Rome."

**NOTRE RESURRECTION N'EST PAS TOUT
ENTIERE DANS LE FUTUR, ELLE EST AUSSI
EN NOUS, ELLE COMMENCE, ELLE A DEJA
COMMENCE.**

**OUR RESURRECTION DOES NOT LIE
WHOLLY IN THE FUTURE; IT IS ALSO
WITHIN US, IT IS STARTING NOW, IT HAS
ALREADY HAPPENED.   Paul Claude.**

CHAPTER XI

THE VATICAN, 1997

"It was March 1,1967 when, according to Dr.
Stewart, Miriam Sharone kissed her parents good-by at
the airport and as Alex expected, they were all in tears.
Rebekah and David were very emotional knowing that
their only child would be gone overseas for the entire
summer but, at the same time, they were relieved that
she would be far away from the influences of her
friends. They were also very grateful that Miriam
would not be travelling alone and they expressed their
gratitude to Alex with a gift," explained Cardinal
DeGroot as he related the events.

"Alex, there is no way that we could express our
gratitude to you for offering to fly over with Miriam.
Rebekah and I bought you a movie camera because we
thought that it would be helpful to you on the
excavation site in Israel. It's the latest model and it runs

on batteries, plus it's small so you won't get tired when you carry it around," explained David as he handed the box to Alex.

Alex was surprised and appreciative, "This a is great gift! And, I can practice using it with Miriam while we're sightseeing in Rome. It'll give her some great memories of the trip and I know that it will be an asset on the site. The camera that I'm using now can be considered as one of the ancient artifacts because it's so old and out-dated! I never had the time to replace it so your gift is really perfect. Thanks!"

"Use it in good health and I hope it helps with your research," added Rebekah hugging and kissing Miriam for the last time before she and Alex ran to board their flight to Rome.

On the plane, Miriam was more relaxed and eager to see the Vatican. She enjoyed Alex's company and his easy-going manner made her feel comfortable. When she looked at Alex, Miriam had a difficult time believing that he was more than twenty years older than she. He certainly looked and acted much younger and she surmised that it was due to the fact that he was always around college-age kids.

Miriam looked over at Alex and smiled to herself and she knew that she liked what she saw. Alex certainly was an attractive man. He wore his dark hair stylishly long and his cornflower blue eyes were kind and gentle, but she detected a look of sadness in them at times. Alex's six foot frame was muscular and well proportioned as a result of the physical work required on a dig site and it made him look much younger than forty. Miriam was very content and comfortable with him and realized that he was very easy to talk to and his conversation about work relaxed her even more.

Miriam knew Alex well because, after all, she had met him so many times before in her dreams.

Alex sat next to her on the plane and couldn't help but stare at her as she got settled in her seat. Miriam's beauty struck him and he couldn't seem to take his eyes off her. When he thought about it after their first meeting, he tried to rationalize his initial feelings. Miriam was only nineteen, yet he had to keep reminding himself of that fact because she was appeared mature compared to his typical students. There was something else about her, something innocent and mystical, he just couldn't figure it out. He began to tell her about his work and his father and when he looked at her, he regretted the fact that he was forty.

Cardinal DeGroot continued to confess in a tired, monotone voice. He explained to the Holy Father that much of his recollection of the past events were told to him by others and he hoped that Pontiff would be able to follow his complicated confession.

"Paul, are you getting tired? Perhaps you need to rest. You do not have to include so much detail if it is too much for you," remarked the Holy Father with concern.

"I'm sorry, Your Holiness, but I must include everything. I'll try to be as brief as possible, but many of the details are necessary so that you could understand the unexplainable events that happened later," apologized Cardinal DeGroot as he once again drifted into the past.

"When do you think we'll get there?" asked Miriam.

"We should be in Rome by dinner time so we are spared from eating the airplane food!" joked Alex. "After we have dinner at the Vatican, I have a meeting with some of the Cardinals. These guys are the most powerful men in the Vatican and the Church except, of course, for the Pope."

"I hate to sound really stupid, but I'm a bit nervous. How do I address a Cardinal? And, do you think that they'll let me take some movies of the Vatican?"

"Just relax. You can address them as Cardinal "so and so," their last name or as "Your Eminence." It's no big deal, they won't hang you if you make a mistake!" laughed Alex. "And as far as taking movies of them, why not? They must love being the center of attention. Just look at how they dress. By the way, how are you feeling? You look like you could use a nap. Put your seat back and relax, if you fall asleep, I'll wake you before we land," suggested Alex.

"I guess I am tired. I didn't sleep too well last night. I had some crazy dreams, so maybe I can catch up on some sleep now," answered Miriam with a yawn.

"What kind of dreams?" asked Alex.

"I'm too tired to tell you right now, maybe some day," she answered with a smile.

Within fifteen minutes, Miriam was sound asleep and Alex was able to attend to his paper work. Miriam woke just as the plane began circled the Rome airport and when she sat up, she looked refreshed. As the couple entered the terminal, they were directed toward customs. Finally after being checked and questioned by the customs agent, Miriam and Alex were greeted by a young handsome man in a chauffeur's uniform.

"*Buon Giorno,* Dr. Stewart, it is good to see you again, and this must be *Sra*. Sharone? I am here to take you to the Vatican. Please follow me, I will have your bags taken to the limousine," greeted the chauffeur with a heavy Italian accent.

"How does he know who we are?" whispered Miriam.

"Don't forget, I've been here before!" chuckled Alex. "Buon Giorno, Pietro. Miriam, this is Pietro Carzana, the official chauffeur for the Vatican. He is also the nephew of one of the most powerful cardinals in the Vatican, Cardinal Brazini. You'll meet him tonight at dinner," explained Alex as he made the introductions. Pietro smiled proudly at Alex's reference to his powerful uncle, "*Piacere, Sra. Sharone.*"

"*Buon giorno, Pietro, como sta*?" asked Miriam practicing her Italian.

"*Bene, grazie,*" answered Pietro with a slight bow.

Within the hour, they arrived at the Vatican Palace and were surprised to see Cardinal Antonio Brazini.

"*Buon guorno, como sta*, Alex? And this must be Miriam Sharone, the young woman you told us about. Welcome to the Vatican, my dear. I hope that your visit here is a memorable one. I also hope that my nephew, Pietro, has taken good care of you. He is a good boy and is very loyal to me and to his job. He is a credit to his mother, my sister. *Arrivederci*, Pietro," he called to his nephew as he left the room.

"Oh, Your Eminence, Pietro was wonderful. Very prompt and professional as usual."

"That's good to hear. Now, how was your flight? I am sure that both of you are famished. Our cook has prepared a special meal for us. My fellow Cardinals and I did not have dinner since we wanted to be able to have a relaxing meal with you and Miriam," commented Brazini.

"Grazie, Your Eminence, we forced ourselves to sacrifice eating the plane food, so we really are hungry!" joked Alex. "I know that whatever Luigi prepares will be superb!"

Cardinal DeGroot continued to ramble on with his story, "I remember that evening so well. When Brazini, Alex and Miriam entered the dining room, Antonio introduced Miriam to the rest of us. The poor girl seemed overwhelmed at meeting us and was quite fascinated with the decor and paintings in the room. We were drawn to her instantly. Her beauty was radiant and she was very gracious as she greeted each one of us. When we sat down, we said grace and enjoyed an excellent meal. About two hours later, while dessert was being served, Michael entered the room. Cardinal Brazini introduced the Bishop to Miriam. He sat down next to Alex and they began discussing Alex's work at Masada in Qumran. During their conversation, I noticed that Michael kept looking at Miriam and she must have felt uncomfortable because she turned toward Chinua Belawa and began to talk to him. It was getting late and Cardinal Belawa excused himself and told Alex and Miriam that it was time for evening prayer. When we heard the time, we said good-night to the couple and began to disperse," reminisced Cardinal DeGroot as he continued.

"As Miriam stood up to bid us good-night, she fell to the floor. Alex and Michael rushed over to her and Michael immediately felt for a pulse. He looked up at the rest of us gathered around the poor girl and began to issue orders. He told Rene to have the staff prepare a room in the Vatican infirmary for her and within minutes, several young priests rushed in and carried Miriam to the infirmary on a stretcher."

"Do you think she had too much wine with dinner?" Alex asked Michael nervously as they carried

Miriam out of the room. "I keep forgetting that she's only nineteen!"

" Relax, Alex, I'm sure that's all it is. The Holy Father wants to meet with you. You go on and I'll stay with Miriam," replied Michael.

"I'm just worried about her seizures. I hope she remembered to take her medication. Do you think she'll be alright?"

"I'm positive. Please remember, I am a doctor. I am sure that all the excitement of being here along with the long air flight has just made her a little weak. I'll make sure that I give you an updated report as soon as you are finished with your meeting. Send my valet, Father Marino to get me and I'll come to your room with a full report on the girl's condition. By the way, Alex, did you tell her anything about her background yet?" questioned Cardinal Bachman.

"Thanks Michael, I'll be looking forward to seeing you later and no, I did not tell her or her parents anything about their genealogy because Ray Pascal told me that he had orders from the Vatican to keep this information quiet for now. He said that you wanted to do some of your own testing before making a statement. As a man of science, that makes sense to me," answered Alex.

"Wonderful," smiled Bachman. "I may have a chance to take the blood tests this evening. This way I will know the definite results within two days. It will make everything a lot easier once I am 100% sure."

"What are you going to tell her once you verify this information," asked Alex. "And what are you planning to do with this information? I mean, what difference does it make who her ancestors are?" asked Alex.

"Well it may not mean much to you as an individual, but it will help to reaffirm the existence of Christ and during these times of trouble, it will be a reinforcement for those who are experiencing doubts about the Church and Catholicism," replied Michael.

Alex left for the papal chambers to meet with Pope Paul VI and he later told me that he felt as if he was abandoning the young girl because he left her alone. When his meeting with the Pope was over, Alex anxiously sent the valet to summon Michael to his room. Fifteen minutes later, Michael was knocking on Alex's door.

"Come in," he said as he held the door opened. "How is Miriam? Can I see her now?" asked Alex.

"Calm down, Alex, she is fine. I left her only about twenty minutes ago and she was resting comfortably. She regained consciousness shortly after you left and we had a nice chat. I did some blood work on her and told her it was a precaution to check the level of her blood sugar since she fainted. She was just amazed that Cardinals were allowed to take blood samples, but I did explain to her that I am also a doctor. Naturally, she was surprised at this. She is doing fine, but if I were you, I would not disturb her tonight. Let her sleep through the night. I will have Mother Angelina stay with her tonight and you can see her first thing in the morning," explained the Cardinal.

"Well, if you say so. I just feel very responsible for her and I feel sorry for her because she's been having such a rough time of it physically and emotionally," answered Alex.

"What do you mean?" questioned Michael in a worried tone.

"Well, according to her parents, she has been experiencing seizures more often recently. Her parents,

Rebekah and David, are convinced that she is on drugs because she goes into trances and has been having all sorts of dreams. Since Miriam has been active in the peace and civil rights marches and has hippie friends, her parents are convinced that she is living the same lifestyle. For the short time I've known her, I cannot believe any of this is true. Besides, all the drug testing has come back negative. The doctors recently put her on meberal to control the seizures and as far as I know, that is the only drug I've ever seen her take. She is a special person, that's all I know. There is something very different about her, something mystical. Does that sound farfetched?" asked Alex.

"I don't know her, so I cannot answer that for you, my friend, all I know about these hippies is what I hear and read in the news. I do know that if her blood tests prove beyond a doubt that she is the person we believe her to be then, you are right, Alex, Miriam is very special. I would like to know more about her physical problems however, and of course, about these dreams. Do you know anything about them?" asked the Cardinal.

"Not much, only that she has them," responded Alex.

"Well, it is getting late, my friend, and I am sure that you are tired from the long flight and all of the excitement. I will leave you now. Get a good rest and I will see you in the morning. Good night, Alex and God Bless," said the Cardinal.

"Thank you, Michael and good night to you. And, by the way, congratulations on your promotion to Cardinal. I only found out recently from Ray. I am very happy for you." said Alex.

81

"Thank you, Alex. The elevation came as a surprise to me and I am honored and very happy with my position." smiled Michael.

As soon as the Cardinal had left, Alex quietly slipped out of his room and went to the infirmary. He gently opened the door and was comforted to see a middle-aged nun sitting by Miriam's bedside reciting her rosary but he was also surprised to see that Miriam was hooked up to an I.V. and was sound asleep. He closed the door and went back to his room and tried to sleep.

The next morning, he rushed to the infirmary and was pleasantly surprised to see Miriam on her feet and fully dressed. "How are you?" Alex inquired. "You sure gave everyone a scare last night. I hope you are feeling better."

"Oh, I'm just fine, except I am a bit embarrassed. It's bad enough that I am a first time visitor to the Vatican but then I start a commotion and pass out after a wonderful dinner! Everyone must think that there is something really wrong with me," answered Miriam.

"Don't be silly. We were worried about you. Did you see a doctor yet this morning? Are you sure that you should be out of the bed?" quizzed Alex.

"Yes, both Dr. Ansilio and Cardinal Bachman were in to see me and both of them gave me a clean bill of health. They told me to have a wonderful day sight-seeing. So let's go," said Miriam.

"O.K. I'm ready." answered Alex. "But let's have some breakfast first, I don't want to have to drag you out of the Sistine Chapel by your heels," he teased as he led her into the dining room.

"Before they left for the airport, Miriam asked permission to take movies of the Vatican. When she and Alex entered the conference room with the movie camera, Michael quickly got up from his seat and apologized as he left the room, stating that he was late for a meeting with the Pope. Cardinal Belawa looked surprised and commented to Milos Kowalsky that he thought that the Holy Father was conducting a private audience with the Bishops from Africa that were assigned to the Vatican II council. Later, Holy Father, I learned that Michael had tampered with the girl's drink and had added a strong potion that caused her to pass out after the dinner. He is a very clever man and he always makes sure that nothing interferes with his plans," added Cardinal DeGroot as he continued to confess.

**TRUTH RESTS WITH GOD ALONE, AND A
LITTLE BIT WITH ME.   Yiddish Proverb**

CHAPTER XII

TEL AVIV, ISRAEL - SIX WEEKS LATER...

Rachel Sharone, Miriam's grandmother, picked up the ringing telephone that was located in the den area of their home.

"Mrs. Sharone, this is Doctor Grossman from the Ben Zion hospital. I just received the test results on your granddaughter and I'm afraid that there are some irregularities. Can you bring her back here tomorrow for some additional testing?"

"Oh, no!" gasped Rachel, "I knew that there was something desperately wrong with her. Does she have Tah Sachs disease?"

"Calm down, Mrs. Sharone, no, we've tested for Tah Sachs and luckily, Miriam doesn't have it. The irregularities may be nothing at all, perhaps some virus. It's just that some of her enzyme levels are a bit raised and we'd like to double check her. Can you have her here by 10:00 tomorrow?"

"Yes, of course, doctor, I'll see you at 10:00," she answered in a concerned voice. As soon as she put down the receiver, she yelled for her husband and told him about the call.

APRIL 18, 1967 - TEL AVIV, THE NEXT DAY

When Benjamin came through the door, he heard his wife crying. He rushed into the bedroom and saw her lying across the bed. He naturally assumed that she was feeling depressed about her physical limitations. He walked over to the bed and sat down next to her and tried to comfort her. But when she looked up at him and he saw her eyes, he knew that something awful had happened. Rachel's face was red and filled with anxiety, but he forced himself to remain calm as he asked her, "What happened? Please tell me what's wrong! Has someone died?" he persisted.

"Oh my God, Ben, what are we going to do? How is this possible? What am I going to tell Rebekah and David?"

"What, What?" What is the what you have to tell them?" yelled Ben. "Calm down so that you can tell me first!"

"No one has died, thank God, but this may be even worse than that! Miriam is pregnant! That's the what!" shouted Rachel near hysteria.

"Who? Miriam? Pregnant? How?" sputtered Ben trying to make some sense out of the news. "Wait a minute! It had to be that no good son-of-a bitch archaeologist, Alex Stewart, the guy who brought her here! Other than him, Miriam hasn't been with any boys, has she?" questioned Ben as he paced the floor. He stopped and stared at Rachel, "I'll kill that bastard!" he yelled as his olive complexion turned purple with fury.

"Oh God, Ben, don't even say the word, "bastard," cried Rachel. "I feel sick, I have to lie down, my head is throbbing! I can't begin to think straight!" she mumbled.

"Yes, you'd better go and rest, Rachel," directed Ben, "but before you do, tell me exactly what the doctor said."

"Just what I already told you! Miriam is about six or seven weeks pregnant! Oh, God, my heart is palpitating, I have to rest," wailed the small, thin woman.

"Wait, where is Miriam now?" questioned Ben impatiently.

"She's helping Sarah at the school. They're organizing the school performance. Why? You're not going to do anything rash, are you?" asked Rachel, who that knew her husband usually acted on impulse. During their forty-five years of marriage, Rachel had always depended on Ben. He was a good husband and an excellent father to David, but at times, he tested her patience because of his impatience and impulsiveness. Everyone who knew Ben knew that he had a bad habit of jumping to conclusions and reacting to his assumptions. Rachel thought it was funny that she turned out to be the one with a bad heart. Over the last five years, she had been in and out of hospitals and knew that the things she loved to do were no longer possible. She couldn't go fishing and hiking with Ben and for a long time, she was depressed. Often Ben would find her crying in their darkened bedroom.

"No, I promise not to do anything rash, just go and rest until you calm down and make sure that you take your medication. I'll think of something," he said as he kissed her. He wanted to reassure her when he saw the anxiety in her large brown eyes. He was furious that he could not do more to protect Rachel from the shock and after forty-five years, he loved her as much, if not more, than the day he married her.

A few minutes later, when he was alone, Ben made a phone call,

"I'd like to speak to Dr. Alex Stewart. It's an emergency. This is Benjamin Sharone calling from Tel Aviv."

"Dr. Stewart is at the dig site, we'll have to patch you through to him. It may be a few minutes, can you hold?" asked a young woman.

"Yes, but hurry and make sure that you tell him that this is an emergency!" barked Ben.

Several minutes later Alex's voice came through, "It's Alex, Ben, what's wrong? Is there something the matter with Miriam?"

"I guess you could say that! She's pregnant, you no good son-of-a-bitch! I want to know what you intend to do about it!" Ben was screaming into the mouthpiece of his phone, "If you were here right now, I swear, I'd kill you! She's just a child! What were you thinking?"

"Pregnant?" asked Alex in a daze. "How in God's name is that possible?"

"Don't be coy, Alex, I'll be expecting you back in Tel Aviv by tomorrow. If you're not here, I'll send someone after you!" shouted Ben Sharone as he slammed the receiver into its cradle.

TEL AVIV - APRIL 19, 1967

"Rachel and Ben, you can't imagine how shocked I am to hear this news," commented Alex as he greeted the elderly couple in their spacious living room.

"You're shocked? How do you think we feel? Miriam is our only grandchild and she's just a child herself! I can't believe that our son entrusted his daughter to your care and you did this to her! I can't believe that you could do such a despicable thing as to take advantage of a young girl like Miriam," screamed Rachel as she began to cry hysterically.

"Rachel, please go and lie down, you shouldn't let yourself get so upset! I'll take care of this," assured Ben as he led his sickly wife into their bedroom.

Alex just stood there in shock and when Ben returned, Alex could see the anger and hatred in his eyes. He decided to defend himself before Ben began his tirade of accusations again, "Ben, there is something very important that I have to tell you. It's something that very few people know. There is no way that I could have fathered Miriam's child. Aside from the fact that I would never even think of taking advantage of her, I couldn't get her pregnant. I'm sterile! I contracted mumps when I was about eighteen and since the risk factor is so high in older males, the doctors have tested me several times over the years and it's been confirmed and medically documented. It's one of the reasons that I never married."

When Alex saw the blank look on Ben's face, he repeated, "Do you understand? I am sterile! Of course it isn't something that I broadcast to everyone I meet. In fact, I'd appreciate it if you kept this information to yourself and, of course, Rachel. If you want to verify what I've just told you, please feel free to call my doctor back in the State. Here's his name and his telephone number," said Alex as he wrote down the information for Ben.

"Oh my God, Alex, I feel terrible, but how did Miriam get pregnant? When could this have happened to her?" questioned Ben perplexed by Alex's news.

"I don't know, but I'm as curious to find out as you are, especially since I was with her for about a week in Rome. How far along is she?"

"From what the doctor told Rachel, about six or seven weeks. After the blood tests were taken, the doctor did a physical exam and that confirmed it."

"Well, I can understand how you assumed that the baby is mine especially since Miriam was with me in Rome about two months ago, but what about her social life here? Is Miriam dating anyone?" questioned Alex apprehensively.

"No, not dating," answered Ben, "she's gone to a few socials but always with Rachel, myself and her cousin, Sarah, who teaches at the local school. But she's never gone on a date alone with any boys here, so I can't understand how she could have become pregnant since she's been in Tel Aviv."

"Where's Miriam now?" asked Alex. "How is she taking all of this?"

"She's with Sarah and it's very strange because she's been unusually calm which is even more upsetting to Rachel and me. She's denied that she's even had relations with anyone, but Rachel and I just thought she was embarrassed or, that she wanted to protect you," rambled Ben. "I must admit, Alex, I'm very sorry that I jumped to conclusions about you. It was difficult to believe that you would do this, but logically, I couldn't come up with anyone else. Rachel and I were really impressed with you when we first met and we were very upset when we thought that you took advantage of Miriam. It's ironic to say that I'm relieved to hear what you've just told me, although, I hope that you understand that I feel badly about your condition," said Ben sheepishly as he patted Alex's shoulder.

"I can understand your reaction, Ben, and I'm sure that if our positions were reversed, I would've reacted the exact same way. If it's O.K. with you, I'd like to talk to Miriam. And, Ben, please remember something, Miriam is not a child. I hope you and Rachel realize that she is a very mature young woman. There are many women Miriam's age who are already married and have children. It's certainly not unusual," admonished Alex.

"I guess you're right, Alex, but you have to realize that in our minds, Miriam is still a little girl. Rachel and I only see her once a year, so it's hard for us to believe that she has grown up. You're right, though, she's not a child anymore. You'll find her with Sarah. They're in school rehearsing for the up-coming performance. Do you know where it is?"

"Yeah, I'll stop in and talk to her now, but I'll be back soon. You'd better check on Rachel and after you explain to her about my medical history, please ask her to keep it to herself. I find it a bit embarrassing," said Alex as he walked out the door.

He found Miriam reading in Hebrew to group of six year old kids sitting on the floor at her feet. It was obvious that they were mesmerized by her. As she read, Miriam continually changed her facial expressions and her voice to fit the different characters in the story. Alex waited until she looked up and when Miriam saw him, she put down the book, quickly said something to the children and ran up to Alex and hugged him.

"Miriam, how are you?" he asked as he held her close. "I just came from your grandparents house and I can understand now why they are so upset. I think we need to talk about this. By the way, I didn't know that you spoke and read Hebrew so well."

"I don't! Alex, remember when we were on the plane to Rome and you asked me about my dreams? Believe it or not, the events that have happened to me over the past two months have not surprised me a bit. But we can talk about this later when we are alone. I'm just so happy that you're back here. I'd like to introduce you to my cousin, Sarah. She does a wonderful job with the children and we've become very good friends since I've been here," said Miriam with a smile.

"Wait a minute! What do you mean that you don't? I just heard you reading and speaking perfect Hebrew," said Alex.

"Oh, Alex, I'll explain all that later. Aren't you more surprised by the fact that I'm pregnant and I've never made love to a man? But let's not talk about this right now, come on, I want you to meet Sarah!" said Miriam as she pulled him over to a pretty dark-haired girl.

"I am thrilled to make your acquaintance. Miriam has only talked of you since she has come here. She told me that you are a very great man. I am happy to see you here," said Sarah in broken English as she smiled and shook Alex's hand.

"Your English is excellent and I am very pleased to make your acquaintance. I'm sure that most of what Miriam told you about me is exaggerated," answered Alex smiling at Sarah as she turned to attend to one of the unruly children. Miriam took this opportunity to pull Alex into a corner.

"I've really missed you, Alex, and I'm glad you're back because I just don't know what to do. My grandparents are so worried and I'm very concerned about my grandmother. She has some heart problems and shouldn't get so upset. If anything happens to her, I'll feel like it's my fault. I guess you know that my grandfather is convinced that you're the baby's father, but there's something that I don't understand. I swear to you, I'm still a virgin," Miriam remarked as she looked directly into his eyes.

"As crazy as it sounds," Alex said, "I do believe you because I don't know what reason you would have to lie to me. But now, I can't wait to hear about your dreams. This whole ordeal is getting more bizarre. I'll only be here for a day or two, because I have to get back to Lebanon. I'm at a crucial point in the dig, but I promise to do some investigating in my free time and try to get to the bottom of this mess. I do believe you, Miriam, but you're smart enough to know that virgin pregnancies are extremely rare. Although it is a medical possibility, a woman still has to have some contact with sperm. Are you sure that you didn't have a boyfriend before we left the States?" questioned Alex with doubt in his voice.

"Alex, I'm not stupid and I'm not naive. I am fully aware of how a girl can become pregnant and I'm telling you the truth! I haven't been close to any guy since I broke up with Isaac when I was seventeen and that was more than two years ago! I've been too concerned with my medical problems to get involved with anyone else. Besides, most of the boys I know are just that- boys!" she exclaimed.

"What about the boys here? Your grandfather said that you've gone to some socials. Did you meet anyone that you like?" inquired Alex cautiously.

"No," said Miriam stubbornly. "Most of the boys here are only interested in joining the Israeli army and all they talk about is taking back the West Bank. You know how I feel about the war!"

"Don't be angry with me, Miriam. I'm just as confused as you are right now. I want to find out what happened to you because I truly care about you and I feel responsible for you. Your parents trusted me to take care of you and look what happened! How the hell am I going to explain this to them?" asked Alex realizing he had no idea what to tell Rebekah and David Sharone.

"Is that what's worrying you? You're only concerned about what you're going to tell my parents? What about me? I'm the one who's pregnant and there doesn't seem to be any medical explanation!" she retorted angrily as tears rolled down her face.

"No, I'm not just worried about your parents. Aren't you listening to me? I care for you a great deal, but I feel that this whole mess is my fault and according to what your grandfather told me, you must have become pregnant during the time you were with me in Rome. Besides, I'm the one who has to break the news to your parents, but before I do, I'm going to find some answers. Hey, let's stop arguing. We're both tired and hungry. Do you want to go somewhere and have a quiet lunch?" suggested Alex looking at the worried look on Miriam's face.

"Yeah, I am getting hungry. I didn't mean to get angry with you, Alex. You know that I like you a lot and I really missed you when you left Qumran. I also wish that you didn't have to go back there so soon. I need your help, Alex, what if this whole thing is a big mistake? Do you think that I should go to another doctor just to make sure?" she suggested as they walked to the cafe.

"That sounds like a good idea, Miriam, but I don't know any gynecologists in Tel Aviv. Maybe Sarah can help you find a doctor and he can run some more tests. I really wish I could stay here too, but I don't have much choice. I have to go back since I am in charge of this dig and it's at a very critical stage right now. We can't count on the weather staying nice and if we get rain or high winds the site could become a disaster, but I'll be back here as soon as possible. Now, calm down and let's order and while we're waiting, you can tell me about your dreams."

"I've changed my mind. I'd rather wait until I see another doctor about the pregnancy before I tell you," she answered.

"I guess that this is a perfect example of a woman's prerogative, huh?" joked Alex. "O.K., have it your way, I can wait."

After lunch, he walked Miriam back to the school and went back to the Sharone's where Alex told Ben everything that Miriam had said. Neither man could come up with a logical solution.

"Do you think she's lying?" asked Ben. "Is this one of the reasons that David and Rebekah sent her here to us? I wondered why, after all this time, they were willing to send Miriam here for a whole summer. They told me that it was to get her away from her friends and their negative influences. Is this what they meant?"

"Calm down, Ben, you're jumping to conclusions again. Rebekah and David did tell me that they were worried about Miriam getting into trouble. Many of Miriam's friends were involved with protesting and taking drugs. I'm sure that her parents told you that she was also active in peace marches and protests but that doesn't necessarily mean that Miriam was a part of the drug culture."

Alex continued to inform him about the situation in the States, "It's a crazy and chaotic time and there's a lot of confusion in the United States right now. It seems that the entire country is in a state of upheaval and any established idea or ideal is being questioned. A lot of the older generation is also involved but the younger generation, like Miriam, are right smack in the middle of it."

"Actually, I can't say that I blame them for their feelings and for some of their actions because I'm very sympathetic to many of their causes, but that's beside the point," explained Alex. "I, for one, don't believe that Miriam is a part of the free love movement. However, I do believe that she is telling us the truth as she knows it and I told you that I am determined to find out how she became pregnant. In the meantime, I think that you and Rachel should try to be as understanding as possible. Miriam is in a very delicate emotional state and she certainly doesn't need to be grilled or accused of lying especially by her grandparents." admonished Alex with concern.

"That's easy for you to say. You're not the one who has to deal with Rachel. You know that she has heart problems and you aren't the one that has to tell my son that his only child is pregnant and no one knows how it happened!" retorted Ben getting visibly upset.

"I can understand your concern, but do me a favor, Ben, hold off calling David and Rebekah for a few days. I told you that I have to go back to Qumran, but I should be able to be back here within a week or two and it really won't make much difference if you wait until then. I'd like to make a few contacts and phone calls before we say anything. Maybe, just maybe, I can come up with some solid answers by the time I see you again. If I do, I promise that I'll take the full responsibility and I will tell Rebekah and David myself. Is it a deal?" asked Alex.

"I hope you know what you're doing. I guess I have to trust your instincts on this because I have no other choices at this point," answered Ben with a worried expression on his face.

When Alex left for Masada in Qumran the following day, he felt an empty feeling come over him as he said good-bye to Miriam. As he got ready to leave, he asked her to try to remember anything else that may have happened during her stay in the Vatican infirmary.

As he hugged Miriam closely, again the feeling that he was abandoning this young and beautiful girl in her greatest time of need came over him. Although he was reluctant to leave her, he knew that he had to fulfill his obligations to the Vatican and the dig site, but he promised himself that he would do all he could to find the answers to this mystery. Something inside of him made him feel that he and Miriam had an unexplainable connection and would meet again soon.

TRUST YOUR HEART...NEVER DENY IT A HEARING. IT IS THE KIND OF HOUSE ORACLE THAT OFTEN FORETELLS THE MOST IMPORTANT.   Balthasar Gracian

CHAPTER XIII

THE DIG SITE IN QUMRAN - APRIL 23, 1967

"Alex," yelled Linda, his assistant, "come quickly, there is a young girl her who says she must see you immediately." She turned to the visitor and said, "Dr. Stewart should be here soon, dear."

Alex looked up from his work and was surprised to see Miriam standing next to Linda at the top of the dig site.

"Oh my God, what are you doing here?" Do your grandparents know that you're here?"

"I rented a car and, no, my grandparents don't know I'm here. I had to come, Alex. My grandfather was driving me crazy with his questions and accusations because he is totally convinced that I'm lying to him and my grandmother is so upset that she's had to stay in bed for the past two days. We need to talk!" blurted Miriam breathless from the climb.

"I'll say we need to talk, but not here," he said as he hugged her. He turned to his pretty blonde assistant and said, "Linda, please take Miriam to my tent and make sure that she has some fresh water to drink and have Aziz get her something to eat. I'll be there as soon as I am finished here. Miriam, you try to rest until I get back," instructed Alex.

2 HOURS LATER

"Miriam," whispered Alex as he entered his tent, "Are you awake?"

"Yes, I guess I did fall asleep for a while. I hope that you are not mad, Alex, but I couldn't stay there another minute. Just looking at my grandfather's accusing eyes made me feel sick. He's so upset that he suggested that I have the baby aborted. And, besides all that, I've missed you," she answered.

"Oh Miriam, I'm, not angry that you're here, in fact, as ridiculous as it sounds, I am happy to see you and I missed you, too. But, how the hell did you find your way here? This place is so remote. Who gave you the directions?" questioned Alex.

"No one gave me directions. When I rented the car, I knew the general direction and as I started out, I somehow knew exactly where to go. It's sounds crazy to say this but maybe the baby is directing me," answered Miriam with a detached expression.

"Miriam, does this mean that you really are pregnant?"

"Yes, Sarah took me to her gynecologist and he confirmed it. I'm due in the early part of December," she answered.

"Since your grandfather suggested an abortion, how do you feel about it?" asked Alex apprehensively.

"Alex, I can't even think about it! I don't believe in abortion even if a person is raped. I truly believe that we're given the gift of life for a reason, so you see, I can't get rid of this baby. I also feel beyond a doubt, that I was meant to have this child. Don't ask me to explain it but I just have a feeling that everything is going to be alright," answered Miriam in a soft voice.

"I'm glad that you've accepted the whole situation as calmly as you have. I guess I can understand how you feel about aborting the baby, but I wish I knew what the hell is really going on. I can't figure out how you found this place, but I am so happy that you got here in one piece. You really are a walking mystery, Miriam. By the way, have you been able to remember anything that happened while you were in the Vatican infirmary?" Alex asked as he looked at her and realized that this young girl had no one else but him to help her.

"As a matter of fact, I do remember something. When you told me before you left Tel Aviv to try to think of anything that I didn't tell you, I kept going over the entire incident. I'm not sure if this is anything important, but I remember having a dream while I was in the Vatican infirmary."

"What?" asked Alex, anxiously, "What kind of dream?"

"Actually, I'm not even sure if it was a dream, I may have been half awake but it was so weird that I just assumed that I was dreaming." said Miriam in a confused tone.

"Will you tell me what it was, already?" said Alex impatiently.

"Alright! When I was lying in the infirmary, I could have sworn that I heard two voices whispering near the bed. I remember opening my eyes, or at least I thought I did, and I saw two men dressed like Cardinals. I'm not sure if they were part of our dinner group, but one of them had a heavy Italian accent, but the other spoke English very well. I think I heard them refer to me as the Chosen One. But that doesn't make any sense. What would I be chosen for? Oh God, this is getting more and more confusing," exclaimed Miriam anxiously.

"Why would the Cardinals speak in English and not Italian? Was anyone else in the room at the time?" asked Alex curiously.

"Yes, that nun that sat with me all night," answered Miriam.

"That doesn't explain much, but why would they refer to you as the "Chosen One? The only thing that I know about you and your family is that I was commissioned by the Vatican to trace the genealogy of the House of David and it led to your parents and you. If my findings are correct, Miriam, you are the most recent descendent from the House of David on your father's side of the family. Do you understand what that means?" Alex asked waiting for her reaction to this news.

"Of course I understand what it means! I've studied my religion since I was a young child land I know that Jesus Christ was from the lineage of King David. So, if I am from that same line, that means that I am the direct descendent of Jesus Christ's family. How long have you known this? Didn't you say that you've been working on this for the Vatican? Why didn't you mention this to me sooner and why does the Vatican care who I am?" demanded Miriam as she impatiently waited for answers to her questions.

"Slow down, Miriam, according to what we know so far, you are from the same blood line as Christ," repeated Alex as he tried to dodge the other questions.

"Alex, cut it out! Why the secrecy?" she asked her voice starting to rise in anger. "I want to know everything!"

"O.K., just calm down. I'll try to answer your questions as best as I can in a few minutes. I have to make an important phone call first. Before I can explain everything to you, I need some answers, so just be patient and wait here until I get back. I'll have Linda come and keep you company while I'm gone. You can help her to catch up on the outside world. She's been at the dig so long, she gets really out of touch! If you need or want anything, ask her and she'll get it for you. Promise me that you'll just stay here until I get back. I won't be gone long," promised Alex as he turned to leave the tent.

"I hope not, you're starting to scare me, Alex. Hurry back," she added, close to tears.

NOTHING IS MORE UNPLEASANT THAN A VIRTUOUS PERSON WITH A MEAN MIND.
                                         Walter Bagehot

CHAPTER XIV

"This is Alex Stewart calling from Qumran. Please get Bishop Pascal to the phone immediately. It's extremely urgent that I speak with him."

One moment, Dr. Stewart," answered Father Sean Ryan, the Bishop's valet.

"Hello, Alex," greeted Raymond Pascal, "How the heck are you and what kind of emergency are you having now?"

"Listen, Raymond, this is serious, very serious. I am desperate and you are the only one who I can talk to and the only one I can trust."

"Slow down, Alex, it must be serious because you haven't called me Raymie. What gives?" questioned Alex's friend with a worried tone.

"Well, wait until you hear this bombshell! Miriam is pregnant!"

"What? How and by whom? Wait, never mind the first question, or the second, it's none of my business. I heard what you said and I can figure out the first, but are congratulations in order, to whom?"

"Well, not to me, my friend. I was working at the site when her grandparents called me in hysterics. They are not happy about this and her grandfather even suggested an abortion! Naturally, they accused me of being the father especially since the doctor told them

that Miriam is about six or seven weeks pregnant.
Besides all of that, Miriam is insisting that she is still a
virgin! I don't know whom to believe! All I know is
that something really strange is going on and I didn't
bargain for all of this when I agreed to take on this
assignment. In fact, I'm really beginning to get very
suspicious of our friends in Rome."

"Alex, what do you mean by that? What
happened in Rome to make you suspicious?" inquired
the Bishop getting upset by Alex's innuendoes. "And
where is Miriam now?"

"She's here with me. She couldn't stand being
with her grandparents any longer because her
grandfather kept badgering her about the baby's father.
He also kept accusing her of lying to them. Miriam told
me that he grilled her whenever he got the chance, so
she just picked up and left and came here."

"Well, at least she's alright. I hope she's not
considering an abortion, Alex, please try to talk to her.
You know that abortion is murder!" exclaimed Pascal.

"No, Ray, she won't even think about an abortion,
but she's confused to say the least. Miriam insists that
she's pregnant for a reason and she rambles on about
the baby directing her to the dig site. I still can't figure
out how she found her way here alone, but I don't have
time for that right now. What should I do?"

"You still didn't answer my question. What
happened in Rome to make you so suspicious?"
pressed Ray.

A number of strange things happened in Rome.
For one thing, Miriam passed out after dinner and was
taken to the Vatican infirmary where she stayed the
night. I thought that she was ill from all of the
excitement and that she had too much wine to drink
with dinner. But, today Miriam tells me that she

remembers something. At first, she thought it was a dream, but I'm convinced it really happened. Miriam claims she saw and overheard two cardinals whispering in the room in English. One of them had a heavy Italian accent and the other spoke English quite well, but she did detect some sort of foreign accent. She said that she overheard them refer to her as the Chosen One. Now, what the hell does all of it mean? How moral are these Cardinals, Bishop?" interrogated Alex with anger in his voice.

"Come on, Alex, these are Cardinals - Princes of the Church! Your intimations are absurd! Why would they risk their careers, their power and their prestige by committing a scandal? Your accusations are bordering on being sacrilegious! Do you know what I think? I think that you've been out in the hot sun for too long!" admonished the Bishop.

"Bull shit, Bishop!" yelled Alex, Princes of the Church or not, they are also men and Miriam is a very attractive woman. I want to know what the hell is going on. Don't protect them anymore, Ray, just tell me the truth!" demanded Alex.

"I don't know the truth, Alex, I wish I did! I understand that you are upset, but are you thinking straight? You sound as if you're getting more involved with Miriam that you even realize. Just relax if you can and you know that I will help the both of you all I can. But, remember, this is a delicate and complex situation, one that cannot be solved over the telephone while I'm in Scranton and you're in Israel. I'll make arrangements to leave for Rome early next week and I'll meet with you when I get back. Hopefully, I'll have some information from the Vatican. Is Miriam sure that no one else came into the room?" asked Ray.

"Just Cardinal Bachman and a Dr. Ansilio who helped Michael take care of her. But Ray, don't bother trying to reach me at the Masada dig site because you won't find us here. I can't explain it, but I have an uneasy feeling about this whole ordeal and all of a sudden, I don't feel too safe in Israel. I'll call you at the Chancellory within the next two or three weeks. I really appreciate your help, Ray. Oh, before you hang up, what did you mean when you said that I was getting involved with Miriam?"

"Chill out, Alex, I'm not implying that you've done anything wrong! It just sounds to me like you're falling for this girl. And, to think your dad and I were convinced that you're a confirmed bachelor!" laughed Pascal.

"Always the joker, Bishop," chuckled Alex, "I'll call you soon. And thanks for everything."

THERE ARE BAD PEOPLE WHO WOULD BE LESS DANGEROUS IF THEY WERE QUITE DEVOID OF GOODNESS.   La Rouchefoucauld

CHAPTER XV

THE VATICAN - MAY 2, 1967

Pietro Carzana, the Vatican chauffeur, was waiting at the airport with the limousine when Bishop Pascal arrived. As soon as the Bishop cleared customs, the gleaming black limousine carrying the Papal seal, made its way through the busy streets. When Ray arrived at the Vatican, he was met by Cardinal LeBlanc who immediately took him into the conference room where the other five Cardinals were waiting.

"Once again, we welcome you to the Vatican, Bishop Pascal," greeted Cardinal Kowalsky. His English was excellent in spite of his Polish accent. "It is always a pleasure to see you."

Ray took the old man's hand, kissed his ring and said, "Thank you Your Eminence, it is likewise a pleasure to see you, again. Unfortunately, I am here to try to solve a very distressing problem. I received a call from Dr. Alex Stewart about a week ago from the dig site in Qumran and he had some upsetting news."

"What is it, Raymond, please do not keep us in suspense," said Cardinal Acietuno anxiously.

"Miriam Sharone is pregnant. Alex is bewildered and the girl's grandparents are furious! Naturally, they want answers as to how this could have happened."

"What are you implying?" questioned Cardinal Brazini angrily.

"I'm not implying anything, Your Eminence, I am only relating to you what Alex told me. Something very strange has happened and Alex would like to know what went on in the Vatican infirmary when Miriam was here. Needless to say, the poor girl is emotionally distraught and had been insisting all along that she is still a virgin. Since she can't identify the baby's father, her grandfather has suggested that she abort the baby. Can anyone of you shed some light on what's happened?" asked Pascal.

"No! She cannot and must not have an abortion!" shouted Cardinal Brazini.

Raymond was startled by his adamant outburst and when Brazini saw the surprised look on the Bishop's face, he quickly added in a subdued tone, "You know as well as I do, Raymond, that abortion is murder! It goes against all teachings of the Catholic Church. She must not even consider aborting the child! By the way, how well do you know your friend, Dr. Stewart?"

Bishop Pascal could not help but give him an angry look, "Well enough to know that he would never make up a story like this even as a cover-up for something that he might have done. He's an honest and decent man and I know that he would never, ever take advantage of the girl, Cardinal. As for an abortion, Miriam will not even consider it. She wants the baby."

"Let's all stay calm," pleaded Cardinal Kowalsky, "We will not accomplish anything if we become angry and accusatory."

"You are right, Milos," answered Cardinal Belawa, "Raymond, there were only two people that were in the infirmary room with Miriam, other than Mother Angelina - Cardinal Bachman and Dr. Ansilio, who attended to her medical needs. Surely, you are not suggesting that they did anything scandalous to the girl?"

"I am not suggesting anything, Your Eminence, however, how well do you and the others know this Dr. Ansilio? Do you think that he is capable of doing something immoral? Who is he and where is he from? Perhaps we should question him." asked Pascal looking at all six of them.

"Raymond, do you think that it was possible for Dr. Ansilio to rape the girl? Don't forget, Mother Angelina was in the room with her the entire night," said Cardinal Brazini. "I think we should call Cardinal Bachman and hear what he has to say."

Cardinal Acietuno quickly left the room and when he returned with Michael, Ray repeated his story. When he heard about Miriam's pregnancy, Michael snickered and looked at Ray as though he was emotionally unbalanced.

"Your story is very interesting, Bishop Pascal, but how do you propose to substantiate it? No one is ever going to believe that the girl was raped by a Cardinal in the Vatican."

"I am sorry that you are taking this personally, Michael. I am not implying that you are responsible, but perhaps this Dr. Ansilio should be investigated," he suggested.

"Very well, Bishop, we will do our part to satisfy this inquiry. We will have Dr. Ansilio investigated and we will also question Mother Angelina if you wish," answered Bachman in short tone.

"May I speak with Mother Angelina?" asked Pascal.

"Only if you speak Italian fluently, she does not speak or understand a word of English." answered Bachman with a slight smile.

THE MALEVOLENT HAVE SECRET TEETH
Publius Syrus

CHAPTER XVI

Bishop Pascal looked at Cardinal Bachman and asked, "In that case, I guess I'll have to question her through an interpreter. Can you make the arrangements as soon as possible, Michael?"

"If you insist, Bishop, however, I still do not see the point of all this nonsense."

"It may seem like nonsense to you, Michael, but my friend's reputation and a young girl's physical and emotional welfare are at stake. I certainly do not consider either one of these nonsense," retorted the Bishop.

"As you wish. My valet, Father Valmi, will interpret for you and please feel free to use my private chambers. Father Valmi will bring Mother Angelina to you within a few minutes and I will make sure that you have the privacy you need," answered the Cardinal graciously.

Ray thanked him and waited for the young Italian priest and the nun to arrive. A few minutes later, Father Valmi entered the room and introduced himself and Mother Angelina, a pleasant old nun, to Bishop Pascal. They immediately sat down at a rectangular table in Cardinal Bachman's spacious apartment. Ray told Father Valmi that he wanted to ask Mother Angelina about the events that occurred in the Vatican infirmary the night that Miriam was ill. Father Valmi agreed and Ray checked his notes.

"Please ask Mother Angelina what time she was called to sit with the young girl," instructed Pascal to the young priest.

"About 10:00 PM, Your Excellency," answered Mother Angelina through her interpreter.

"Did she see anything unusual while she was in the room?"

"No, the doctor and Cardinal Bachman were just finishing some tests on the poor girl when I arrived."

"Ask her if she knows what type of tests they were doing?"

"I know they did blood tests. I also saw a very long needle but I did not see them use it because the curtain was pulled closed for about fifteen minutes after I arrived," interpreted the priest.

"How did she know that they did blood tests?" asked Pascal in English as he looked over at Father Valmi.

"I saw the vials of blood in Cardinal Bachman's hand and the doctor had the long needle in his hand when they finally opened the curtain. I don't think that they heard me come into the room because both men looked surprised when they saw me," explained the old nun in Italian to the interpreter.

"Ask her if either man said anything to her when they saw that she was in the room."

"Yes, Dr. Ansilio told me that I was as quiet as a mouse. He told me that he and Cardinal Bachman just finished some necessary tests on the girl and that she would probably sleep for the rest of the night. Cardinal Bachman thanked me for helping them by watching over her during the night. I told him that I was glad to do it and that it would give me a chance to pray in peace. Before they left the room, Cardinal Bachman blessed me and told me that if the girl awoke, to call him immediately. I told them that I would and the two men left the room."

"Did anyone else come into the room that night?" inquired Pascal.

"Cardinal Bachman came back in about an hour later to check on her and Cardinal Brazini was with him, but they did not stay long," she responded in Italian.

"Please ask her if Cardinal Bachman or Cardinal Brazini said or did anything to the girl while they were there."

"I didn't see them perform any more tests. Cardinal Bachman did check the girl's I.V. tube. When they stood at the girl's bedside, I could hear them whispering, but I could not understand them because they spoke in English. I did see the man who brought the girl to the Vatican look through the door at about 11:30 PM. I remember the time because I had just looked at my watch. The man opened the door and looked into the room, but when he was that the girl was asleep, he did not come in, he waved to me and left."

"Ask her if there is anything else that she can remember."

"No, Your Excellency, except that I prayed fifteen decades of my rosary." answered the old nun with a smile.

"Did she fall asleep at all during the night?"

"No, I stayed awake all night, but I was not tired because I had taken a long nap earlier in the day."

"I guess that is good enough, Father Valmi, please thank Mother Angelina for me and tell her that she was very helpful. And you, Father, were a tremendous asset. My Italian is very elementary. I wish I had taken the opportunity to practice it more often. Now, I will bless both of you and you can return to your duties."

Both Father Valmi and Mother Angelina kissed the Bishop's ring and thanked him for his blessing before leaving the Cardinal's chambers. When Pascal was finally alone, he began to mull over the events that the old nun had just related. As he went over his notes, he was deeply disturbed by the fact that Michael Bachman and Dr. Ansilio were alone with Miriam for an undetermined amount of time. He was positive that Alex told him that Miriam was taken to the infirmary at about 8:00 that evening. Yet, the nun said that they were behind the closed curtain for about fifteen minutes after she entered the room at 9:45. He wondered just how long Michael and Dr. Ansilio were in the room alone with Miriam before the nun came in for her private duty. His thoughts turned to the long needle that the nun mentioned and made a note to ask Doug or Alex if they knew what type of test required an instrument like that. Just then, Cardinal Bachman opened the door and walked in.

"Father Valmi told me that had finished. I trust that he did a good job for you."

"Yes, he's an excellent interpreter and he did a wonderful job. Thank you for suggesting him."

"Did questioning Mother Angelina help your investigation?"

"I'm not really sure, Michael. It will be sometime before I can gather all of the information together. However, I do have a question or two that you may be able to answer, if you have a few minutes."

"Truthfully, that's about all the time I have right now. I'm scheduled to meet with an envoy from Belgium in a few minutes, but I'll do what I can to help you," answered Michael.

"Well, when the nun came into the room, she said that the curtain was pulled closed and remained that way for about fifteen minutes. What were you and Dr. Ansilio doing behind the curtain?" inquired Ray Pascal.

Michael's face remained stoic, but his eyes betrayed his anger and impatience with Ray, "I hope that you have not forgotten that I am a medical doctor! Dr. Ansilio and I were performing the normal routine blood tests on the girl. We drew some samples so that we could test Miriam's blood count and glucose levels. We also hooked up an I.V. containing saline solution to keep her hydrated during the night. Does that satisfy your curiosity, Bishop?" responded Michael.

"Yes, I suppose so," hesitated Ray.

When Michael saw his hesitation, he quickly added, "You know that there is an easier way to prove whether or not she was raped by someone in the Vatican. As a geneticist, all I have to do is a simple blood test to check the paternity of the child. Where is Miriam now?"

"That's the problem, Michael, I have no idea where she is."

"What do you mean? Didn't you tell me that she was with Stewart in Qumran?"

"Yes, but Alex didn't want to stay in the Middle East for some reason. He told me that he was leaving, but refused to tell me where he was headed," answered Pascal.

"How are you supposed to get in touch with him?" asked Michael visibly irritated at this new development.

"I'm not. He's going to call me within the next week or so and I promised him that I would relay any information I could collect from the Vatican which may help solve the mystery of Miriam's pregnancy. By the way, how can you do a paternity test? Don't you need

Miriam's blood and a sample of the baby's blood to determine paternity?"

"Yes, but when you speak with Alex, perhaps you can suggest that he have Miriam and the fetus tested where ever he is and send me a copy of the results. I can test some of the people here, especially Dr. Ansilio and compare the results. Does that sound reasonable to you, Bishop?"

"Yes, Michael, it sound like a very logical idea to me."

"Good," answered the Cardinal, "then it's all settled. I guess that you'll be able to return home to your duties much sooner than you thought possible," said Michael with a smile.

"I suppose it does," responded Pascal as he and Bachman walked toward the door, "I had no other reason for coming, but since I am in Italy, I would like to visit an old friend before I leave."

"Oh? An old friend in the Vatican?" inquired Michael.

"No, not in the Vatican, in Turin. Bishop Taglia and I studied together while I was in Rome and he's currently the Guardian of the Shroud. Since I'm here for a few days, I thought I'd call and pay him a visit before I leave for the States. By the way, Michael, how is your research progressing on the Shroud? Are you still testing the cloth?"

"What? Oh, yes, the Shroud. Actually, I haven't had much time to do much testing recently, but I am hoping to run some new genetic tests in the near future since there have been so many advances in this field of science. But, why do you ask? I didn't know that you had an interest in science, especially sindonology," answered Michael as though he was preoccupied.

"I'm not overly interested in the scientific study of the Shroud, Michael, but, like most Christians, I'm curious as to whether or not the cloth can actually prove the existence of Christ. Also the Church can really use some positive publicity right now, especially in the United States," responded Ray Pascal.

"I agree with you. Proving the Shroud as the authentic relic would certainly erase the doubts and ease the restlessness of the American Church. But now, I must leave, Raymond, as I an sure that I'm late for my meeting. Have a nice visit with your friend and give Bishop Taglia my regards. I hope you have a safe journey home," remarked Michael as he quickly left Ray alone in the foyer.

Ray, troubled by Michael's reaction to Miriam's pregnancy, went into the Sistine Chapel and began to pray for Miriam and his friend, Alex. Ray slowly walked around the Chapel and contemplated the beautiful scenes that were the reminders of his faith. However, even these reminders couldn't calm his nerves and no matter how he tried, Ray couldn't quite put a finger on why he felt so disturbed. Deep within his heart and mind, he knew that there was much more to Miriam's pregnancy than Michael Bachman or any of the other Cardinals were willing to divulge. He couldn't seem to make the pieces fit together. Ray knew that he was intimidated by the Cardinals' power, especially here in the Vatican, but as he knelt down before the altar of God, he became determined to find the strength he needed to help Miriam and Alex. In the quiet Chapel, the bishop begged God to help him by dispelling his mounting doubts and fears of his brothers in Christ.

LIFE IN ITSELF IS NEITHER A GOOD NOR AN EVIL, IT IS THE SCENE OF GOOD AND EVIL.
Seneca

CHAPTER XVII

QUEBEC, CANADA - MAY 23, 1967

"Dad, it's Alex, how are you?"

"Alex, my long lost son! I'm fine, but where are you, still in Qumran?" asked Douglas Stewart.

"No, Dad, I'm in Quebec, Canada. Listen, I need your help."

"What the hell are you doing in Canada? I thought you were still working at Masada, what happened, were you fired?"

"No, Dad, I was not fired! Will you please stop talking and listen to me? I need you to go to the site in Qumran and bring back all of my personal logs and belongings. I'm not sure how long I will have to be away, but tell Linda and Aziz that I'll be back as soon as I'm able. Also tell them to continue with the Carbon 14 dating of the latest artifacts until I return. Did you get all of that, Dad?"

"Is Linda the pretty blond?" asked his father.

"Dad, were you listening to me? I'm serious! I need you to get my stuff and bring it to Quebec!" yelled Alex impatiently.

"Hold on, son, I'm not deaf or senile yet. I heard every word you told me. Are you going to tell me what's really going on or is this another one of your famous mysteries?"

"I promise that I will fill you in on all the delicious details as soon as you bring my stuff to Quebec. It's not something that I can talk about over the phone. By the way, I may need your help on this one, are you free?"

"As free as a bird. I finally completed my work at Stonehenge. You should have been there, Alex, there was a large group of hippies that were interested in the magical forces that are supposedly connected with the place."

"That's real nice, Dad, but can we talk about this when you get here? Can you make it sometime this week?" urged Alex.

"You always were a demanding child. I'll try hard. In the meantime, try to stay out of trouble," chuckled his father.

"Thanks, Dad, I owe you one. I'll see you soon."

"Actually, Alex, you owe me more than one!" retorted his father, a world renown archaeologist and ancient language specialist as he hung up the phone.

Douglas Stewart was not just Alex's father, but his mentor as well. Both father and son worked closely together over the years and Doug gave his son the training that no text book could possibly teach. Even though they argued bitterly at times over their work, Doug and Alex always remained close friends and they knew they could always depend on each other for anything.

QUEBEC, CANADA - ONE WEEK LATER

Alex was waiting at the Quebec airport when his father's flight landed. "Dad, I'm over here," he called to his father, a tall distinguished looking man with gray hair.

The elder Dr. Stewart gave his son a bear hug and commented on his beard, "Well, son, you look like something out of the Old Testament! I guess working in the Middle East is rubbing off on you!" joked his father, his blue eyes twinkled as he smiled at his only child.

"Yeah, Dad, I thought I'd try it. Besides, it fits in the style today and there's nothing like keeping current."

"Especially for guys like us who live in the past!" laughed his father who prided himself on the fact that he had a repertoire of jokes to fit any occasion.

"Promise me that you won't start on your corny archaeology jokes, Dad, at least not right now. There's someone who I want you to meet and I also need your help in solving a puzzle. Just sit back and listen to what I'm about to tell you and don't interrupt until you hear the whole story," instructed Alex as they began the drive back to the rented cottage.

Alex was finishing the details of his story as he turned into the cottage driveway, "Miriam is very perplexed because she doesn't understand how she could have become pregnant. Quite frankly, I have my suspicions, but I can't make the pieces fit. What do you think?"

"I think that I'm starving!" responded Doug Stewart. But, wait one minute before we go in, son, I have to say one thing."

"What is it, Dad, or do you just want to know what we're having for dinner?" asked Alex sarcastically.

"No, son, but I hope it's something I like. I only want to say that I hope you're not going to be stupid and marry this girl just because she's pregnant and you feel responsible for her," commented his father.

Alex gave his father a startled look, "No, Dad, I'm not that stupid, I'd probably marry her because I think that she's a wonderful person and I admire her courage, but why did you even bring up marriage?"

"Ah, son, I can hear it in your voice and I can see that look on your face when you talk about her. You're in love with her, aren't you?" chuckled Doug.

"I guess I am. I can't really explain it, but from the second I saw her, I knew that she was special and I guess I fell in love with her when we were still in Rome," admitted Alex.

"Oh, well, that's a totally different story. I think it's high time that you do get married, but tell me something, what happened to the confirmed bachelor theory?" teased Doug.

"You know, Dad, you and Ray Pascal should do a vaudeville act together."

"How is the old Bishop? I haven't seen him in a while."

"You may see him soon. I'll be in touch with Ray this week. He went to the Vatican recently to check some things out for me and I supposed to call him and get the information he gathered. Maybe I'll give him a call tomorrow," explained Alex.

As they approached the porch, Miriam opened the door to the small white cottage and the elder Dr. Stewart was immediately impressed with what he saw,

"Well, hello, I'm Douglas Stewart, Alex's younger brother," he quipped.

Miriam laughed as she shook his hand. Alex just rolled his eyes as he told Miriam that she was in for a weekend to remember especially once his father started on his corny jokes.

"I love corny jokes," she answered.

"Ah, a girl of my own heart," responded Doug and he took her arm and walked her into the kitchen. "And what is that fabulous aroma I smell?"

"Our dinner and I hope you'll like it and I hope you're both hungry. I made a roast beef, whipped potatoes, corn, fresh green beans and a blueberry pie for dessert. Alex told me it was your favorite meal and I hope he told me the truth. Dinner should be ready in about a half an hour, so that will give you time to freshen up and relax, Dr. Stewart," said Miriam as she started to set the table.

"Please, call me Doug!" he yelled as he headed toward the bathroom. "Alex did tell you the truth, it sounds like the perfect meal!"

When he came into the living room, he said to Alex, "She is absolutely breath-taking son, but she is young. I hope you know what you're doing."

"Don't worry, Dad, she's young in years, but she's much more mature than she looks," answered Alex.

"Ah, just the opposite of you!" quipped his father.

Later, during dinner, Doug dominated the conversation with his stories of the places he's been and the many discoveries that he's made.

When he asked Alex about the progress he was making at Qumran, he remembered the photograph that he found with Alex's papers, "By the way, son, I found an old photo with your personal belongings."

Doug checked his bag and found the photo, "Here it is," he said as he handed it to Alex, "Where was that taken?"

Alex looked at it and he immediately answered, "Oh, it was taken in the Vatican in 1945. Ray asked someone to take the picture and he sent me this copy. Why, dad?"

"Who is the man standing next to you, Alex?"

"He's the young guy that Ray helped to rescue from Germany. He was studying to become a priest when Hitler closed the seminaries and Hitler forced him to attend medical school and work for the Fatherland. The Vatican found out about him and they wanted to help get him out. The Curia located him through their underground connections and sent Ray into Germany to meet him and bring him back to Rome. In turn, Michael helped Ray to recover some of the Church's treasures so that they could return them to the Vatican. Why are you so interested in him?"

Miriam excused herself and said, "I'm really sorry to interrupt, but I am really exhausted. Do you mind if I leave the two of you alone to talk shop? I really have to lie down."

"No, how inconsiderate of us. Go right ahead, but are you sure that you're O.K.? Can I get you anything? Are you sure that you'll be alright?" asked Alex with concern in his voice.

"No thanks, I'm just tired. I'll be fine by morning."

"The spare bedroom is ready for you and there's an extra blanket on the chair if you need it. Good-night, Dr. Stewart, Oh, I mean Doug, I really enjoyed meeting you and I hope you have a restful night."

"Likewise, my dear. Please take care of yourself. I'll see you at breakfast and be prepared for a treat, I'm going to cook!"

"Oh, no," moaned Alex.

"What's wrong, son? I haven't poisoned you yet."

"Not exactly, Dad, but I'll make a deal with you, I'll cook and you can make the toast. Good-night, Miriam, sleep well,"

When she was out of the room, Alex turned a worried face to his father and asked, "Dad, do you think she's going to be alright?"

"Yes, son, she's pregnant, she's not terminal! Your mother was tired for the entire nine months that she carried you, but then again, that's no surprise. Even now, you can't sit still! But now, let's get back to that photograph. Do you know who he is?" asked his father in a very serious tone of voice as he pointed to the man next to Ray.

"Yeah, Dad, I just told you who he is. Of course, now he's a cardinal - Cardinal Michael Bachman," explained Alex.

"Alex, I mean, do you know his true identity?

"What do you mean by his true identity? What are you getting at, Dad?"

"Alex, this man is no Cardinal! This guy is probably the most dangerous Nazi alive!" exclaimed Doug.

"What? How can this be possible? Ray never mentioned this to me!" said Alex, shocked at his father's insinuations.

"Cardinal Michael Bachman, what a convenient and perfect cover-up," commented Doug lost in his thoughts. "I'm positive that this is the same man that I met when I was in Germany. He's real name is Rupert Bertram and he is no holy man or Prince of the Church!

He's probably one of the most intelligent, yet evil men that the world had ever known. When I was there, I heard that he was working on the cloning process for his lunatic boss, Hitler. So, I guess you can say that your Cardinal Bachman has more in common with the Prince of Darkness!"

"Cloning!" yelled Alex. "What the hell are you talking about?"

"Just that - cloning. From what I remember, he was working on the process of cloning genes so that an identical person can be made from the DNA of a living person. It was one of Hitler's crazy schemes to try to make himself immortal," explained Doug.

"Dad, that's impossible," exclaimed Alex. "Cloning research didn't start until about ten years ago. In the early '40's, it was not even thought of."

"That goes to show how much you know. During the late 1930's and early '40's, I was in Germany doing some work for the Vatican. Pope Pius wanted me to track the exact route that the Holy Shroud took into France after the Crusades. I happened to meet with several of the German officials and one of them was Dr. Rupert Bertram. I remember that he was very young, but an absolute genius. The man's intelligence was scary and I recall that he had the habit of looking at a person very intensely. When he looked at me, I felt as though he was boring through my very soul and that he could read my thoughts. It's funny because I still shudder when I remember those cold colorless eyes. I also recall that he asked me a lot of questions about the Shroud and he wanted to know if I honestly believed it to be authentic."

"What did you tell him?" asked Alex fascinated by his father's revelations.

"I told him that I never doubted things that were beyond my realm of proving, especially religious articles. He just laughed and commented that religion was invented for the ignorant. Needless to say, I was not amused by his insinuations."

"I'm sure you weren't, Dad, but tell me something, this Bachman or Bertram or whatever his name is, did he ever complete his research?"

"That I don't know. Even though I had the Vatican diplomatic immunity that allowed me to travel unharmed, I was not about to stay in Europe any longer than I had to. I never did find out how far his research progressed or what happened to him until now. He looks different than I remember him. He's hair is dark in the photo and I don't think he wore glasses, but I'll bet my last dollar that Cardinal Michael Bachman and Dr. Rupert Bertram are one and the same."

"Well, this is getting more interesting. I can't wait to tell Ray about this. Poor Raymie thinks that he's a hero for saving Bachman's life and soul for the Church. I hope that the shock won't be too much for him. I'll try to call him tomorrow, he should be back from Rome by now. But, Dad, are you sure that he's the same man that you met in Germany?"

"Son, that was a long time ago and I can't swear to it, but this man in the photo certainly bears a very strong resemblance to Bertram. I think that it's worth looking into."

JUNE 11, 1967

"Raymie, it's Alex, how was Rome?"

"I knew it was you, who else calls me Raymie? You sound more chipper than during our last conversation. Rome was interesting. Where are you?" asked Bishop Pascal.

"I'm in Quebec. Guess who's here with me."

"Miriam, of course."

"Yep, and my father," answered Alex.

"Your dad! How is the old goat? Tell him I send my warmest regards. When is he coming to the States again?" inquired Ray.

"Sooner than you think. Can you meet us in Wyalusing? We can meet at Marie Antoinette's hide out. There's a great restaurant nearby and we can stay in my uncle's cabin. We really need to talk. By the way, Ray, my dad said to bring your fishing gear."

"This is getting more interesting all the time. Tell your father that I'm putting up five dollars an inch for the biggest trout. Before I forget. what's the name of the restaurant?" asked Ray.

"You're going to love this place, Raymie. It's called the Gravestone Inn and it's not exactly a formal place so don't wear your Bishop's robes, dress is very casual," laughed Alex.

"I'm almost afraid to ask, but why is it named the Gravestone Inn?"

"Well, actually, it's right next to a very old graveyard."

"Now, I know I'm going to hate myself for asking this next question, but is the graveyard full of former customers?" asked Ray apprehensively.

"I honestly don't know, but I've eaten there several times and I'm still kicking! Don't be such a coward, just be there on Wednesday at 6:00 PM. Dad and I will be waiting for you."

"Yeah, I'll be there, I only hope that you're kidding about this place. See you on Wednesday and this better not be one of your goofy practical jokes, Alex," warned the Bishop as he hung up the phone.

**EVERY GREAT LEADER, WHETHER GOOD
OR EVIL, WHO HAS EVER WALKED THE
EARTH HAS ALWAYS LEFT SOMETHNG OF
HIMSELF BEHIND TO DOCUMENT HIS
EXISTENCE.   D.V.L.**

CHAPTER XVIII

WEDNESDAY - JUNE 14, 1967

Alex waved to Ray when he saw him slowly enter the Gravestone Inn, "Hey Raymie, over here. We've got the best seats in the house."

"Douglas, you old goat, you look marvelous, digging up old stuff must really agree with you." greeted the Bishop shaking his hand. He turned to Alex and asked, "And, how are you doing, Alex?"

"Well, thanks for the compliment, Ray, but you should be grateful that I'm not digging you up from some grave site. No offense, but you look a bit haggard, What's wrong?" asked Doug Stewart.

The trip to Rome was really draining. I've got a lot to tell you, but it can wait. Let's have dinner first," suggested Ray. "You know, you guys really didn't exaggerate about this place! What made you want to meet here?" he asked as he looked around the room and digested the decor.

"Don't you know anything about history?" quizzed Alex. "Marie Antoinette was supposed to come here to a prepared hideout in order to escape the guillotine. In exactly one month, the French will celebrate their Independence Day - Bastille Day, the beginning of the French Revolution. The heads began to roll and unfortunately for Marie Antoinette, so did hers! She never did get out of France. The locals celebrate Bastille Day because there are so many people of French ancestry that did come here to escape the revolution. See, Bishop, you learned something new today!" teased Alex.

"Talking about heads, where did all of these animal heads come from?" asked Ray as he checked out the collection of animal heads on the walls.

"What do you think you're going to be eating?" quipped Alex.

"Oh, no, you guys are not serious, are you?" asked Ray with a worried look.

"No, we're not serious," laughed Doug as he rolled his eyes making sure that Ray saw him.

'Chill out, Raymie, if one of us doesn't make it through dinner, at least the other two won't have far to carry him. Did you notice the graveyard, next door?" asked Alex.

"Yeah, how could anyone miss it? What's the story with it being so close? It's not filled with former customers, is it?" inquired Ray.

Nah, let's eat, I'm starving!" announced Doug.

"You can't be that hungry, dad, you just ate less than two hours ago!" laughed Alex.

By the way, where's Miriam? I though she'd be here with you so I'd get a chance to meet her," inquired Ray.

"You will, she was very tired so we left her at the cabin. She's going to take a nap, so we told her that we'd bring her something to eat."

"From here?" questioned Ray, laughing.

"Yeah, why not? Let's order!" commanded Doug.

The three men ordered Beaver Chili, Elk Steak and Rattler Stew and Ray was pleasantly surprised. The food was excellent and plentiful. The men were quiet as they concentrated on their plates and when the meal was finished, Alex began to question Ray about his trip to the Vatican. Ray told Alex and Doug that Bachman persisted in trying to get some information about Miriam's location. Ray also related Bachman's suggestion about having blood test done on Miriam and the unborn baby in order to prove the paternity of the child. He continued his account of his trip by telling Alex and Doug about his interview with the old nun.

"Mother Angelina claims that Cardinals Bachman and Brazini were the only people other than Dr. Ansilio who were in her room. She did say that you opened the door and looked in on Miriam at about 11:30 that night, Alex."

"Yeah, I did, but what did she have to say about the two Cardinals?"

"Only that they came in to check on her and since Miriam was asleep, they didn't disturb her, but stood near her bed for a few minutes whispering. She said that she had no idea what they were saying because they only spoke in English, which she does not speak or understand," reported Ray.

"Oh my God, then Miriam wasn't dreaming after all!" exclaimed Alex.

"What are you talking about, son?" asked Doug.

"I guess I forgot to mention it to you the other day, dad. Miriam must have been sedated because she couldn't be sure if she was awake or not. She thought she saw two Cardinal near her bed and she said that she heard them whispering in English. She remembers that one of them had a very heavy Italian accent, but the other spoke English quite well. Miriam had no idea who they were because she couldn't stay awake or focus on them." explained Alex.

"The Cardinals were Bachman and Brazini?" asked Doug.

"None other, now you know why I look so worried and haggard," answered Ray in a tired tone.

"Well, what of it? What did Miriam hear?" asked Doug impatiently.

"She said she heard them refer to her as the Chosen One," Alex paused for a moment and then his face took on a frightened expression.
"Are you thinking what I'm thinking, dad?"

"The Chosen One! Oh my God!" whispered Doug in an astonished voice.

"Wait a minute, guys, you lost me! What's going on?" demanded Ray.

"Do you want to tell him or should I?" asked Doug looking at his son.

"You tell him, Dad, I need a few minutes to digest this information and sort things out in my head. It's all starting to make me dizzy!" commented Alex in a weak voice.

"Maybe it's the Beaver Chili you ate!" quipped his father, trying to make light of the situation. Doug turned toward Ray and proceeded to fill him in on their suspicions about Bachman's true identity. After Doug supplied the details, the Bishop's tanned complexion became pale. He looked worse than when he came into the Gravestone Inn.

"Are you feeling O.K.?" asked Alex when he saw Ray's face become blanched. "You don't look too well, in fact, you look as though you're ready to cash in."

"I'm fine, it's just been a bit of a shock. I'm not ready to be dragged outside, if that's what you're hinting," answered Ray pointing to the cemetery. "Do you realize what all of this means? If Bachman is the man your father claims he is, and Miriam is pregnant and still claiming to be a virgin..."

"Oh Christ, not Hitler!" interrupted Alex with a look of horror.

"That, my friend, is the other possibility," finished the Bishop in a quiet but frightened tone.

LOVE IS A THING THAT'S NEVER OUT OF SEASON.   **Barry Cornwall**

CHAPTER XIX

"Ray, if I understand what you just said, and if Bachman is the man we think he is, then the question is, can Michael Bachman possibly be carrying out Hitler's plan to have himself cloned? Or, are you saying that you believe Michael may have actually have the ability to clone Jesus Christ? How could he possibly do this and what would be his motive?" questioned Alex with a stunned expression.

"Well, for one thing, all prodigies like Bachman need to prove their genius and satisfy their superior intellect. Maybe he wants to clone Christ because he wants to meet his Maker on his own terms, or maybe he just wants to prove to the world that he can be equal to God, who knows? Do men like Bachman need a reason? If you want my guess, he may be doing this as payment for the protection that the Church has provided him. If so, we must be extra cautious around that tight group of Cardinals, especially Brazini." concluded Pascal.

"Listen to us. Do you hear yourself? This whole mess sounds like something out of a science fiction novel, and Ray, you sound like a heretic!" remarked Alex. "Miriam's pregnancy is why we are here, right? I don't believe in this whole nonsensical science fiction bullshit! I believe that Miriam was raped by one of

those bastards and we have to find out who did it!"
raged Alex in a loud voice.

"Alex, calm down and lower your voice. I know
that you're upset, but let me remind you that I haven't
even met Miriam, but I did hear my old friend tell me
that he believed her when she told him that she's never
had sexual relations. I don't really believe that Miriam
was raped in the Vatican. For one thing, it would be
too risky and for another, why would they pounce on
her? There have been many other female visitors in the
Vatican and I never heard of anything like this
happening before!"

"You, know, Alex, you've spent a life-time
documenting facts and I know that you wouldn't have
believed Miriam's statement unless you based it on
some evidence. Guys like you and your dad are trained
to trust their instincts and the first instinct usually
proves to be the correct one. Besides, while you were
gone to the men's room, your father informed me that
you're in love with Miriam. Is that true?" asked Ray,
looking directly at Alex.

"Well, thanks to the town crier, I guess everyone
must know how I feel," said Alex as he gave his father
a dirty look.

"Hey, Alex, if you do love her, then I know that
you believe what she's told you. We just have to put
our heads together and get to the bottom of this mystery
for both your sakes."

"What about the possibility that Miriam was raped
before the old nun came into the room. You said that
Bachman and Dr. Ansilio were with her for some time
before the nun got there." commented Doug.

"I guess it is possible, but why would Michael
suggest a blood test to try to prove the paternity if he or
Ansilio were guilty? It doesn't make sense!" said Ray.

"Ray, don't be stupid! He's a doctor, a geneticist!
He could falsify the results of any test and get away
with it!" answered Alex with anger.

"I guess you're right, Alex, but you can't blame
Miriam for this. The poor girl needs someone she can
trust and someone who can support her through this
ordeal right now. Don't forget, it can't be easy for her
to realize that she's going to have a baby when she has
no idea in hell how she even got pregnant!" lectured
Ray. "Have you told her that you love her, yet or are
you waiting until you're an old goat like your dad?"

"Hey, I may be an old goat, Bishop, but at least I
took the plunge! Mr. "I'm a confirmed Bachelor" here
is just about over the hill. He'd better hurry before he
starts rolling down the other side!" chuckled Doug.

"Will you two give me a break? I need some time
to think about this! I haven't said anything to Miriam
and maybe I should just wait until all of this is settled."

"Well, I think Miriam already knows that you
love her, son, so don't wait too long. Your mother
always claimed that she knew things long before I did
and she attributed it to woman's intuition. She said that
all women know about love before the men do. I really
think that Miriam knows you love her and I think she's
waiting for you to make the first move. I can see the
way she looks at you, trust me, Alex, I may be an old
goat, but I know about love," encouraged Doug in a
wistful tone.

"Do you intend to marry her even though she's
carrying this child?
I mean, if she'll have you?" asked Ray.

"I'm not concerned that the child isn't mine but, I
am concerned about the baby's paternity. It's funny,
though, I would marry Miriam in a minute and I
wouldn't give a second thought to the baby's father, but

I don't think I have to worry about that. Don't forget, she's just going to be twenty and I'm forty. I'm much too old for her!" admitted Alex miserably.

"Big deal! It's been done before! What about the old geezers in their eighties that marry women in their twenties! At least you're a little better off!" teased Ray. "Just ask her and set a date. I'll celebrate the ceremony!"

"Thanks a lot! First you compare me to an eighty-year old and now you're rushing me into a ceremony! You religious really know how to rush things!" exclaimed Alex nervously. 'What if she says no?"

"Hey, Alex, I know she'll accept, I've got an "in" with God!" teased the Bishop. "You know, the old saying is true, there is something good to be found in everything and a reason for everything that happens."

"Spoken like a true man of God, Raymie! I'll make a deal with you, you can perform the ceremony only if you promise not to preach for an hour." quipped Alex.

"Agreed! Besides, I couldn't find that many nice things to say about you!" retorted Ray.

"Ten points for that shot, Raymie, but beware, I'll get even when you least expect it!" joked Alex.

"Alex, let's get back to the problem at hand. Do Miriam's parents know anything yet?" asked Doug with concern.

"No, Dad, we haven't told them yet and I asked Ben and Rachel not to say anything either. I wanted to wait until I had a chance to give them a reason for all of this, but I guess time is running out. I don't think that we can keep the news from them much longer. I dread calling them because they entrusted Miriam's care and safety to me. What a mess! And, to top it off, Miriam is their only child!" lamented Alex as he looked over at his own father. "Dad, you're awfully quiet, I hope you don't have indigestion from the Elk Steak that you wolfed down!"

"Are you kidding? The steak was excellent. No, I've just been thinking about Bertram or Bachman or whoever that madman claims to be. We have to get to the bottom of this and the sooner the better!" exclaimed Doug in a serious tone.

"I agree, Doug. But first things first. Alex, would you like me to contact Miriam's parents and break the news?" asked Ray trying to be helpful.

"No, Raymie, that's my job. I appreciate the offer, though. Her parents entrusted Miriam to me and I should be the one to give them the news. I plan to call them as soon as I can."

"Well, don't wait too long. Remember, a pregnancy is something that can't be hidden for too long and besides, I'm sure that her parents and grandparents are worried about her. When did she speak to them last?" asked Ray.

"I guess it was about a month ago, just before we left Israel. But, you're right Raymie, I'll call them soon," agreed Alex. "In the meantime, maybe you and dad can try to find out whatever you can about Bachman and about what's going on in the Vatican. But, I'm not sure where you would even start! Any ideas, Dad?"

"In my opinion, the best start is to go back to the beginning and in Cardinal Michael Bachman's case, I'll bet it's Germany. I can fly over there and meet up with some old friends that will be glad to help me dig up some information on a guy like Bachman. Hopefully, we'll be able to come up with enough evidence to prove his true identity." suggested Doug enthusiastically.

"That's sounds like a terrific start, dad. Ray, do you have any other connections in the Vatican other than our buddies the Cardinals? Maybe you can find out some inside information on what they have been up to." suggested Alex.

"I'll see what I can do. I do have one friend in particular, Bishop Taglia. I had hoped to see him this last time I was there, but he was not in town. I do plan to call him. As soon as I get back to Scranton, I'll check my schedule. Maybe I can go back to Rome to do some snooping on my own. I'm really curious to know what role the Cardinals played in all of this."

"Just be careful, Raymie, even though they are the Princes of the Church, they can be dangerous!" cautioned Alex. "But, answer this, what do we do if and when we find out what Bachman and Brazini and the others are up to? If dad is right about Bachman or Bertram and he's perfected the cloning procedure, what do I tell poor Miriam?" asked Alex as he covered his face with his hands.

"Unfortunately, Alex, there isn't too much you can do right now. Take my advice. Don't tell Miriam anything yet. In her condition, she shouldn't have to worry about something we really can't prove. What do you think, Doug?" asked Ray as he looked at his old friend.

"For once, Bishop, I think you are making a lot of sense!" responded Doug. "Miriam sure as hell doesn't need to worry about a theory that may prove to be false!"

**WHEN I SAID THAT I WOULD DIE A
BACHELOR, I DID NOT THINK I SHOULD
LIVE TILL I WERE MARRIED.**
William Shakespeare

CHAPTER XX

THURSDAY, JUNE 15, 1967

The following morning, Alex took Miriam for a walk through the woods behind the cottage and told her about his meeting with Bishop Pascal the previous evening.

"Unfortunately, Miriam, there's nothing new that I can tell you about the people who took care of you in the Vatican infirmary. According to Ray's report, the only ones who were taking care of you were Cardinal Bachman, Mother Angelina and Dr. Ansilio. Ray did have some information that should make you feel a little better. Remember when you told me that you thought you heard two men talking at your bedside? Well, you weren't dreaming. Mother Angelina told Ray that Cardinal Bachman and Cardinal Brazini stopped in to check on you and you must have overheard their conversation when they referred to you as the Chose One. Evidently, Bachman's blood test was the final proof that the Vatican needed to confirm that you are indeed a direct descendant from the House of David."

"Alex, I asked you before this question before, but I never got an answer from you, why is this information so important to them? I mean, what difference does it make to a group of Cardinals in the Vatican if I'm a direct descendant of Christ?" she asked with a perplexed expression.

"I know that I didn't answer you before, Miriam, but I was told by the Cardinals that any information I gathered was to be kept secret. But, at this point, I don't give a damn what they've told me about keeping it confidential! From what I've been told, this information will help the Church to authenticate the Shroud of Turin as the true burial cloth of Jesus Christ. The Cardinals are hoping that this will help to stabilize the beliefs of the Church laity," explained Alex.

"I still don't get it. I thought that the Catholic faith was based on just that - faith! But Alex, this still doesn't explain my pregnancy," Miriam stated looking at him and waiting for an answer.

"Miriam, I've learned one thing from this whole ordeal - the Church hierarchy only tells you what they choose to tell you! In any event, you certainly are a very special person and not only to the Church, but because of what you mean to me. I have to tell you that since the first day I met you, I haven't been able to think of much else."

Miriam looked at him and smiled. He looked in her eyes and took a deep breath as he continued, "I guess I shouldn't be telling you this because I'm old enough to be your father," Alex winced at the words, "but, I'm in love with you. You can't imagine how difficult it was for me to leave you when I had to get back to the dig site in Qumran. I tried to bury myself in my work just so I could fill the empty void I felt. When your grandfather called to tell me about the pregnancy, I was actually happy because I knew that I'd get to see you again! Hell, your grandfather could've put a bullet through me, but I doubt if I'd feel a thing! I was numb with anticipation of seeing you! And when I had to leave you again, I felt physically sick."

Alex paused for a few seconds and Miriam started to say something, but he put his fingers on her soft lips and said, "Miriam, wait, before you say anything, let me finish. I want you to know that I'll never forget how happy I was to see you when you arrived at the dig site. I know that I'm probably not making much sense, so I'm just going to blurt it out, I love you and I want to spend the rest of my life with you," he rambled as he wiped the sweat from his forehead and took a deep breath.

"Alex, have you just proposed to me?" laughed Miriam.

"Yes, Why? Why are you laughing? Do you think that it's that funny? I mean the two of us getting married? Do you think I'm too old for you?" he asked with a pained expression.

"No!" exclaimed Miriam.

"No, you won't marry me? I'm really sorry, Miriam, I should've known better, please forgive me, I should never have put you in this awful predicament!" mumbled Alex getting more embarrassed.

"Alex, be quiet and listen to me!" exclaimed Miriam in a stern voice. "I meant that I don't think that you're too old for me or that there's anything funny about us getting married!"

"You don't? Then, why did you laugh?" he asked still reeling from her reaction.

"Because you look like someone threw you in a shower! You're drenched in sweat and it's cool out here! Were you so sure that I'd refuse? Believe it or not, I knew right from the first moment we met that I was going to spend my life with you!" she said looking into his eyes. "Yes, I'll marry you, no matter how old you are, you old goat!" laughed Miriam using his favorite term for his father as she threw her arms around him and covered his face with kisses.

"Talking about old goats, my father was right! He told me that he knew that you loved me just by the way you looked at me. I wonder how he does it?" asked Alex chuckling.

"Well, Alex, he's a smart guy and he's been in love, so I guess he can read the signs! You should really listen to him more often," teased Miriam. By the way, do you remember when you asked me about my dreams when we were on the plane to Rome? I guess this is as good a time as any to tell you. When all my medical problems began, so did my dreams. And, you, my love, were always the major character in them!" she explained as she kissed him.

Alex kissed her back and then held her by her shoulders as he looked into her face and asked, "What do you mean? How could I have been a major character in your dreams when you only met me a few months ago?"

Miriam saw the confused expression on his face and smiled, "You never met me before, but I knew who you were because I had dreams about you and the baby for a long time. When I first met you, I was afraid and shocked because you are exactly as I saw you in my dreams. I tried convincing myself that it was only a crazy coincidence, but then when I found out that I'm pregnant, I knew that we were destined to be together."

Alex's face betrayed his thoughts. "What? Are you telling me that your dreams can predict the future?"

"I know it sounds freaky, Alex, and I know that you may not understand all of this, because, quite honestly, I don't fully understand it myself. But, I do know that for some reason, we are meant to be together.

And, I know that my son will be a very special person," answered Miriam a bit out of breath.

"Miriam, are you telling me that you're a visionary and can see into the future?" Alex asked again hoping that what she said would finally make sense.

"Well, I really can't predict anyone else's future, just ours, that is, if you still want to be a part of my future after hearing all of this. You don't think I'm crazy do you? Remember, just because you're the man in my dreams, it doesn't mean that you're forced to marry me," she said apprehensively as she looked at him with a worried expression waiting for his response.

Alex didn't bother to answer with words. He gathered her into his arms and continued to kiss her passionately.

A few minutes later, Miriam looked at him and asked, "Alex, did you know that your name, Alexander, means 'helper of men'"

Alex looked at her and laughed, "Yep, I do, it's part of my job to know, but just in case you're wondering, the best part of the definition includes a special woman - you!" he mumbled as he kissed her again.

They finally realized that it was beginning to rain and as they ran toward the cottage hand in hand, Alex suggested that they get married as soon as possible.

"Ray can marry us as soon as we get all the paperwork settled. If it's O.K. with you, we can have a private ceremony with just our parents.

"That's sounds fine with me, but I think if we try calling my parents, it's only going to delay and complicated everything. Don't forget, I'm their only child and when I left Kingston, I wasn't pregnant! By the way, what about the baby, Alex?" she asked.

"Miriam, I promise you that I'll love that child as my own. After all we've been through, I feel as though the baby already is a part of me. Everything will be alright as long as we are together," he promised as he held her close as if he was trying to shield her from all the evils in the world.

MARRIAGES ARE MADE IN HEAVEN.
Proverb

CHAPTER XXI

SCRANTON, PA - JUNE 23, 1967

"Do you, Miriam Diane Sharone, take Alexander Douglas Stewart to be your lawfully wedded husband, for better or worse, for richer or poorer, in sickness and in health, until death do you part?"

"I do," answered Miriam as she looked into Alex's eyes and smiled.

"With the power invested in me, I now pronounce you man and wife. What God has joined together, let no man put asunder. Go in peace and congratulations!" smiled Ray as he kissed the bride and gave Alex a bear hug.

"Congratulations, to you both. I never thought I'd live to see this day! The old bachelor finally hitched and to someone as beautiful as you, Miriam!" said Doug as he hugged his daughter-in-law and kissed her on the cheek. "Son, treat Miriam well, she's a great cook!" he joked. "And now that all the formalities are over, let's eat, I'm starved!"

"Not so fast, Doug, I have a special surprise for Alex and Miriam. Look up in the balcony, instructed Ray.

Everyone looked up into the cathedral balcony and Miriam squealed with delight. "Mom, you're here!"

she shouted as she ran down the aisle toward the balcony stairs. Rebekah, crying and laughing at the same time, started down the steps to meet her daughter. As they met half way, they hugged on the steps. A few seconds later, Alex approached them and cautioned them to come down before they fell down.

As both women reached the bottom of the steps, they hugged and kissed again and Alex reached out to Rebekah and hugged her, too.

"Congratulations, Alex and welcome into our family," said Rebekah coolly as she turned to her daughter, "Miriam, you look beautiful, where did you find that dress? It's perfect for you!" exclaimed her mother.

"Thanks, Mom, Alex helped me pick it out. I'm glad you like it. I'm just so happy that you're here! Who told you and where's Daddy?" surprised that he wasn't there.

"Honey, Daddy didn't come today because he's very upset about everything. Bishop Pascal came to the house a few days ago and told us about the ceremony and about the baby. Needless to say, your father is very hurt and angry. You really should have called us yourself to tell us about the baby and the wedding. Both Daddy and I feel badly that you felt you couldn't confide in us," admonished her mother with a hurt expression.

"Mom, we wanted to tell you, but we figured that you and Dad wouldn't understand the situation and we didn't want to delay our plans any longer," said Miriam trying to justify her actions to her Mother.

"Miriam, what's not to understand? You and Alex are going to have a baby and you decided to get married. It's happened to other couples before, it's just that Daddy and I didn't think it would happen to you.

You know how your Father can be, he still thinks you're a little girl in pig-tails!" explained Rebekah.

"Mom, I don't think you and Daddy understand something very important. Alex is not the father of my baby! He is too much of a man to do anything to hurt me, physically or emotionally. In fact, he's never so much as suggested anything all the time that we were together in Rome," exclaimed Miriam.

"Oh my God, then who is the father?" shouted Rebekah in total shock.

"I don't know! You have to believe me when I tell you that I have no idea how I got pregnant!"

"What are you saying? How could you not know the father of your baby? What have you been doing? What do you mean that you have no idea how you became pregnant?" yelled Rebekah at her daughter.

Ray interrupted, "Rebekah, Miriam, calm down! Take a deep breath and relax. Let's go into the rectory and sit down and try to talk this through."

"Just a minute, Ray, I want my mother to know one thing. I love Alex and I know that he loves me. We did not get married because we felt that we had to, we got married because we truly love each other! Alex is also willing to accept this baby as his own," exclaimed Miriam through her tears.

"Calm down, Miriam, you'll make yourself sick," cautioned her mother, "I'm sorry that I got so upset, but you have to bear with me. I'm having a hard time understanding how you can tell me that you don't know who the father is and how you became pregnant! This is 1967 and I know we had our Mother-Daughter talk, so please, enlighten me!" begged Rebekah.

"Ray's right, Mom, let's go over to the Chancellory and have something to eat. We can sit for awhile and talk. I realize that you're confused, but believe me, so am I!" admitted Miriam.

"What time is it? I have to be home by 5:00. You're father doesn't know that I'm here. I have to back home before he gets there," explained Rebekah as she walked over to the large building holding her daughter's hand.

After the exchange between the two women, Alex finally got the opportunity to introduce his father to Miriam's mother. When they were all seated at the long dining room table, Doug stood and gave the toast.

"Alex and Miriam, I would like to toast you as newlyweds. I am almost as happy as my son is today, because he has brought a most welcome addition into our family - the very beautiful, radiant and special woman, Miriam. Raise your glasses to Miriam and Alex," he instructed as he began his toast,

"May you always be surrounded by those who love you, may you be blessed with good fortune and many happy, healthy and prosperous years and may your lives together be filled with laughter and joy. I love you both very much!" he said in a choked voice as he lifted his champagne glass to his lips.

"Thanks, Dad, we love you, too. Don't tell me that those are tears I see!" teased Alex his voice husky with emotion.

"Yeah, son, but there for Miriam. Now she has to worry about you and take care of you!" laughed Doug.

"Hey, Dad, behave yourself! You're going to give my bride the wrong impression! In spite of your corny jokes, I want to thank you for being a great father!" quipped Alex. "I also want to thank Raymie for the beautiful ceremony and for inviting Rebekah here to share our special day, but most of all, I want to thank

Miriam for making me the happiest man alive!" he said as he looked at Miriam and kissed her.

As they began their meal at the perfectly set table, Rebekah asked her new son-in-law where they planned to live.

"Miriam and I are leaving for Canada later this afternoon, but we hope that you and eventually, David, will come and visit us often," said Alex.

"Canada!" exclaimed Rebekah, "why so far?"

"It's not that far! You should know that after living there yourself," laughed Alex. "Right now, Miriam and I think it best if not too many people know where we are for awhile," he explained.

"What do you mean? You sound as if you two are hiding from someone. I'm really starting to get worried!" answered Rebekah as she gave Alex a confused look.

"I didn't mean to worry you or frighten you, Rebekah, it's just that after what happened to Miriam, we'd like some time to sort things out without any interference. We're not sure what happened to her when she was in the Vatican infirmary and, right now, we are not really sure whom we can trust. I hope you can bear with us for now, because we really don't have anymore to offer than that." Alex saw Rebekah's concerned expression and added, "As soon as we get to the bottom of this mystery, you and David will the first to know."

"I guess I have no choice but to agree with you, but I hope that I will get to see you two often. Please try to call me a few times a week, Miriam, you know that I'll be worried if I don't hear from you. You can't imagine how worried we were when you didn't call after leaving your grandparents'. Promise me that you'll never do that again!" chastised Rebekah.

"Oh, Mom, I promise and I'm sorry for making you and Daddy worry so much, but everything happened so quickly that I didn't know what to tell you! You know that I love you both very much and I'll try not to make you worry again!" smiled Miriam as she hugged her mother tightly. "Honey, I think we should think about getting started. It's getting late," she said to Alex.

"Wow! I didn't realize it was so late! I've got to get home before your father does. Please be careful driving and call me when you get there. I hope that you don't plan on driving all night!" worried Rebekah.

"No, Mom," laughed Miriam, "we'll stop somewhere tonight and I promise to call you as soon as we get settled in Quebec."

"Don't forget!" reminded Rebekah and she turned to Ray and said, "Bishop Pascal, thank you for everything, it was a wonderful day and the meal was superb. I only wish that David was here and that we could have had a real wedding for Miriam and Alex. Maybe in the near future, we'll be able to have a reception for them," she added hopefully.

"I'm so happy that you were here, Rebekah, I would have felt badly if you missed you daughter's wedding day! Please keep in touch and I hope we get together again soon, only I hope that David will join us next time," responded Ray.

Rebekah turned to Doug, "Douglas, it certainly was a pleasure to meet you and I am looking forward to being in your company often now that we are family. And, I just want you to know that I enjoyed every one of your corny jokes!"

"Like mother, like daughter! Not only beautiful, but they both have excellent taste in humor!" laughed Doug as he gave his son a smug look. He gave

Rebekah a hug and kissed her cheek as he wished her a safe drive home.

"Come on, Mom, I'll walk you to your car," said Miriam as she put her arms around her mother and left the room.

When the women left, Ray asked Doug about his up-coming trip to Germany. He mentioned that he was leaving for Rome next week and suggested that they schedule their flights together. Doug agreed and thought it give them a chance to plan their investigations that would hopefully solve Miriam's mysterious pregnancy.

As soon as he had the chance, Alex interrupted the two men's conversation about their flight plans and said, "I'm glad that we have a few minutes alone. I need to tell you guys something before Miriam and I leave and don't want her to hear. When I proposed to Miriam, she told me something very strange," he whispered nervously.

"What? That you're too old for her?" laughed Doug.

"No, Dad, and cut out the jokes!" admonished Alex, "this is serious and I don't have much time! Miriam told me that she knew that she was going to marry me because she's had dreams about me long before she even met me!"

"Oh, brother! Now, I've heard it all! I always knew you had a super large ego, Alex, but this is ridiculous! Are you telling us that you're the man of her dreams?" teased Ray.

"Will you guys shut-up and be serious for a few minutes. This isn't a joke! Miriam told me that she was really surprised when she met me because she already knew me from her dreams! And, get this, Miriam said that she also knew that she was going to have a baby, but, she can't explain how she got pregnant!   Since you're a man of religion, what do you make of it, Ray, do you think she's telling me the truth?" whispered Alex as he heard Miriam say good-by to Rebekah.

"Alex, if what Miriam has told you is true, then this whole thing is more of a mystery than we thought. It seems to be coming more complex and dare I say, more frightening. I really wish I had some answers for you, my friend, but I can't give you a reasonable explanation. I'm not above telling you that I believe her especially as a man of religion. You should know that in any religion, there are things that just have to be accepted on faith alone."

"Son, do you think that Miriam is a visionary, or do you think it's just a crazy coincidence?" asked Doug who was surprised with this latest revelation.

Before Alex had the opportunity to answer him, Miriam walked back into the room. They said their good-byes and left for Canada.

THREE WEEKS LATER...QUEBEC, CANADA

"Alex, do you realize that we've been married three whole weeks already! Isn't that wonderful!" "Yea, but three weeks isn't all that long!" laughed Alex. "Are you happy?"

"Nope, I'm ecstatic!" she proclaimed. "I'm married to the greatest guy in the world and, he happens to be the smartest and the most handsome!" she gushed as she smothered him in kisses.

"Well, don't stop there!" he urged, returning her kisses, "You are free to continue with your truthful comments about me," he teased. "I'll have to add that my mother thought the same thing about me!"

Miriam gave him a playful swat. You know, you've never told me too much about your mom, what was she like?"

"Marilyn was funny, happy-go-lucky and very patient with my father and his life-style. She was also very supportive of me when I chose to do the same thing as dad. I know that he misses her as much as I do. I know that you would have gotten along with her," he answered with sadness.

"What did she look like? Do you have any pictures of her?" asked Miriam as she plopped down on Alex's lap.

"Yeah, I do in my wallet." Alex pulled out an old wallet-size photo of his mother. She had beautiful auburn hair, green eyes, and classic features. "I loved to sit on her lap and rub her cheek. I remember that her skin as almost as soft as yours," he added as he gently caressed Miriam's cheek.

"What did she do? I remember you told me one time that she taught school, but I don't think you told me what subject she taught."

"My mom had a Ph.D. in Medieval Literature so she taught college courses. She also told the most wonderful stories, so I guess it's no wonder that I turned out to be an archaeologist. Having parents who specialized in the past, I grew up living and the breathing the past. You know sometimes I wonder if I ever lived in the present," he said in a low thoughtful voice, as if he was thinking aloud.

"How did she die, Alex?" asked Miriam in a soft voice.

"She had breast cancer. It devastated both my Dad and me when she died because she was only forty-five and so full of life," he answered with sadness.

"I'm so sorry, honey, I didn't mean to depress you, but you never told me and I was curious."

"It's O.K., Miriam, it's just that it was a difficult time for us because we felt so helpless. There wasn't much we could do for her, except to try to keep her comfortable towards the end."

"Well, I think that you're parents did a marvelous job with you. And, I think your background is what makes you so attractive. For one thing, you still have an old-fashioned sense of manners and compassion," consoled Miriam as she hugged him.

"How did you get to be so smart, so beautiful and so right?" he joked, laughing as he broke out of his somber mood. "Go and get ready! I'm taking you out to dinner to celebrate our three week anniversary!"

"Wow! I don't have to cook! I'll be ready in ten minutes!" shouted Miriam as she jumped up from his lap and ran into the bedroom to change. "I wonder how your dad is making out in Germany," she yelled to Alex.

"I was just thinking the same thing! I guess it's true when they say married couples start to think alike. Or, maybe you're having one of your visions!" he teased.

"I heard that!" she yelled.

"Just joking, Dear," he called back. "I hope my father doesn't get himself into any trouble because he seems to have a knack for saying the wrong thing or being in the wrong place at the wrong time!" he said as she came back into the living room.

"Have your tried calling him? Oh, Oh, I'm really getting fat! Do you think this skirt is getting too tight?"

Miriam asked as she turned around and waited for his opinion.

"Hell no! You look beautiful! You're not fat, you're voluptuous!" he said as he grabbed her close. "You are not only voluptuous, but you're glowing! In fact, if you glow anymore, we won't need electricity!" he mumbled as he nuzzled her neck.

"Alex, you're tickling me, cut it out," she said laughing and trying to push him away. "You didn't answer me, did you try calling your father?"

"I'll try tomorrow, I don't want to talk about all that right now," he said as he continued to whisper in her ear.

"That's enough, you'll tickle me to death!" she squirmed out of his hold, giggling.

"You're no fun!" he protested, "but I have a present for you anyway."

"A present! For me? Oh, Alex, what is it? I feel terrible, because I didn't get you anything!" she said feeling guilty.

"Don't worry about me, just remember, you owe me, big time!" he joked. "Now, my dear, follow me into the kitchen and close your eyes," he said in a luring voice.

When Miriam opened her eyes, she screamed in delight, "Oh! A puppy! He's so little and so cute and cuddly! I just love him, what's his name?" she babbled excitedly as she picked up the furry German Shepherd puppy.

"I didn't name him yet, I thought I'd let you do the honors."

"I'm going to name him, it is a "him," isn't it?" she asked.

"Yep, it's a "him," Alex answered with a laugh.

"I've got it! I'm going to name to name him Zak," decided Miriam.

"Zak? What the heck kind of a name is that for a dog? What happened to Spot or Killer?"

"Alex! For one thing, he doesn't have spots and for another, I like Zak. It's a good strong name for a puppy that will probably grow to be a big strong dog," she proclaimed as she cuddled the ball of fur. "I think he's the best gift ever! Thank you, Honey!"

"Hey, don't I get a hug and a kiss? I hope that I'm not going to have to share all my hugs and kisses with Zak!" exclaimed Alex pretending to be jealous.

"Don't be so silly!" Miriam chastised as she kissed his cheek.

"That wasn't much of a kiss! But, I'll let it pass for now. Put Zak in his cage and let's get going. I'm starving!"

"You sound like you're father!" she laughed. "I hate to put him down. Do you think he'll be too lonely while we're gone?"

"Miriam, the puppy will be fine! I put a ticking clock and a hot-water bottle in his cage. The man at the pet store said that Zak will think it's another puppy. Look! See how he's snuggling next to it? Come on, let's go, we won't be gone that long," he urged.

"O.K. but let's hurry back!" answered Miriam finally agreeing to leave the puppy.

BY DOUBTING WE COME AT THE TRUTH
Cicero

CHAPTER XXII

ROME, ITALY - AUGUST 18, 1967

Dr. Douglas Stewart realized that his research into Rupert Bertram's past was at a dead end for the present time. He was tired and anxious to meet with Raymond Pascal to compare their findings.

"It'll be great to see a friendly face again," he said to himself as he thought of his old friend, Ray. As soon as the plane had landed in Rome, Doug hurried through customs and phoned the Vatican and asked to speak with Ray.

"Ray, it's Doug, How are you? My flight just landed and I'm still at the airport, but I'd like to talk to you as soon as possible. I don't want to come to the Vatican, do you think you can meet me at Pirandello's for dinner in about an hour?" inquired Doug. Ray agreed and expressed curiosity about Doug's sense of urgency, but was only told to be patient.

After he finished his conversation with Ray, Doug made reservations for dinner at the popular restaurant and then made reservations at the nearest hotel. He collected his bags and decided to go directly to Pirandello's and wait for Ray. In the taxi, he reflected on his latest visit to Germany, but his thoughts were interrupted by the shouts of the irate cab driver. As usual, traffic was congested and the middle-aged driver cursed and swore in Italian as he served in and out of the traffic lanes.

When Doug arrived at the restaurant, he found an empty seat at the crowded bar and ordered a rye and ginger-ale. Even before his drink was served, Doug began to attack the antipasto that the bartender put down in front of him. While he waited for Ray, he, again, tried to review the information he learned in Germany and tried to make them fit with the events that happened over the last several months.

Doug was deep in thought when a noisy group entered the restaurant and he glanced at the doorway to see what was going on. When he did, he was surprised to see a familiar face staring straight into his eyes. A few seconds elapsed before Doug was able to connect the face with the name. When he realized that it was Cardinal Brazini's nephew, the Vatican chauffeur, Doug quickly got up from his barstool and went over to the doorway to greet him. As he walked toward the door, a waiter with a dessert cart passed in front of him and cut him off. By the time his path to the doorway was free, the chauffeur was nowhere in sight.

Doug thought it was strange that Brazini's nephew didn't come over to say hello to him. He had been such a frequent visitor to the Vatican because of his work for Church, that he was sure that the young man recognized him. Doug unconsciously shrugged his shoulders and went back to the bar and was glad that his seat was not taken. The restaurant was filling up and when Ray arrived a few minutes later, Doug was glad to see him. The men shook hands and Doug ordered a round of drinks just as the maitre d' called his name for their table.

Both men enjoyed Pirandello's, not only for it's excellent food, but for the atmosphere. Reproductions of many of the famous Italian artists hung on every wall. A huge marble statue of Bacchus, the God of Wine, was appropriately positioned in the center of the floor, reminders of Italy's illustrious past.

"I'm glad we're in a corner," remarked Doug, "I feel like we have a little more privacy."

"I agree. "It's been a long three weeks for me. How was Germany?" asked Ray as he sipped his Bourbon.

"Actually, Ray, I'd prefer not to say too much about my trip while we're still in Rome," answered Doug cryptically eyeing the waiter who had approached the table to take their orders.

"What's with you? You're acting like you belong in a bad spy movie," commented Ray as soon as the waiter was out of sight.

"Very funny, Ray, but things are not as simple and safe as we make think. I'm afraid that we have to watch our backs and become suspicious of everyone. Aside from you, my son and Miriam, I am not about to trust anyone, especially here in Rome!" he remarked with a serious expression. "Oh, by the way, guess whom I just saw while I was sitting at the bar waiting for you?

"Who? Humphrey Bogart?" joked Ray. "You know, Doug, you're starting to get paranoid with all this spy stuff and I have to admit, you're starting to worry me."

"I'm not paranoid, I'm being cautious, there's a big difference!" retorted Doug. "I saw, what's his name? - the Vatican chauffeur, the one who's related to Brazini. Geez, I can never remember that guy's name!" said Doug shaking his head.

"Pietro Carzana? What the hell was he doing here? He left the Vatican before I did. He was on his way to the airport to pick up Bishop Collins. Are you sure, Doug? Maybe it was someone who just looked like Carzana."

"Look, Ray, I may be getting older, but I'm not totally gone, yet. I'm not very good at remembering names but I never forget a face. I know that it was Carzana, in fact, he had his chauffeur's uniform on. Now, that I think about it, I'm sure that he quickly high-tailed it out of here when he realized that I was coming over to talk to him. What do you make of it Ray?" inquired Doug.

"I don't really know what to think at this point, but you may be right. Things are getting pretty weird around the Vatican lately," commented Ray waiting until their salads were served before he continued. "When are you planning to leave Rome for the States?"

"As soon as possible. How about you?" asked Doug between mouthfuls.

"I'm ready to leave now. After dinner, I'll call the airport and make reservations. We'll be able to relax and talk in peace on the flight home. I can see that you're too nervous to make much sense while we're still in Rome. Where are you staying tonight?" asked Ray.

The hotel right near the airport. I'm in room 439. You can call me when you make the reservations and I'll take a taxi straight to the airport. Just say a novena that I arrive in one piece! These taxi-drivers are ruthless!" laughed Doug.

"Don't worry, I have an in with God!" joked Ray. "Are you staying at La Casa Roma, I know exactly where it is. I'll call you as soon as I make the reservations. Hopefully, we can get out of here within the next two days or so. By the way, have you spoken to Alex and Miriam lately?"

"Yeah, I phoned them just before I left Germany. They're doing fine. Alex bought Miriam a German Shepherd puppy and she named him Zak! I talked to her for a few minutes and she assured me that she feels wonderful and she's thrilled with her puppy. I hope the rest of her pregnancy goes as well. What a name for a dog!" exclaimed Doug.

"What's with you? You of all people should know that Zak is a great name for a German Shepherd since it's a Germanic name! Doug, are you slipping up or what?" teased Ray. "You know, I'm glad that Alex got a dog, not only for Miriam, but for himself. I had a German Shepherd when I was growing up in Berlin. Her name was Gretchen and she never left my side. I still miss that dog! They make excellent guard dogs. I wonder if that's what Alex had in mind when he bought her the puppy?" commented Ray.

"Touche, my friend, I guess Zak is a perfect name after all. You're right about German Shepherds making great guard dogs. I'll never forget when I was in Germany and I had the opportunity to watch the SS train Hitler's personal guard dogs. Believe me, I wouldn't ever want to tangle with one of them. You're probably right, Ray, Alex may be worried or just thinking ahead. I think it's a smart move. A guard dog is a good idea for both of them. Ah, finally, our dinner is here. I'm starved!" exclaimed Doug as the waiter served their meal.

"When they finished their demi-tasse, both men admitted to being tired and parted ways at the front of the restaurant. Ray took a cab back to the Vatican and Doug went to the hotel. It was after 10:00 PM and Doug realized that he was both mentally and physically exhausted. He quickly undressed for bed, got into his pajamas and began to go over his notes before getting into bed. Just as he reached over to turn out the light, the hotel phone rang. *"Ciau",* he greeted when he picked up the receiver. "Oh, Ray, it's you. Did you call the airport? Really? Tomorrow at 11:00 AM? That's sounds great to me. I can't wait to get home. Meet me by 8:30 and I'll spring for breakfast. There's a restaurant downstairs and the hotel is only about ten minutes from the airport. Great! I'll see you at 8:30 in the lobby. Good-night, Ray."

AUGUST 19, 1967 - 11:45 AM

"We're finally on our way home and I never thought I'd say this, but I'm really glad to be leaving Rome. You know, Doug, I never felt this way any other time that I was here, but this time there is so much tension and the undertones vibrating throughout the Vatican that I was a nervous-wreck the whole time. I need a relaxing fishing trip. First thing I'm going to do when I get back home, is call my favorite fishing buddy, Jim. I need a day on the creek!" commented Ray as he settled into his seat.

"I agree with you about getting home. I've traveled so much my entire life, that now, I really look forward to spending some quiet time at home. I can imagine that there is tension in the Vatican. You know, Cardinal Bachman has covered his tracks extremely well. In fact, he covered them so well, it's like he never existed," reported Doug.

"What do you mean? Are you saying that you can't find any traces of his real identity?"

"I searched the archives in Germany for the past three weeks and I found out that Rupert Bertram is listed as having committed suicide along with Hitler and his henchman. There were no known photographs taken of him during his adult life when he was a part of the Third Reich. He's one smart bastard, I have to give him credit for that." explained Doug.

"Well, did you find out anything about his past that will help us figure out this mess?" asked Ray impatiently.

"Will you keep quiet and let me finish?" admonished Doug. "The story gets better. The records clearly show that his fingerprints were documented by the Allies when they removed the bodies from the bunker. According to all of the official documents and records, Rupert Bertram died with Hitler on April 30, 1945.

"Damn it!" muttered Ray. "Does this mean that the search leads to a dead end?"

"You really are impatient, aren't you? I did manage to find a photo of Bertram from some old church records. He attended the St. Nicholas Catholic High School for boys and I found a class picture but unfortunately, the no good son-of-a-bitch was only twelve years old when it was taken. Before you think I made a mistake, don't forget that this guy is a really prodigy. He graduated from high school by the time he was twelve and according to the records, his scores in every subject were perfect!"

"Do you have the photo with you?" asked Ray excitedly.

"Yeah, but it's locked in my briefcase. I didn't want to take any chances. If you can sit still long enough, I'll show it to you as soon as we are settled in the States. The photograph is in black and white and

imprinted on a medal oval frame. I'm not sure that it'll
be much help, however, I know that it is Bertram. I can
never forget those cold light blue eyes. Those eyes
always reminded me of something diabolical and
whenever Bertram looked at me, I honestly felt as if my
soul became frozen." admitted Doug with a shiver.

"I agree, I'll never forget the first time I met him
in Berlin. He took his sunglasses off when we were
introduced and I couldn't help but stare because I've
never seen eyes like his before or since. Now, I know
why he wears those tinted glasses. They hide the fact
that his eye color is so unusual. What about your
meeting with him, how well did you actually know him
when you were in Germany for the Vatican?" inquired
Ray.

"I knew him well enough. I also found out
through some people in the underground that he was
doing top-secret genetic research exclusively for
Hitler." disclosed Doug. "I also heard that it had
something to do with cloning.

"Yeah, you mentioned that when we were in the
famous or should I say infamous Gravestone Inn, but to
be very honest, Doug, I really don't understand the
cloning procedure. Are you sure that he was involved
with this cloning stuff?" questioned Ray.

"Well, my sources told me that Bertram
discovered a scientific process that would enable him to
extract the DNA, the genetic blueprints of a person and
insert another's DNA into a fertilized cell. In this way,
by taking a sample of a person's DNA and injecting it
into a fertilized egg from which the original DNA has
been extracted, the result is an identical copy of the
DNA donor." explained Doug.

Doug continued as Ray sat quietly with a
confused expression. "According to what I found out,

Bertram never got the opportunity to try it on a human being, but he did have great success with his animal experiments."

"What the hell are you talking about? Is this even possible, let alone plausible?" asked Ray in a disbelieving tone. This sounds like something you just made up, Doug! I had a hard time understanding it when you first mentioned it and I still can't believe that anyone is capable of creating an identical human being!"

"Well, Ray, you know a lot about religion, but as a man of science, believe me when I tell you that the general public has no idea about what science has done and what it is capable of doing. This DNA transfer is entirely possible and really not that difficult if done under the proper conditions by someone who knows exactly what he's doing." retorted Doug.

"You mean someone who is a genius and an expert in genetics, like Bertram?" insinuated Ray.

"You said it, my friend. For someone like our buddy, the Cardinal, genetic transfer of the DNA would be a piece of cake. Just think about the possibilities. Or, better yet, don't think about them! It is truly frightening and he is a frightening man, Ray, certainly one who cannot be dealt with lightly. I'm really concerned about Miriam's pregnancy and as much as I hate to admit it, maybe it will be a blessing if we find out that she was raped in the Vatican rather than think of the other possibilities. It's going to take some real planning to figure out where we go from here. Can you meet with Alex and me in the very near future? I plan to call Alex as soon as we land and maybe we can set a date. What do you think?" asked Doug.

"Of course, I can. I may need a day or two to clear up some backed up appointments and paperwork but my valet, Father Ryan, is more than efficient. I'll be glad to do whatever I can to help you and Alex solve this whole mess, especially for Miriam's sake. I really feel for her and I hope and pray that she and Alex will be strong enough to get through whatever it is that we uncover," commented Pascal.

"I truly believe that Miriam is a special person in more ways than one. Although she doesn't appear to be strong physically, I think that she is a very strong and determined person mentally. I have a feeling that she'll need all the strength and stamina she can muster before this whole mess is settled," remarked Doug.

Ray agreed with his observations and listened as he continued.

"In any event, I know that Alex will protect her, support her and do whatever is in his power to keep her from any harm. Ray, I am literally exhausted, do you mind if I try to get some sleep? I know that you have some important information that you'd like to share, but in all honesty, I don't think I could assimilate any of it right now. The last few weeks have been so hectic, that I feel like a spinning top!" admitted Doug with a yawn.

Ray looked at his friend and could see the haggard look on his face, "Doug, you deserve a nice nap. I'll fill you in about the Vatican later. Put your seat back and try to sleep. If you snore too loudly, I'll plug up your nose!" laughed Ray as he handed him a pillow.

"Thanks, Ray, you're a true friend! Wake me up before we land."

Doug was sound asleep within a few minutes and once again, Ray was overcome by a strong need to pray for his friends.

SEVERAL HOURS LATER - IN PHILADELPHIA

"Doug, wake up! The plane is about to land. Fasten your seatbelt. You've been asleep for about three hours, in fact, I dozed for awhile, too. Do you feel better, now?" asked Ray.

"Yeah," yawned Doug. "I'm glad that I got a chance to sleep. I guess the trip to Germany really tired me out. I'm hungry. Let's stop and have dinner when we get out of the airport. Or, were you planning to drive back to Scranton tonight?"

"Actually, I'm thinking about waiting until tomorrow morning. I'm hungry, too and I know that after I eat, I'll be tool tired. Besides, I'd like to linger over dinner and discuss Germany and Rome and decide on the next step in dealing with Bachman. We also have to decide what and how to tell Alex. Where do you want to have dinner?" asked Ray.

"You know the Philadelphia area better than I do. Pick a place that has a good menu selection and one that is quiet so we can talk without being overheard or disturbed," suggested Doug.

"Well, if your stomach can wait, I'll drive into Medea because there are some good restaurants and hotels there. What do you think? Will you starve within the next hour or so?" joked Ray.

"I guess I can make it. I'll buy some cheese crackers and a candy bar in the airport to hold me over," said Doug.

"I still think you're the ninth wonder of the world because I can't figure out where you put all that food. You must have a super metabolism!" commented Ray.

"For one thing, I never sit in one place for too long, so I guess I do burn it up. In any case, eating is my favorite hobby. You get the bags and I'll get the snacks. I'll meet you by the front exit."

"Don't get lost, Doug, and hurry up!" called Ray as Doug was almost out of earshot.

Within an half hour, Doug and Ray were on their way out of the Philadelphia airport.

"This traffic is terrible. I'm glad you're driving because I'm sure that I'd get lost." commented Doug.

"I'm sure you would, too. I'm always amazed that you're able to travel all over the world and into the most remote parts of an area to dig for artifacts and you never bothered to learn to get around you own area. You were born around here, weren't you?" chuckled Ray.

"Yeah, I grew up in the Allentown area which isn't too far from Philadelphia. I just don't like to travel in traffic, I guess I'm much better in remote areas." admitted Doug.

"Well, isn't that coincidental. My fishing buddy, Jim, is from Allentown. He grew up in Wilkes-Barre which is only about twenty minutes outside of Scranton, but he moved to Allentown about seventeen years ago. Whenever he comes to visit his parents, he comes to visit or calls, usually to tell me how many fish he's caught!" said Ray.

"See it is a small world!" laughed Doug.

They arrived at the restaurant about an hour an a half later and after they ordered their meals, Doug handed Ray an old metal photograph.

"Here, I promised to show you the photograph of our friend, the Cardinal. What do you think? Can you pick him out of the class?" asked Doug as he handed it to Ray.

"I would bet my life that this is Bachman here. The third one from the left," indicated Ray pointing to a young boy who was much shorter than the others. "Not only is he the youngest looking one, but he's eyes are very similar to Michael's, don't you think? In fact, the resemblance is really quiet remarkable!" observed Ray.

"Oh, I won't argue with you, there, Ray. I totally agree and I don't think that anyone can deny the resemblance. However, it will be hard to prove beyond a reasonable doubt. I'm the only other person who knew him as an adult in Germany and it's his word against mine. After all, the kid in this photo is only twelve and Bachman should be between forty-four and forty-eight years old if are assumptions are correct," added Doug.

"If I were to guess, I'd say the age is about right. I remember when I went into Germany for him, he was only about my age, which surprised me because from what I was told l by the Cardinals, I did expect someone much older than twenty-four. That was about twenty-two years ago, so we can't be too far off. He looks much younger, don't you think?" asked Ray.

"Yeah, for all we know, though, this Nazi bastard has probably found the secret to eternal youth along with immortality!" remarked Doug sarcastically. "Don't laugh, Ray, I wouldn't put too much past his genius.

"You're probably right again, Doug, but the problem is, where do we go from here? We feel sure that this kid is Bertram or Bachman, but what good does it do us? This guy hasn't committed any crime that we can prove. By the way, you didn't steal this photograph, did you, Doug?" questioned Ray.

"No, Bishop, the priest at St. Nicholas church was willing to part with it when I offered them a hefty donation. Father Stukart did mention that many of the birth and death records were destroyed during the war, so, he didn't seem the least bit surprised that there were no other records found for Rupert Bertram. Actually, he was rather surprised that the photo was intact and kept in the files, especially since Bertram was so closely affiliated with Hitler. I guess you could say that the fact that it exists at all is really a stroke of luck!"

"More like a miracle, which in a way, is ironic. Think about this whole ordeal. We go from dealing with lost records and the Third Reich to the Catholic Church! Don't forget Doug, that the six most influential and powerful Cardinals were the ones who gave Bachman sanctuary in the Vatican! No one will ever convince me in a thousand years that those guys didn't really know what they were dealing with and who they were saving!" blurted Ray in anger. "I know one thing for sure, that even if some of the Cardinals were unaware of Bachman's true identity, Brazini knew all along. He was like a brick wall when I tried to get information out of him. In fact, the guy whom I thought was a dedicated man of God, turned out to be cold and vicious. He acted like our twenty-five year friendship never existed," exclaimed Ray, pausing for breath.

"Ray, calm down, don't get yourself sick over this. Besides, I need you to help me solve this thing!" said Doug trying to ease his friend's anger.

"Listen, Doug, I have to purge myself, if I don't I know I'll feel worse. You weren't there, so you have no idea how condescending this guy was. He indirectly let me know that I was only an American Bishop who was out of my league on his turf. I must say that not only was I shocked, but I was and still am very hurt."

"Did he give you any reason or satisfaction as to what is going on concerning Miriam's pregnancy? Is he aware that the poor girl is maintaining that she has no idea how this happened to her?" inquired Doug.

"Well, I didn't want you to get upset, but Cardinal Brazini's answer to Miriam's pregnancy is Alex. He claims that Alex is really the father of the child, but that he is refusing to admit it in order to save face, especially in lieu of his friendship with the Holy Father. However, Brazini is livid because he fears a lawsuit by Rebekah and David Sharone. And, along with Brazini's reaction, I had to deal with Bachman's snide remarks. He told me that all of this was total nonsense and that no one would ever believe that a Cardinal committed rape within the walls of the Vatican. I did catch the old boy in a lie, however," Ray paused to finish his dinner.

"Hurry up!" yelled Doug impatiently, "are you going to tell me the best part or not?"

"Chill out, Doug, you're always telling me that I'm impatient! Anyway, when I questioned Michael about his work on the Shroud, he told me that he hasn't done much testing on it for a long while. But, when I called my old friend, Bishop Taglia, who happens to be the Guardian of the Shroud of Turin, he told me a different story. Vincenzo told me that Michael has been working feverishly on the Shroud and is close to proving that the dried fluid on the cloth is actually blood! In other words, Doug, I didn't get too far inside the Vatican except it did make me realize that something is not kosher! No pun intended!" reported Ray.

"I'll say something's not kosher! Miriam's pregnancy for one thing, and the Cardinals' reaction for another. Brazini has a lot of nerve to slush off all the blame on my son. No wonder why Alex is so upset about this whole thing! And, why would Bachman deliberately lie about his research? Thank God that you do have some friends outside of the Vatican because

I'm beginning to get the feeling that we are dealing with much more than we originally thought. By the way, how did you ever get chosen to bring Bachman out of Germany?" inquired Doug.

"You know, I often wondered about it over the years, and at the time, I thought I was very blessed to be able to serve the Holy Father and the Cardinals. I was really flattered that Rome would even notice a small fry priest like me and that they would choose me to claim the Church's treasures. More importantly, I was really flattered that they entrusted me to save a man from Hitler's grip. As it turns out, I lived in Berlin until I was fifteen because my father had a government job and was stationed there. Just before things got really bad, my father requested a transfer back to the States. But while I lived there, my mom taught English to a group of kids from wealthy families. As a result, I learned to speak German if I wanted to communicate with my friends until they learned enough English! Anyway, before we left Berlin, I spoke German like a native Berliner!" recalled Ray.

"Alex did tell me that you spent some time in Germany, but I didn't realize that it was fifteen years!"

"Yeah, and my language ability along with my knowledge of the area and my youth and innocence made me the perfect patsy for the job! And, to think that for years I felt favored and special. Now, I realize how dangerous the whole mission really was. I was only a tool for their dirty work! They all knew how treacherous their scheme was, yet they were still willing to risk my life. The only thing I ever got out of it was a photograph, and of course, they eventually named me a Bishop," vented Ray in a tired tone.

"Don't get discouraged and don't feel bad, Ray. You did get to make some true friends out of the whole experience! You met Alex because of the Vatican and later, me, didn't you," commented Doug trying to cheer him up.

"Ah, yes, that is true! And, for truer friends, no man could ask! Now that I've purged myself, I guess it's time to figure out how to handle this mess from here. First of all, what do we tell Alex and when?"

"Well, I think the best thing we can do is to tell him everything. He's got to be prepared for the worst - between the baby and the Cardinals, especially Bachman. And, we have to meet with Alex as soon as possible. How's your schedule? Do you think you can get away this week?" asked Doug with a sense of urgency.

"I told you before that I'd be there for Alex. Let's call him after dinner and set a date. I'll check my calendar when I get back to the Chancellory tomorrow and I'll call you and we can set a definite date. Are you planning on dessert after that lobster dinner?" inquired Ray with an amazed look.

"Why do you ask stupid questions? Of course I'm going to have dessert! I'm partial to cheesecake. Do you want anything?"

"Are you kidding? I'll have to buy an extra large cassock! I'll just have coffee. Am I safe in assuming that you know that Gluttony is one of the seven Deadly Cardinal Sins?" teased Ray.

"You know, I really think that you've been hanging around me too long. Your puns are getting worse than mine, Bishop! It's not gluttony, I do stop eating when I'm full," chuckled Doug as he gave the waiter his dessert order.

"Whatever you say, but I still think that you can pack an amazing amount of food into that body. But, Doug, something has been bothering me all evening," said Ray getting very serious. "How are we going to prove to anyone that Cardinal Michael Bachman is really a former Nazi scientist and that he's true identity is Dr. Rupert Bertram?"

Doug looked at Ray and didn't answer for a few seconds, "Ray, that's not our biggest worry right now. Let's hypothetically assume that Miriam wasn't raped and that Bachman has perfected the cloning process. The logical question is, just who is that bastard really working for? The Church or the Third Reich? The follow-up question is, if he did perfect the cloning process, did he have enough time to perform the DNA transfer while Miriam was in the Vatican infirmary?"

Ray turned pale as he stared at Doug, "Oh my God, now I realize why I felt so uneasy after interviewing the old nun. I'm sure that he had time, Doug, because there was a time-span of about two hours from when the nun claims that she entered the room at 9:45 PM and when Alex told me that Miriam was taken into the infirmary at about 8:00 PM. The old nun also said that Bachman and Dr. Ansilio were behind the closed curtain for about fifteen minutes after she came into the room. Do you think they could have had time to do this cloning thing?"

"From what we've learned about Bachman's abilities so far, and from the fact that he had the help of another doctor, I'd say that there was plenty of time! Remember, Ray, all of this must have been planned well in advance because Brazini was very eager to get Miriam into the Vatican. In fact, you were the one who helped to get her there, weren't you?" asked Doug.

"Thanks for reminding me, but wait a minute, I almost forgot something!" exclaimed Ray as he pulled his notebook out of his briefcase. "The nun specifically mentioned that Bachman had several vials of blood in his hand when he left the room and that Dr. Ansilio was carrying a syringe with a long thin needle.   I kept forgetting to ask you or Alex what kind of test would require a syringe like that. Do you have any ideas?"

"Are you positive that she described the syringe the right way?"

"Yeah, listen to my notes," instructed Ray as he read them back to Doug.

"Dear God, Ray, he must have used that syringe to extract and replace Miriam's egg after he injected the DNA into it! But, who's DNA was it?" asked Doug visibly upset.

"Well, it seems to me that we've already narrowed it down to two possibilities when we discussed this at the Gravestone Inn, namely Christ or Hitler! I'm telling you, Doug, that I can't begin to imagine the repercussions from either choice," moaned Ray, shaking his head.

"Right now, my biggest concern is how to tell Alex what we actually suspect. He's convinced that Miriam was raped and I really believe that he's blocked out any insinuations that were mentioned in the Gravestone that night. The poor guy will be devastated!" worried Doug.

"Not only do we have to tell Alex, but how do we convince others that what Bachman has possibly done will change the world, and the way I see it, not for the better! Doug, how does a geneticist actually extract the DNA, I mean, what does he need to get the DNA?" asked Ray perplexed.

"All he'd need is a blood sample, why?"

"Would dry blood work or do you think it has to be fresh blood?" inquired Ray.

"I'm not really sure, Ray, please remember that I'm not a medical doctor, I only know as much as I do about genetic testing and cloning from my work in archaeology and from my own reading interests. But, I guess blood is blood. I guarantee that I'll find out as soon as possible." assured Doug.

"Remember what Bishop Taglia told me. Bachman is close to proving that the dried fluid on the Shroud is really blood!" exclaimed Ray.

Doug's face registered the shock that he felt, but he managed to ask, "Wait, Ray, if Bachman did clone Christ, are you saying that having Christ on earth again will be a bad thing? I'm surprised, Ray, a man of the cloth and you have such a negative attitude!" remarked Doug seriously.

"Doug, are you Bible illiterate or what? Haven't you read the Book of Revelations? The apocalyptic message states that the Parousia will occur at the end of the world. Michael may have unleashed someone or something that he is not ready to bargain with. I don't think I'm ready to deal with this!" admitted Ray.

"Ah, yes, Parousia. Greek for the Second Coming. I certainly do remember the Book of Revelations and the predictions of what is to happen before Christ returns to earth. Eschatology has always fascinated me, but Ray, do you honestly believe that the Rapture and the 'Little Season' are really going to come to pass?" questioned Doug.

"I honestly believe in the Rapture because I know that those who have lived a good life will be rewarded. As for the idea of the 'Little Season,' or 'Satan unchained,' it has been equated with a time of prosperity before Christ comes again. The question is, do we look at the events today as coincidences or as actual signs of the coming of the end? Look around at the world today. We are in a time of prosperity as the world-wide economy is fairly stable, but there are some awful things that are happening in the world, too. Are they the prophesized signs from God, or are they mere coincidences? Think of the wars, the political and social unrest, the so-called freaks of nature like the famines, the droughts, and the untreatable diseases of epidemic proportions, just to mention a few occurrences. According to the scandal sheets at the newsstands, the end of the world is just around the corner. I guess what I'm trying to say, is that much of it is hype, but much of it can also be interpreted as the signs predicted for the Parousia in the Book of Revelations. All I know for sure is what I feel and my instincts tell me that Michael Bachman is an evil man and we must do whatever we can to stop him," preached Ray in a weak voice.

"But, Ray, how can we stop a pregnancy, except to abort the child," asked Doug pragmatically.

"We can't kill the child! It would be murder! Good Lord, Doug, I just don't know, but maybe all of this is happening because it is exactly what God had intended all along," whispered the Bishop in a frightened tone.

**MANY A TIME I HAVE WANTED TO STOP
TALKING AND FIND OUT WHAT I REALLY
BELIEVE.** Walter Lippmann

CHAPTER XXIII

AUGUST 20, 1967

When Doug and Ray arrived in Scranton the next
day, they called Alex before Doug left for home.

"Alex, it's Dad, how are you and Miriam?"

"Dad, I'm really happy to hear your voice! We're
both fine, but how are you? You sound exhausted!"

"I am son, but I'm also happy to be back in the
States. I need you to listen carefully, Alex and try to
follow the conversation. Do you remember the
restaurant where we had dinner shortly after you
moved?"

"Of course I remember, why Dad, don't you?"
asked Alex, worried that his father's memory was
failing.

"Alex, don't mention the name of the place, just
go there in a half hour and I'll call you there. Please
don't ask me a lot of questions right now, just do what I
tell you and wait for my call," instructed Doug.

"O.K., Dad, but are you alright?" asked Alex
anxiously.

"I'm fine, get going, will you! I'll talk to you
soon."

Thirty minutes later, Alex arrived at the Loire
Valley Restaurant and waited nervously at the bar. He

father got himself into this time. Ten minutes elapsed and it seemed like an eternity. When the phone rang and the bartender called his name, Alex almost jumped. He motioned to the bartender who handed him the receiver.

"Dad? What the hell is going on? Why all the secret service stuff? You have me worried! Are you in trouble?"

"Sorry Alex, I know that you don't need anymore stress right now, but after what Ray and I found out, we can't be too cautious. Ray's here now and we're calling from a pay phone because neither one of us trust anything or anyone but each other and you at the moment."

"Well, are you going to tell me what's going on, or not?"

"Actually, not! I can't tell you anything over the phone, but I'll be around to see you within the next week or so. In the meantime, I think you and Miriam should leave the cottage and find another place to live. In fact, I strongly urge you to move as soon as possible. Maybe you can try the area where we went fishing several times, you know, the place where I caught the big Rainbow. Are you following me?" asked Doug cryptically.

"Yeah, Dad, I know exactly where you mean and I also know that you're scaring the hell out of me. Is it really as bad as you're insinuating?" asked Alex looking around the bar nervously.

"Believe me, Alex, I would never put you and Miriam through all of this if I didn't think that it was urgent and necessary. When you move, try hard not to leave any kind of trail. Just take the bare necessities and get out of there as soon as you can. I'll leave a number where you can reach me and only use a pay number where you can reach me and only use a pay phone to call. I'm not sure what you should tell Miriam about all of this, but I'll leave it to your good judgement. Maybe you can tell her that it's something to do with work. In the meantime, keep her calm," suggested Doug.

"Dad, stop!" exclaimed Alex louder than he realized. He noticed that several people seated at the bar were staring at him. He lowered his voice to a whisper, "Is all of this really necessary, or are you and Ray just becoming paranoid?"

"Alex, you can think what you want, but in the meantime, follow my directions if you value Miriam's well being and your own! I hope to see you in a few days and I'll explain everything. Maybe you should use your mother's maiden name for any legal transactions. You can tell Miriam that it's for work purposes and has something to do with discovery laws. I've got to go now, but I'll be waiting to hear from you. The telephone number is 555-987-4063, leave a message and a number for me and I'll call you back within five minutes. I love you, son. Give my love to Miriam and please, be careful," warned Doug.

ONE WEEK LATER - AUG. 27, 1967

Alex dialed the number that his father had given him. He left the number of the pay phone, hung up and waited. While he waited, he thought about the past week and about how hectic the move was. He thought of Miriam and how patient she was despite the secrecy. For some reason, Alex always had the feeling that she was very much aware of what was going on even though she didn't talk about it. Within five minutes, the shrill ring of the phone brought him back to the present. Alex answered and when he was sure that it was his father, he asked, "Dad, what the hell is going on? When are you going to be here?"

"Whoa, hold on a minute. Let me catch my breath. How's Miriam, did she ask a lot of questions? I hope the move wasn't too much for her condition."

"Miriam is fine, Dad, she's not a porcelain doll, in fact, she' tough. She's a bit tired right now, but she's resting and Zak is in his normal spot, right at her feet. We found a great place on the Muncy and it's completely furnished and it's much larger than the cottage we had. I know you'll like it, but now, I want to hear your story, Dad."

"Alex, I'd feel a lot better telling you all of this in person. Do you remember the little General Store near the Splash Dam On Covered Bridge Road?"

"How could I could I ever forget it when it's on a road with a name like that?"

"Can you meet me there on Monday at 1:00?" asked Doug.

"Sure, Dad, should I bring my fishing pole?"

"You know, Alex, that sometimes you ask stupid questions," quipped Doug. "I know I'll have mine with me and I'm not letting you use it, so I guess you'd better bring yours! What about Miriam, will she be alright if she's alone?"

"She won't be alone, our neighbors, Joe and Andrea Perrins, are great! Andrea is also expecting a baby in January, so she and Miriam have a lot in common. In fact, they've been talking about a shopping trip so that they could look for baby things. I'll offer to drop them off at the local shopping center for a few

"That's sounds like a good plan and I'm glad that Miriam won't be alone. By the way, how's that dog, what's his name working out?"

"Zak, Dad, and he's working out just fine. Miriam loves him and he feels the same way about her. They're inseparable! Miriam claims that he understands everything she tells him. Getting Zak was a good idea because it makes both of us feel more secure, especially living in a remote area like this."

"I agree. Listen, I've got to go, someone wants to use the phone. Just remember, Monday at 1:00 on Splash Dam On Covered Bridge Road. See you then, son."

MONDAY, AUG. 30, 1967 - THE GENERAL STORE

"Hey, Doc, how ya bin?" yelled Willard Jones when he spotted Doug at the doorway. "Don't tell me ya brung yar kid witchya? I ain't seen him since about two years or so! How ya bin, Alex boy?" The heavy set old man grabbed Alex's hand in a tight grip and shook it vigorously.

"Hey Willard, great to see you again. We decided to take a break from digging up bones and we want to try our luck on the creek. How're they biting today?" smiled Alex through the pain from the old man's vice-like grip.

"They're jest 'bout jumpin' inta the creels! There's a ton of Natives in this here crick, but I ain't tellin you boys nothin' new. You two guys're old pros. 'Member that there big Rainbow ya caught the las time you was here, Doc, didya ever get that beauty mounted?"

that there big Rainbow ya caught the las time you was here, Doc, didya ever get that beauty mounted?"

"As a matter of fact, I did and you're right, that was the last time Alex and I were fishing here together. I think that you'll be seeing a lot more of us though. How'd you like that, Willard?" laughed Doug as he checked out the bait in the old refrigerator.

"Hey, sounds good ta me. You boy're good customers and good frien's. Anythin' ya need, ya jest hafta yell fer ole Willard. If I cain't take care o' ya, I know somebody who can. What kinda bait ya boys lookin' fer? How 'bout some grubs? The guys on the crick says that them there Natives are goin' fer 'em like candy!" yelled Willard throwing his arms around as he talked. "Hey, youse guys hungry? The Mrs. jest put together some fresh hoagies, only $1.99 each, and they're loaded wit meat! Whadda think: Kin I sell ya two?" asked Willard with a big smile.

"Umm, fresh hoagies, I remember your wife's hoagies. They are the best I've ever tasted! Better give me two, what do you want, Alex? asked Doug.

"Dad, those things are huge! Just one for me, Willard, but you'd better throw in a six-pack of soda and a big bag of chips. We don't want Dad to starve on the creek!" laughed Alex as he gave Willard the order.

"Comin' right up, boy and I'll git ya yer bait, too. Need anythin' else?"

"Yeah, Willard, do you have a map of this area?" asked Alex.

"Sure do, I'll even throw it in for nothin' 'cause I like youse guys!" chuckled the old man.

"Thanks Willard, we'll be seeing you again real soon. Tell the Mrs. we sent our best! You take care of yourself," said Doug as he and Alex started walking toward the car.

"Why did you want a map, Alex?" asked Doug.

"To tell you the truth, Dad, you've got me so paranoid that I figured I should play it safe and become familiar with all of the roads in case I have to high tail it out of here."

"You know, you're a smart guy, you must take after your father," quipped Doug chuckling to himself.

"O.K., Dad, enough beating around the bush. What gives? Tell me the whole story from beginning to end. I need to know what's going on," demanded Alex impatiently.

"Well, Alex, it's a mess and it looks like we're up against something that doesn't seem possible, but here goes. According to German WW II archives, Rupert Bertram committed suicide with Hitler in his bunker on April 30, 1947, just after the Allies were entering Berlin. According to the records, Bertram's body was later identified from the dental charts that were found in the school files. Unfortunately, it seems as though everything about Rupert Bertram died with him and his boss, Hitler on that fateful day. But, you know me, I continued to dig and found an old priest, Father Stukart from St. Nicholas Church in Bonn. The old guy had some records stored away in the church basement and as it turns out, Bertram graduated from St. Nicholas High School, at the age of twelve, no less! So you were right on target when you said that you were impressed with his intellect the first time you met him. From the evidence, Bertram is a genius, especially in genetics, but I'm getting ahead of myself. I managed to donate a decent sum of money to Father Stukart's church renovation fund and he let me have this picture. Here, what do you think? Can you see any resemblance to our Cardinal Bachman?" asked Doug as he handed the old photo to Alex.

"Geez, it's not hard to pick out a twelve year old among seventeen and eighteen year olds, but Dad, look at those eyes! They are definitely Michael's eyes! You really can't mistake them, very light colored and cold as ice!" exclaimed Alex as he handed the picture back to his father. "Did you show it to Ray, and if so, what does he think about all of this?"

"Slow down, son! Yes, I did show it to Ray and he believes that the kid in the photograph is Bachman, too. He has his own news to tell you about his trip to Rome. But first, let me finish. Not only did I manage to dig up this photograph, but I continued searching through as many old library records and medical records that I could find. Actually, I was surprised that any records of the experiments still existed, especially after the bombings and pillages that went on after the Third Reich fell. I did manage to discover that our Dr. Rupert Bertram was doing some heavy duty research in cloning. Apparently the plan was to save the DNA from Hitler so that he could be cloned at a later date. Bertram, I guess, became obsessed with the fact that he could play God and create another human being, especially one as charismatic and powerful as Hitler. The dumb bastard obviously believed whole-heartedly in Hitler's master race and master plan to rule the world," reported Doug as he glanced at Alex.

"Alex!" yelled Doug, "are you alright? You don't look so good, in fact, you look like you're going to faint! Come and sit down on this big rock over here. I'll open a can of soda for you. Here, have a few sips, you'll feel better!" rambled Doug with a worried look.

"Dad, calm down and stop hovering over me like a wet hen. I just can't believe that what we suspected maybe true! I guess I knew it could be possible, but I tried hard to convince myself that it was just a farfetched idea. Oh, Christ, what the hell am I going to do with Miriam and this baby? Nobody is going to tell me that Miriam's baby is an ordinary child! But, who is it?"

"I wish I could give you an answer, Alex, but I don't know what to think myself," responded Doug shaking his head and feeling badly for his son.

"When we met Ray in the Gravestone that night, I was sure that Bertram was trying to resurrect Christ because of his research on the Shroud of Turin, but after hearing what you found out in Germany, I just don't know! I'm scared to death that that genius bastard might be crazy enough to resurrect the devil himself! Dad, what the hell am I going to do? Do you honestly think that Bertram brought Hitler's DNA out of Germany when he came to Rome with Pascal? My God! What are we going to do?" mumbled Alex as he held his head in his hands.

"Alex, stop! We have to keep our heads clear if we want to get to the truth and stop this lunatic from doing anything else!" yelled Doug, trying to snap Alex out of his mood. "Let's try to figure this whole thing through. I still have friends in Germany who will continue to dig for me and hopefully, come up with some survivor who may have known Bertram during his heyday. Believe me, Alex, if Bertram or Bachman is the man we think he is, you and Miriam are in great danger!"

"Gee, Dad, thanks for telling me something I don't already know!" answered Alex sarcastically.

"Well, I'm just trying to put things in perspective, but one thing still bothers me. Bertram is a genius, a perfectionist and a Nazi, so there must be a reason why he and the Cardinals insisted on Miriam as their choice for carrying this child. Why would he choose her, a

185

young Jewish woman, to bear the clone of Hitler? And, if he has impregnated Miriam with Hitler's DNA, you can be sure that he's not going to let her out of his sight for too much longer. The baby will be born sometime in December which doesn't give us much time to figure out a plan. These 'Princes of the Church' are smart and powerful men. If I were you, I wouldn't trust them or anyone else for that matter. We really don't know what length they'll go through to find the child once it is born," said Doug in a serious tone.

"Dad, I hope I have the brains and the stamina to sort through all of this, especially for Miriam's sake. Even though I don't understand what happened to her, Miriam is excited about the baby. I just don't know how or what to tell her. Do you have any suggestions?" asked Alex with an anguished look.

"I wish I had an easy answer for you, but before I forget, remember one of Hitler's parents was of Jewish decent. For right now, Ray and I feel that the less you tell Miriam in her condition, the better off she'll be. I know it'll be difficult for you, but until we know the truth, it's probably best to say as little as possible. Besides, how can we explain everything to her when we don't know ourselves? I know this is easier said than done, but you can't make yourself crazy with this whole thing. Try to relax, Alex, things usually have a way of working out," advised Doug patting his son's shoulder.

"Speaking of Ray, what did he find out in Italy?"

"To be honest, he didn't come up with too much more, only some gut feelings and conjecture. He was very upset with the way Cardinal Brazini treated him during his stay at the Vatican. You know that up to this point, Ray and Brazini had a good relationship," reported Doug.

"What happened to change it?"

"Ray told me that when he tried to question Brazini about Miriam's pregnancy and about the Shroud of Turin, Brazini turned on him and became infuriated. Ray said that it scared the hell out of him when he saw how quickly Brazini's anger surfaced when Ray probed for an answer and he was even more surprised at the change in Brazini's demeanor. Brazini informed Ray never to question him about anything, especially about things that don't concern him. Brazini very curtly reminded Ray that he is only a mere Bishop and Ray's power in the Church will never compare to his or the other Cardinals. Needless to say, Ray was shocked and hurt by Brazini's cold and hostile treatment and he also said that the tension among all the Cardinals was unbelievable," reported Doug.

"Hell, I feel bad for Ray. He's always been faithful to the Vatican and the Church in general. It always amazes me that people could treat others so badly in the name of religion. Is Ray still planning to meet with us so we can discuss our next step?"

"Yeah, and he's also going to get in touch with Miriam's parents and her Rabbi and explain why its necessary for you to stay isolated, at least until the baby is born. He did mention that Brazini was very interested in whether or not he knew where you and Miriam are now. That's what convinced Ray and me that the both of you must stay out of sight for awhile."

"Well now, it's beginning to make more sense and it probably is the best thing especially after what you've told me. At least we're happy here, it's so quiet and peaceful and Miriam is content to spend time with her new friend, Andrea, and her husband, Joe. He's made a great fishing buddy for me, " said Alex.

"I'm glad that Miriam likes this area, you always did when you were a kid. By the way, since I'm semi-retired, I've been thinking about settling down. Maybe I'll buy a lot and build a small house around here, what do you think? It'll give us more time to spend together and I'd get to know Miriam better. And, when the baby is born, I can spend time with him or her. You'd get free babysitting!"

"You know, Dad, every once in awhile, you come up with a good idea. I'd feel very comfortable having you nearby and I'm sure Miriam will, too. She really cares a lot for you, Dad, and she needs someone especially now since her father is still keeping his distance. It'll also help to take the strain off my shoulders whenever I have to make a trip to the dig site. Miriam won't be able to come with me because of her condition and I still have an obligation to the staff at Qumran. I'm lucky to have Linda and the rest of my crew because they're well trained and get along well. Never the less, I still have to go back to the site to check the artifacts before they're shipped to Rome. If you're nearby, it'll be much easier on both Miriam and me."

"Then it's settled, I'm going to check out a piece of land I saw near your place. There's a small cabin on it that needs some renovations, but I know that old Willard will find someone to help and when you get back, I can put you to work, too," said Doug smiling.

"No rest for the wicked, huh Dad?" laughed Alex as he cast his line into the swift moving creek.

NOVEMBER 28, 1967 - THANKSGIVING DAY

"What a meal!" exclaimed Doug, "I'll have to loosen my belt. Heck, Miriam, I probably look as pregnant as you do!"

"Gee, thanks, Dad, but I think that my stomach is still bigger than yours, even after that meal. In fact, I not only feel like a beached whale, I feel like I've been pregnant forever!" laughed Miriam.

"Actually, you look great!" remarked Alex as he hugged her. "The only problem is, you're not as close as you used to be when I hug you!"

"Thanks honey, but after that smart remark, you and your dad can do the dishes. I think I'd better sit down and put my feet up for awhile. My ankles no longer look like ankles! They are so swollen that my shoes look like they're ready to burst," answered Miriam as she headed for the recliner.

"No problem, my lady, we shall do your bidding. Dad, you dry and I'll wash," directed Alex as he threw him a towel.

"Why do I always have to dry? I'd rather wash," complained Doug.

"No way, Dad! We need some dishes for tomorrow. You have a knack for breaking three or four dishes or glasses per wash cycle," quipped Alex heading for the kitchen.

Zak sat at Miriam's feet while she rested and about an hour later, Doug and Alex finished the dishes and came into the dining room with dessert.

"Honey, do you want a piece of apple or pumpkin?" asked Alex as he juggled the pies and plates.

"'Umm, maybe I'll try a tiny piece of each. What the heck, I can't get much bigger than I am!" she laughed.

"That's a great idea!" said Doug. "I'll have the same, only don't make my pieces too tiny! Who made the pies? The look delicious!"

"Mrs. Jones, Willard's wife., sent them over with her grandson yesterday. She's quite a character and she's been a great help to Miriam. She worries about her and makes sure that Miriam is alright."

"I agree, she and old Willard are the cream of the crop. They would do anything to help someone out," remarked Doug as he filled his plate with a chunk of each kind of pie. He sat down next to Miriam and asked, "Have you two decided on a name for the baby, yet?"

"As a matter of fact, we tried a few names, but the one we both like is Nathan. I'm partial to it because it means 'Gift of God' which is more than fitting for him, don't you think? I mean under the circumstances and all," Miriam asked Doug.

"Nathan? That's a nice name, but how do you know it's going to be a boy? What are you going to do if it turns out to be a 'she'?" teased Doug.

"Well, we did the old-fashioned wedding ring test that Mrs. Jones showed us and every time we did it, the results come up with a boy," said Alex.

"Spoken like a true man of science, don't you think, Miriam?" joked Doug.

"Actually, Dad, I've had several strange dreams and I just know from these dreams and from my intuition that this baby is going to be a 'Nathan'," responded Miriam with a content look.

"Oh, more scientific proof?" exclaimed Doug.

"By the way, Dad, did we tell you that we're planning on having the baby at home?" questioned Miriam.

"What? Are you serious? You want to have this baby here? What's wrong with doing it the normal way, in the hospital? What if there are complications! I don't think it's a very safe idea!" rambled Doug getting upset.

"Relax, Dad, the doctor will be here to deliver the baby. It's nothing that hasn't been done before. Miriam said that she'll feel more comfortable here and I can't blame her. Andrea and Mrs. Jones are nearby to help and Dr. Riofsky is only twenty minutes away. It's not going to happen that quickly," admonished Alex. "The doctor told us that it is rare to have a first baby be born very quickly."

"He's right, Dad, I'll be fine. A lot of woman have midwives deliver their babies. I'm going to have an obstetrician here. I'm sure that Dr. Riofsky will be fully prepared and I know that I'll be much more relaxed at home," added Miriam.

"I can see that I'm outvoted, so I guess I have no choice but to agree with the set-up, but I'll still be worried. What about the weather? Have you two heard the latest weather report? The guy on Channel 16 is predicting about four feet of snow for this weekend. Looks like we're going to get hit with a real blizzard. You know, this weather has been crazy lately. What if the doctor can't get here?" questioned Doug nervously.

"Dad, will you chill out? The doctor has a jeep and he can get here in almost any kind of weather and besides, Miriam's due date is not until next week!" added Alex.

"Well, it's not that far away. Sometimes babies decide to come early, just like you did! Two weeks early, by the way!" disclosed Doug.

"Relax, Dad, eat your pie and drink your coffee before it gets cold," advised Alex trying to change the subject.

**LIFE IS A FLAME THAT IS ALWAYS BURNING
ITSELF OUT, BUT CATCHES FIRE AGAIN
EVERYTIME A CHILD IS BORN.   G.B. Shaw**

CHAPTER XXIV

DECEMBER 16, 1967

Miriam awoke with a feeling of dread. She slowly
became aware of the absolute silence. As she became
fully awake, Miriam realized that she was drenched
from perspiration and her skin felt as if it was on fire.
She sat up and tried to remember her nightmare and
without warning, the pain hit. She gasped and felt as
though she couldn't catch her breath. Then she realized,
she was in labor! She looked at the clock and
remembered that she was supposed to time the pains.
Another one hit and then she felt the baby kick. "The
last pain was only ten minutes ago," she thought. She
got out of bed to get a drink of water and as she walked
into the bathroom, Miriam felt something trickling
down her legs. "Oh, my God, my water just broke!"
she said to herself out loud. She grabbed some heavy
towels, drank a glass of water, and headed back to the
bed. Another pain hit. Only seven minutes apart.
Miriam realized that it was going much quicker than it
should and she knew that she should not wait much
longer. Miriam roughly shook Alex from a dead sleep,
"Honey wake up! It's time! Wake up, Alex, the baby's
coming!" shouted Miriam with panic in her voice.

"What? What time is it?" Alex asked in a groggy voice.

"Three thirty in the morning. I think you'd better call Dr. Riofsky and make it quick. Then, call your dad," instructed Miriam.

"What do you mean? The doctor told me that with a first baby, there's no urgency. We should have plenty of time."

"Listen, Alex, the pains are getting worse and coming faster! My water just broke and I feel tremendous pressure to push! This is my first baby and I'm telling you that you're going to have to deliver him! He's not going to wait much longer! Stop sitting there arguing with me, call the doctor!" she ordered in a desperate voice as another pain hit.

"I'm already dialing! Dr. Riofsky, it's Alex Stewart. I think the baby is coming! Can you get here soon? How soon? Please hurry, Miriam feels like she has to push!"

"He'll be here within fifteen or twenty minutes, Miriam. He said you should just breathe with the pain and try to rest and relax in between the contractions. Do you want me to do anything for you?" asked Alex feeling helpless.

"Oh, yes, please rub my back, it's killing me! Did you call your father, yet?"

"Yes, he told me that it's snowing like crazy. He said that there's close to a foot on the ground already. I hope to hell that the doctor gets here soon."

"Well, so do I! Oh, God, Alex, I really have to push! The pressure is getting worse. What should I do?" panted Miriam through the pain.

"I have no idea! Oh my God, just don't push yet! I forgot everything that we went over with the doctor!

Do you remember anything?" he asked close to hysteria.

"Stop babbling! I feel like have to push! Oh, the pain is unbelievable," cried Miriam, "Do something!"

"Oh God, Miriam, I don't know what to do! Just hold on, honey, Zak is going crazy! Someone is here and I hope to hell that it's the doctor! Stay calm and breathe, I'm just going to open the door and I'll be right back!"

"Oh, damn it, it's only you, Dad, but I'm glad you're here! Hurry up!" yelled Alex as he closed the door behind his father.

"Gee, I'm glad to see you too, son, the weather is terrible! But you don't seem too excited to see me, what's the rush?"

"Dad, Miriam is ready to have the baby! I've got to get back in there! Do you know what to do? The doctor isn't here yet!" shouted Alex as he ran into the bedroom to help Miriam.

"Good grief, Alex, how would I know what to do? When you were born, they wouldn't let me near the delivery room. I guess I should boil some water or something. I tried telling you that this was a bad idea! Where the hell is that doctor? Are you sure you remembered to call him?"

"Of course I called him, Dad, you're starting to ramble. Just stay calm and get me some towels from the bathroom," ordered Alex as he heard Miriam's urgent call.

"Oh no! The baby's head is out! Dad! Hurry with those towels!" shouted Alex.

"Zak is going nuts again! The doctor must be here! Thank God! Dad, give me those towels and go and open the door!"

"Hurry up, Doc, the baby isn't bothering to wait for you," remarked Doug as he opened the front door.

"Sorry, but I was held up because of the weather. Move out of the way, Alex. Miriam, hang on dear, the baby is almost here. Give a good hard push! Good, good! Take a deep breath and push again! His shoulders are almost out! Great! Relax and take a deep breath! Alex, get me more towels! A deep breath, Miriam and one more good push! Ah, he's here! And, it is a he! Miriam, dear, you have a beautiful baby boy! Congratulations! Now, relax a minute while I cut the cord," instructed the doctor.

"Oh, thank God you got here when you did! I couldn't hold out a minute longer! Let me see my son!" whispered Miriam in an exhausted voice.

"I did it!" shouted Alex. "The baby's here and it's a boy, Dad!"

"What the heck are you yelling about? You didn't do anything! Miriam's the one who had the baby!" laughed Doug.

"Honey, are you alright? Isn't it wonderful?" asked Alex tearfully.

"Oh, Alex, he is beautiful, isn't he? Thank you for being you and for helping me. I'm just so glad that it's all over! I'm really tired, but I want you to know that you did a great job. I didn't think he'd be born so quickly, did you?" asked Miriam softly as she looked at her crying baby son.

"No, I thought we'd have a few hours at least. But, to be truthful, I don't think I could've lasted much longer," admitted Alex seriously.

"Well, you were wonderful, Honey. Did the doctor check the baby, yet? Is he alright?" Miriam asked worried. "I don't hear him crying."

"He's fine, Honey, relax, he's not crying because he's sound asleep. I guess he's tired out, too. As soon as the doctor finishes checking you, you should try to get some sleep. I'll get the doctor and my dad something to eat and drink and later, when you're rested, we'll give your parents a call. Don't forget it's only about 6:15 AM, so they're probably still sound asleep. Here, Honey, drink some water and try to rest awhile. We'll listen for the baby," he said as he leaned into the bassinet to kiss the baby's head. "I love you, Miriam, you were wonderful and our son is beautiful!

"I love you, too, Alex, more than you'll ever know. I'll call you when I wake up. Will the doctor stay here for awhile?" she asked in a sleepy voice.

"I'll make sure that he does, and if I don't, this weather will. The baby sure picked a heck of a time to arrive. There's more than a foot and a half of snow on the ground. We're having a real blizzard!" said Alex smiling at the sleeping baby. When he looked over at Miriam, he saw that she was sound asleep, too.

About an hour later, Alex heard the baby crying. He went into the bedroom and called the doctor before he gently woke Miriam. "Honey, the baby's hungry, I think, anyway, he's crying. The doctor's coming in to get him out of the bassinet. I don't know how to pick him up!" admitted Alex sheepishly.

Doctor Riofsky and Doug walked into the room and saw the look of panic on Alex's face as he stood over the bassinet.

"What's wrong, Pop, don't you know how to pick him up?" laughed the doctor as he saw Alex. "Come here, this is your first lesson in fatherhood. Put your hand underneath his head and the other one underneath his body and pick him up. He won't break, just remember to always support his head and neck," instructed Dr. Riofsky.

"Are you sure that I'm ready for this?" asked Alex, pale and nervous.

"Alex, stop being so afraid. I used to pick you up and I knew less than you do. Besides, I never dropped you, that I can remember, anyway," remarked Doug thoughtfully.

"Thanks for those encouraging words, Dad. I guess I'll get the hang of this. Here, Honey, here's our son and it sounds like he's really hungry. The doctor said that he'll help you to get started with the nursing. We'll leave you alone so that you can relax. Call us when you're finished feeding him. Wow! He sure is a big, handsome baby, isn't he, Doc?"

"I'd say he weighs close to eight pounds. He looks like a very healthy baby boy to me. Listen, while I get Miriam started on the nursing procedures, you guys clean off the table and find a deck of cards. When I checked last, the snow was coming down harder than before, so it looks as though I'll be camping here tonight," stated Dr. Riofsky.

"That's O.K. with us, Doc, we'll get the card table ready. You just take care of my beautiful wife and son," he said as he kissed Miriam's cheek and then, kissed the baby's head.

"He really is beautiful, Miriam, Alex was all red and wrinkly when I first saw him. But Nathan is just smooth and rosy. Try to rest for now, I'll be in again when you finish feeding the baby," said Doug as he kissed his daughter-in-law's cheek.

'Thanks guys, I really appreciate all you've done! Both of you were very brave! I'm so glad that you are here with me. I feel very safe and secure. By the way, where is Zak?" asked Miriam.

"He's out here with us, Honey, I don't think he should be in there with the baby, yet. What do you think, Doc?"

"Let the dog out there for now, maybe he can come in for a visit when Miriam finishes nursing. Now, scram, you two, this little guy is starving," said the doctor as he pushed them out the door.

As Alex looked at Miriam and Nathan one last time before closing the door, he realized how much his life had changed within a year and he knew how lucky he was. Nathan was a healthy baby with a head of thick, dark hair, pink cheeks and a loud healthy cry. As Alex admired the typical mother/child scene, Alex's feelings of contentment were abruptly interrupted by a loud crack of thunder. The loud noise made Miriam jump and the baby started to cry louder than before. As Alex closed the door to the bedroom, he sadly realized that the baby was not part of him and for some reason, he suddenly felt very apprehensive about the true identity of the child.

"Hey, Dad, did you see that? Lightning and thunder and during a blizzard! This sure is strange weather," observed Alex as he set up the card table.

"According to the prophecies of Nostrodamus, the weather will become very strange and violent," remarked Doug.

"Dad, cut it out! You always come up with your crazy hocus-pocus theories, the world isn't ending. Miriam and I are just beginning our lives together, especially now with our new baby,"

"Relax, son, you really are too tense. Let's play cards! By the way, are there any left-overs?"

DECEMBER 16, 1967 - THE VATICAN

"Paul, it has happened! The child has been born! I saw the signs!" exclaimed Cardinal Brazini as he entered Cardinal DeGroot's private chambers.

"I could not sleep last night because I had a strange feeling all evening. I went out and sat on my terrace for a while and watched the sky and without warning, I saw the sign! I saw the comet, Halley's Comet! According to what Michael told us, Halley's Comet would announce the birth of the child. The Comet is not to appear again until 1986, but Michael did tell us that it would appear out of the time sequence when the child was born."

"Antonio, calm down, my friend. You are too worked up over this. How do you know that it was Halley's Comet that you saw and not just a shooting star?"

"I know it in my heart! Besides, Paul, I know the difference between a comet and a shooting star. I am sure that the astrologists and astronomists will confirm that it was indeed Halley's Comet. Let's listen to the morning news, or better yet, let's call Michael and hear what he has to say. I am telling you, Paul, that the signs are going to appear just as they were prophesized. Our plans have taken root. He has come again!" smiled Brazini as he picked up the phone and started to dial.

DECEMBER 16, 1967 - MUNCY, PA - 10:00 AM

"Miriam, I'm going to call your parents. Do you think it's tool early?" asked Alex yawning.

"Honey, haven't you been to sleep yet?

"Well, not really. Doc, my dad and I got caught up in our card game and then we started to talk about the weather and the baby. I just never got to sleep. The doctor finally fell asleep on the couch and my dad is asleep in the guest room. Let's call your parents now before the baby wakes up again."

"O.K." answered Miriam as she dialed the phone. "Mom, it's Miriam, guess what? You're a grandma! I had the baby early this morning and his name is Nathan. He can't wait to meet his grandparents! Yes, Mom, I'm fine, but the weather isn't! It's been snowing like crazy up here. There must be more than two feet of snow on the ground and it's still coming down! Yes, Mom, the doctor made it just in time, but Alex was wonderful until he got here. He didn't even faint!" laughed Miriam as she continued chattering and giving her mother all of the details of the early morning birth.

"Ask them when they'll be able to get up here for the Christening"

"Just a minute, Mom, Alex is asking me something. The Christening?" questioned Miriam as she put her hand over the receiver. "What about the Bris? We have to have both, Alex, my parents and I still practice the Jewish traditions. My parents offered to bring Rabbi Rosenthal up here with them.

"That's fine with me, Honey. I'm sure Ray will agree with the arrangements, too. After all, this baby is special," remarked Alex as he kissed her cheek. You finish making plans with your mom, I'll go and wake Dr. Riofsky in case he has other calls. I'll make him and Dad a good breakfast and the doctor will check on you before he leaves. Give your parents my love and warm regards."

"Thanks, Honey, I will. I love you," she whispered to him as he walked out of the room

Alex started the coffee and put some bacon in a pan before he went to wake the doctor and his dad. The three men sat down to eat breakfast after he took a plate to Miriam. He told them that Miriam had called her parents.

"Well, I hope that neither of you has plans for next weekend. According to the Jewish tradition, the baby should be circumcised eight days after the birth. Ray will also be here to baptize Nathan. It'll be quite a ceremony, don't you think?" asked Alex smiling.

"Yeah, quite unusual, isn't it? How do Miriam's parents feel about the fact that a Bishop will baptize the baby after the Rabbi performs the circumcision?" asked Dr. Riofsky.

"Well, Doc, just remember, this is the Age of Aquarius! Where have you been?" laughed Doug. "Actually, it's not so unusual. Miriam and her family are Jewish, but they belong to a sect known as Messianic Jews. They practice all of the traditional Jewish laws, but they believe that Jesus Christ is indeed the Messiah. Although it sounds paradoxical, it works for them."

"I must admit, Nathan is a very special baby!" chuckled Dr. Riofsky.

"More special than you could possibly know," admitted Alex with a thoughtful expression.

"Spoken like a proud father," laughed Doug. "Now it's time to give some solid advice to the proud mother. You boys can clean up and do the dishes, I have an important date with a beautiful woman and my very handsome grandson," he said as he walked toward the bedroom.

"You know, he always finds a way out of work. You think I'd learn his tricks by now!" laughed Alex as he and the doctor started clearing the table.

"Tell Miriam that I'll be in to check on her and Nathan as soon as I'm finished with K.P. duty," called the doctor to Doug.

Doug knocked on the bedroom door and heard Miriam's low response telling him to come in. He looked at her holding her son and immediately, tears blurred his vision. Miriam looked up at him and smiled, "Dad, are you crying?"

"I guess I'm just a bit emotional right now, Miriam. You look so beautiful, so happy and so peaceful lying there holding Nathan. Let me see that bouncing baby boy!"

"Here he is Grandpa!" smiled Miriam as she handed the baby to Doug. "I think you two are going to be good buddies."

"I know we are! I can't wait to take him fishing!"

"Well, Dad, I think you'll have to wait awhile for that!" laughed Miriam as she watched her father-in-law awkwardly holding his grandson.

"Gee, Dad, you look a bit nervous holding Nathan, I thought you were an expert on holding babies!" joked Alex as he entered the room. "And, I just came to tell you that you're off the hook, doc and I finished the dishes. Hand him over, let me hold him for awhile."

"Just be careful, Alex, this is my future fishing buddy," said Doug as he handed the baby to his son.

"Oh, Alex, my mother said that she and my dad will be here on Thursday. My father finally wanted to talk to me and he sounded very excited about his grandson. Dad said that he feels foolish about the way he's been behaving and he asked me to tell you that he apologizes for being so stubborn and for not accepting the whole situation sooner. I told him that all of that is in the past and that we're looking forward to seeing them both on Thursday. I told my mother to call Ray and give him directions to our place, but she said that Ray already knows where we are living. Did you tell him, Alex?"

Alex looked at her with a puzzled and worried expression and then quickly looked at his father, "I don't remember if I did, Hon, did your mother say when she talked to Ray?"

"Mom said that he called her last week to find out how we were and he wanted to know if the baby arrived. She told Ray that she'd call him as soon as she heard any news and she promised to get all the details and directions for him. Ray told her that he already knew where we are living and that he's familiar with the area because he often comes here to fish. What's wrong, Honey, are you upset about something?"

"No, Honey, I'm not upset, I'm just tired. I guess I did tell Ray, but I've forgotten in all the excitement. Oh, oh, Nathan's starting to cry! Does he need a diaper change or is he hungry again?"

"I just changed him, so I guess he takes after Grandpa Doug, he always hungry! You two go and get some sleep, you look like you're ready to fall asleep standing up. Give me the baby and tell the doctor that Nathan is awake if he wants to check him before he leaves, he can do it now. By the way, is the doctor planning on sending a nurse for a few days? He mentioned something about it before, but I don't think it's necessary. I can take care of the baby myself."

"Miriam, I think it might be a good idea for awhile so that you can recuperate. If you were in the hospital, you'd be taken care of for a few days, so just relax and enjoy the service. Besides, the hospital is an hour away and I'll feel more relaxed knowing that someone else is here in case of an emergency," insisted Alex.

"O.K., I know that you're going to arrange it anyway. You are definitely going to spoil me!"

"You deserve to be spoiled. Now, we're going to take a nap and after the doctor checks the baby, you do the same," suggested Alex.

When Alex and Doug were in the living room, Alex quickly turned to his father and Doug noticed the worried expression on his face.

"What's the matter, Alex, you don't look too happy."

"Dad, how the hell does Ray know where we're living? I know damn well that I never told him a thing! I wanted to keep our location a secret because I'm afraid that the wrong people will find out. I hate to say this, Dad, but I'm beginning to get suspicious of the Bishop."

"Alex! What's wrong with you, son?" exclaimed Doug. "Ray had been a trusted friend for years! What makes you think that'd he'd jeopardize your safety? I think that you're just overtired."

"Dad, think about it. Miriam visits the Vatican, becomes pregnant and no one will admit to it, or even attempt to explain how it could possibly happen to her. Ray could have easily been influenced by the Cardinals when he was in Rome investigating this whole mess. If you remember, Dad, he didn't have all that much to offer in the way of information. I just don't like it. I really don't trust any of these guys, the Cardinals, or our friend, the Bishop. You're the one who said that these guys in Rome will go to any length to try to find this baby, especially if what we think happened really did!" exclaimed Alex in an agitated tone.

"Calm down, Alex, Miriam will hear you. Let's wait until the doctor leaves and we'll think this whole thing through. There must be a reasonable explanation. No matter what you say or think about Ray, I still trust him. I've known him for too long to accept the fact that he would betray you even for the Church," scolded Doug.

"I hope you're right, Dad, because I am very angry. If I ever find out that Ray betrayed us, I don't know what I'd do. As soon as Dr. Riofsky leaves, I'm going to give my good buddy, the Bishop a call. In the meantime, you go and lie down. I'll talk to you later and fill you in on my conversation with Ray.

"Just try to stay calm. Getting angry with Ray won't help much at this point. Remember, Alex, that you need all the help you can get to solve this mystery! Ray is your only real connection with the Vatican right now. I still believe that there's a reasonable explanation. Just give him a chance," advised Doug as he walked toward the guest room.

While the doctor went into the bedroom to examine Miriam and the baby, Alex dressed warmly and went out to plow the driveway. Before he got into his jeep, he heard a truck engine and turned to see Willard and his son plowing the road in a beat-up old truck. Alex yelled to them and when they stopped, he shared his happy news about the baby. Willard promised that Mrs. Jones would stop by in a few days to pay a visit and help with the cooking. Alex thanked him, finished plowing the driveway, and went back into the house. Dr. Riofsky was putting on his hat and gloves as Alex came in.

"Miriam and the baby are doing very well. They are both in excellent health so there shouldn't be any problems. Just make sure that Miriam drinks plenty of fluids and eats a healthy diet. If she does, she should have no trouble nursing the baby," the doctor instructed. "The nurse should be here by suppertime. I'm sure that Mrs. Brown will be thrilled with the assignment. She raised four kids and is a terrific pediatric nurse."

"Alex shook the doctor's hand and thanked him as he walked him out the door. He waited on the porch, watching the doctor drive off and when he went back into the house, he checked on Miriam and the baby. Since they were both sound asleep, Alex headed straight for the telephone.

"Ray, it's Alex, how are you?"

"Alex! Congratulations! How are you? Better yet, how are Miriam and the baby?"

"They're both doing fine, Ray, Nathan is healthy and beautiful. But, before I go into any details, we have to talk," answered Alex in a curt tone.

"Alex, what's wrong? Has something happened? You don't sound like yourself. I know something's wrong because you didn't call me Raymie. What's going on?"

"I think that you should tell me what's going on, Ray!"

"What do you mean by that? What are you implying?" questioned the Bishop.

"I'm implying that you were someone that I thought I could trust, but now, I'm not so sure. How the hell do you know where I'm living? Tell me the truth, Ray, are you involved with the Cardinals?" asked Alex angrily.

"Dear God, Alex, calm down! There's a perfectly logical explanation. I'm certainly not plotting against you and Miriam. For heaven's sake, doesn't our friendship mean anything to you? I would never betray you, not even for the Church!"

"Right now, Ray, I'm not sure that I believe that. Cut the crap about our friendship and tell me how you found out where we are!" Alex's voice was filled with anger.

"Listen, Alex, I figured out where you were living because one of my old parishioners has a cabin near you and told me about two guys he met on the stream. He couldn't remember your names, but from the way he described you and Doug and from the topics of you conversations, I put two and two together and I realized that it was you and your dad. Besides, I know that you guys have had a favorite fishing hole up there for years. Did you forget that I was there with the both of you?"

"Oh shit! I feel like a total ass!" exclaimed Alex sheepishly.

"Look, Alex, I'm really sorry that I caused you to worry. I didn't thing anything of it when I told Rebekah that I knew where you were living and it didn't dawn on me that you would become suspicious of me. I'm really sorry about making you worry like this, but I can honesty say that I don't blame you one bit. Do you still want me to come up for the Baptism next weekend?"

"Hell, Raymie, I'm really embarrassed and I don't know what else to say except that I'm really sorry that I doubted your friendship and trust. I should've listened to my father. Although, when he hears this, I'll certainly pay my dues for being wrong. Do you think that you can ever forgive me, Raymie?"

"Alex, don't give it a second thought. Of course I forgive you and I already told you that I'd probably jump to the same conclusions. You had every right to be upset."

"I guess the only excuse that I can give you for my ridiculous behavior, is that I'm so afraid of what can happen to Miriam and Nathan, that I suppose I'm becoming paranoid. Along with all that, I'm exhausted! I haven't slept since the baby's been born. All in all, it's a feeble excuse for treating you the way I did and for being suspicious of my best buddy. Are you sure that you forgive me?" asked Alex still embarrassed.

"Well, my friend, I can forgive you on one condition and it's going to cost you dearly. I think a dinner and a long weekend fishing in your favorite hole is definitely a fitting punishment. How does that sound for penance?" laughed Ray.

"My favorite fishing hole? Gee, that's really is steep penance! I guess that since you are my best friend and I owe you big time, Raymie, I suppose I'm forced to comply. Thanks, Bishop, you truly are a good and trusted friend," said Alex in a sincere tone. "Oh, when you get to the General Store on Splash Dam On Covered Bridge Road, stop in and ask Willard for directions. You remember him, don't you?"

"I sure do remember old Willard. I'll be there on Wednesday or Thursday, if that's alright with you and Miriam. I promise I won't be any trouble. In fact, I think I'll annoy Doug and stay with him," joked Ray.

"Dad will be thrilled to have the company. He'll also be thrilled to find out that he was right and I was wrong, again! Can't wait to see you, Raymie and I can't wait for you to meet my son!"

"Spoken like a typical proud father! Wait until you see the present I bought for the baby, you'll love it! I'll call you and let you know the definite day and time. How's Miriam? I hope she's surviving you and your dad! Take care of her and give her and the baby a kiss from me. Tell the old goat to be ready because I'm going to match him fish for fish. He'd better have a hefty sum of money handy because I plan on catching the biggest one!" teased Ray as he ended his conversation with Alex.

As Ray hung up the telephone, he couldn't help but wonder about Alex and Miriam. Ray knew how easy it was for him to find their hiding place and he came to the realization that Alex, Miriam and the baby would never really be safe. He stood in the same spot for a few moments and wondered if he should warn his old friend. Then, he shook his head and chuckled out loud at his cloak and dagger fears and he finally convinced himself that he was becoming paranoid.

**MEN OF SENSE ARE REALLY ALL OF ONE
RELIGION. BUT MEN OF SENSE WILL NEVER
TELL WHAT IT IS.**   **Shaftesbury**

CHAPTER XXV

SEVEN DAYS LATER...DECEMBER 24, 1967 - 5:00 AM

"At last, Nathan's big day has arrived!"
proclaimed Miriam as she lay the baby back into the
bassinet. "Today he will become a part of the Jewish
and Christian community. Most people would think
that we're crazy to have him circumcised by Rabbi
Rosenthal and Baptized by Bishop Pascal, but it will
bind both of our beliefs. In today's world, I think that
it's necessary for us to learn about other religious
beliefs, don't you?"

"What?" asked Alex. "I'm sorry, dear, I was
preoccupied. When the baby started to cry, I couldn't
go back to sleep, so I decided to read up on the whole
ordeal of circumcision. Do I really have to be there
when the Rabbi does this?"

"Alex, you're the one acting like a baby! Rabbi
Rosenthal has done hundreds of these. You should
know that the *berith milah*, or the circumcision is the
public initiation of the male child into the covenant of
Abraham. There is nothing odd about the ceremony
and the Rabbi will be very careful. I promise!"
laughed Miriam.

"Well, you can laugh! Our poor son may wind up singing soprano for the rest of his life if the old Rabbi slips! I'm really nervous about this whole thing. I don't know how you can stay so calm!" commented Alex.

"Oh, Alex, just go back to sleep for awhile. I'm wide awake so I'll go out and get things ready for the ceremony. I'm sure that everything will turn out fine. You do worry about everything!"

"Maybe you're right. I'll try to sleep for another hour or two, but if you need me for anything, wake me up. O.K.?" said Alex as he kissed her and turned over.

As Miriam closed the door to the bedroom, she could hear that Alex was already snoring. Miriam went into the kitchen, put on a pot of coffee and pulled out the step stool so that she could reach her dishes that were on the top shelf. She wanted to wash them before the party. As Miriam stood on the top of the stool and reached up into the cabinet, she suddenly felt weak and broke into a cold sweat.

"Oh, no," she thought, "I hope I'm not going to have another seizure." Miriam held onto the side of the cabinet and steadied herself. But, instead of passing out, she was overcome with a strange sense of calmness. She was sure that no matter what happened, she would be alright. Miriam thought about Alex and Nathan and was filled with a tremendous feeling of love and contentment. When the aura passed, she counted out the dishes, took them to the sink and began to hum as she washed them.

LATER THAT AFTERNOON

"Alex, somebody just pulled into the driveway," called Miriam as she sat in the rocker nursing Nathan. "Maybe it's my parents."

"It is! I'll go out and help them with their bags,"
called Alex from the living room window and he
hurried to put on his coat and gloves. "Are you almost
finished feeding the baby?"

"Yes, but send my mother in here. I'm sure she'll
want to see Nathan and he's almost asleep again."

Alex opened the door and almost bumped into his
father-in-law. "David!" greeted Alex putting out his
hand, "I can't tell you how happy Miriam and I are that
you're here. Wait until you see your grandson!"

Rebekah came up the porch steps and Alex
hugged her and kissed her cheek, "I have orders from
my boss to tell you to hurry and get inside. Nathan will
be asleep again and Miriam wants you to see him while
he's still awake!" laughed Alex.

"Just try and stop me! I can't wait to see my two
babies!" exclaimed Rebekah in an excited tone.

Alex went to their car and as he carried the bags
to the door, he was surprised to see David waiting for
him on the porch. As he approached his father-in-law,
David sheepishly said, "I know that I've been behaving
like a real fool, Alex, but I hope you understand that
Miriam is my only daughter.   I apologize for the way I
acted and now, maybe we can begin to be a real
family."

"David, you made my day!" exclaimed Alex.
"But, there was no reason to apologize. I know that I
would have reacted in the same exact way, on second
thought, I probably would've behaved worse! Let's go
inside, I'm freezing out here!"

Just as they opened the door, Alex heard another
car and saw a it pull into the driveway.

"What great timing, there's the Rabbi," remarked
David. He and Alex walked towards the car and as the
Rabbi got out, David greeted him.

"Sherman, it's good to see you again. Did you have any trouble finding this place. I hope my directions were clear."

"Sherman? Your name is Sherman?" asked Alex in a surprised tone.

"Yeah, what's wrong with Sherman?" asked David bewildered.

"Don't you like the name?" asked the Rabbi.

"Good God, it has nothing to do with my liking the name, it's just that in Old English, Sherman means a 'shear man' or a 'cutter' and every time I think about what you are going to do to Nathan, I get sick to my stomach!" replied Alex with shudder.

"Relax, Alex," commented David. "I survived and so did many other Jewish boys and we're all intact, believe me! Rabbi Rosenthal, this is my son-in-law, Alex Stewart. Alex, Rabbi Rosenthal," introduced David.

The two men shook hands and David continued to tease Alex about his weak stomach. "I hope you won't hold it against the Rabbi for being named Sherman. How did you know what his name means?"

"All names have a meaning and it's a big part of my job as an archaeologist to know that. For instance, we named the baby Nathan because in Hebrew it means 'a gift.' Miriam and I felt that under the circumstances, it is a perfect name" explained Alex.

"I'd like to talk to you about those circumstances when we get a chance. Maybe later. But now, let's get inside, I'm frozen! Come on, Rabbi, Alex will get those later!" shouted David to the Rabbi who was trying to get his bags out of the trunk. David looked back at Alex, put his hand on his shoulder and said, "I want to thank you for all you've done for my daughter. I realize now, how much you must care for her and the baby."

"David, I do love Miriam. More than mere words could ever express. The funny thing is, we both feel like all that's happened was meant to be and we're very happy together. I want you to know that I'll always love her and protect her for as long as I'm alive," promised Alex looking directly at him.

When they entered the house, David heard the voices coming from the bedroom. He walked quietly to the bedroom door and looked in. His eyes filled with tears as he saw his wife and daughter arm in arm looking into the bassinet.

"Miriam," he whispered.

When she turned around, her eyes opened wide, "Daddy," she cried running toward him.

"Oh, Miriam, I'm so sorry that I've been so stubborn. I was just so confused and upset. You know I love you very much and I hope that you can forgive me for being such a jerk!"

"Oh, Daddy, you're not a jerk! I'm so happy you're here because I've really missed you! Now, let me show you your grandson."

David bent over to look inside the bassinet, "Can I pick him up?" he asked softly.

"David, he's sleeping! Let him alone! You can hold him later," scolded Rebekah. Let's go out to the living room and make sure that Alex isn't forcing the Rabbi to give him a detailed account of the circumcision, " she laughed walking toward the doorway. "The poor guy is a nervous wreck."

"I'll say," chuckled David. "He was even worse when he found out that the Rabbi's first name is Sherman. He proceeded to give us a run-down on what Sherman means. I hope he makes it through the ceremony."

"Well, so what if the Rabbi's name is Sherman," commented Rebekah. "What does it mean?"

"Sherman means 'cutter' now, what are the odds of that?" laughed David as he saw the surprised expressions on his wife's and daughter's faces.

They walked into the living room and Miriam noticed that Alex was listening intently to whatever the Rabbi was telling him. She went over to them and overheard the conversation which was, as she surmised, a detailed account of the circumcision. Miriam could see that Alex's hair was drenched from sweating so she interrupted the conversation, "Excuse me, Honey, but why don't you serve some wine?"

She gave Alex a look and he excused himself and went into the kitchen.

"Rabbi Rosenthal, I'm so happy that you could be here with us today!" she said as she hugged and kissed him. "I hope that Alex hasn't been too rough on you!"

"Not at all, I can understand his nervousness, especially after he found out my name!" laughed the Rabbi good-naturedly.

Alex returned with a tray of wine glasses and a decanter and Miriam asked, "Honey, what time did you tell your dad and Ray to be here? Do you think they got lost? I thought they'd be here by now!"

"I can't wait to meet your father, Alex. I've heard only wonderful things about him from Bishop Pascal. I know that Ray mentioned his field of expertise, but it slipped my mind," commented the Rabbi.

"You'll love this, Rabbi, it's ancient religions and languages! So, I'm sure that you two will have a lot in common."

"How about you? Are you still involved with your project in Israel?" asked the Rabbi interested.

"Yes, but luckily, my crew can handle this phase of the dig. I'll have to get back there in the spring, though, and I hope that Miriam and the baby will be able to adjust to the living conditions on the site."

"What do you mean?" demanded Rebekah. "You can't possibly take a small baby to a place like that!"

"Mom, it's not all that bad. Alex spent his childhood on dig sites and he survived. Alex, I hear a car door, I hope it's your father and Ray," said Miriam, happy to have a diversion from her mother's comments.

"I'll run and out and check," responded Alex putting on his coat.

As Alex closed the door behind him, David looked at Miriam and smiled. "You know, Honey, I think that you and Alex are very well matched. You seem to be made for each other."

"Thanks, Dad, what a nice thing to say! It really means a lot to me. I knew that you and Alex would get along and I know that he's the perfect guy for me, maybe because he's so much like you!" remarked Miriam as she got up to kiss her father.

"Good Lord, it's snowing again!" yelled Doug as he stamped his feet on the rug. "It sure nice and warm in here. Hello, again, Rebekah, you look wonderful! You, sir, must be the very lucky husband and father of these two gorgeous women," he remarked as he offered his hand to David. "I'm Douglas Stewart, one of the proud grandpas."

"I've certainly heard a lot about you, and yes, I'm David, the other proud grandpa! I'm very happy to meet you."

"Hello, Doug," said Rebekah kissing his cheek, "it's wonderful to see you again. I was just telling the Rabbi about your great jokes. I hope you have more of them for today! You know, I laughed all the way home after the wedding!"

"Rebekah!" exclaimed Alex shaking his head, "I warned you not to encourage him!"

"Dad, this is Rabbi Rosenthal," said Miriam as she introduced her father-in-law. "Rabbi, this is Doug and this is Bishop Pascal."

"Sherman, how are you?" greeted Ray Pascal. "I haven't seen you in awhile. You're looking great!"

"Oh, I forgot that you two know each other!" laughed Miriam.

"Yep, we're in the same business!" joked Ray. "By the way, has this guy started calling you Shermie, yet?"

"Funny you should ask," chuckled Sherman, "he's been avoiding my first name ever since I arrived. He knows what Sherman means and now, he's really nervous!"

"Well, what does it mean? Don't forget guys, I'm not a language expert," remarked Ray.

"You would have to ask, Raymie. Sherman means 'shear man' or 'cutter' in Old English. Now, you know why I'm nervous," answered Alex as he paled again.

"I can't believe it! This is too funny!" laughed Ray.

"Let's change the subject!" commented Alex. "Have you decided who's going first, the Rabbi or the Bishop?"

"Well, the way I see it, I'd better Baptize the kid before the Rabbi makes his cut, what do you think Sherman?" teased Ray.

"Yeah, maybe you're right, Ray, I've been feeling a little shaky lately," responded the Rabbi winking at Miriam.

"Oh, brother, you guys are too much! Mom, come with me and help me get Nathan ready. By the way, Rabbi, your drinks are cut off until after the ceremony, especially since you're scheduled to go first!" joked Miriam as she and Rebekah headed toward the bedroom.

"Miriam, don't say 'cut'!" Alex called after her. "I think that I need another glass of wine, but I agree with Miriam, Rabbi, you'd better wait until after the ceremony!"

By 4:00 PM everything was ready for the ceremony, including little Nathan who appeared to be well fed and content in his mother's arm. Rabbi Rosenthal began to chant the Hebrew prayers and as he prepared to make the incision, Miriam heard a loud thud. When she looked up from the baby's face, she realized that Alex wasn't next to her, but was passed out cold on the floor. Doug and David quickly roused him and made him sit in the recliner for the remainder of the ceremony. As soon as Miriam realized that he was fine, she couldn't help but laugh.

"I guess he really was nervous about this whole thing. I wonder how he's going to get through the rest of the baby's childhood!" remarked the Rabbi, laughing. "May God give him strength! He'll need it more when Nathan becomes a teenager!"

By 4:45, little Nathan was part of the Jewish covenant and the circumcision was completed without a problem except for Alex's bruised head.

At 5:00 PM, Bishop Pascal began the Baptism and Doug stood in as godfather to the baby. As Ray began to pour the holy water over the baby's head and say the words, "I baptize you in the name of the Father, the Son, and the Holy Ghost..." Nathan opened his eyes and stared directly into the eyes of the Bishop and smiled.

When Ray finished reciting the words, lightning flashed and thunder rumbled so loud that the small house shook.

Ray was stunned and it was a few moments before he could regain his composure and continue on with the ceremony.

"Now, that's what I call good timing!" he laughed, but at the same time, he was overcome by a strange and troubling feeling. He could never forget the look that the baby had given him. Nathan's eyes were definitely not the eyes of an eight day old child, but the eyes of an adult who had lived a lifetime. And, the baby's smile seemed to indicate that the child knew exactly what was going on around him.

As soon as the ceremony was completed, Miriam handed the baby to Alex. "Here, Daddy, you baby-sit while Mom and I get the dinner on the table. Doug, would you please pour the wine? Dad, will you light the candles on the table?"

"What can I do, Miriam?" asked Ray.

"Nothing! You and Rabbi Rosenthal did a wonderful job. It's your turn to just sit and relax. You are both going to say the prayers at dinner so now, you can enjoy that glass of wine!" Miriam answered.

After dinner, Rebekah brought a New York cheesecake and raspberry sauce to the table. As Miriam finished serving the dessert, Nathan started to cry.

"Come on, Miriam, no rest for mommies. I'll keep you company while you feed him and when you're finished, I'll give him a bath. I hope I remember how it's done! It's been a long time since I bathed a baby!"

"I'm sure you'll remember, dear," said David to his wife as she carried her dessert to the bedroom. "Call me when you're finished so I can kiss my grandson good-night," he requested.

While Miriam and Rebekah tended to Nathan, the men sat at the dinner table while Doug passed out brandy glasses and filled them as he commented, "This sure has been an eventful day."

"I'll have to agree with that. I found the lightning and thunder to be remarkable, especially since it happened just as Ray was baptizing the baby. You know, we've been having some really strange weather lately. The scandal sheets are filled with stories that the signs are beginning," commented the Rabbi.

"What do you mean by that? You can't mean those silly prophecies by those fly-by-night seers that write for those papers," commented Ray.

"Actually, Ray, I think that the prophecies of Nostrodamus deal with the signs that are supposed to occur before the Second Coming! interjected Doug.

"Yeah," added Alex, "they predict changes in the normal weather pattern, wars, famine, drought, plagues or pestilence, and all sorts of strange but inexplicable happenings or signs."

"Well, think about it, gentlemen, what's happening right now? We're experiencing thunder and lightning during a snow storm in December, the war in Viet Nam is raging and our young men are dying by the thousands. Jack and Bobby Kennedy have been assassinated and the famine and drought in Africa is no closer to an end. Add to that the outbreak of the E-boli virus in Africa that has the potential to become a world-wide epidemic. Consider the poverty, hunger, and natural disasters in South America and the horrible unrest in the Middle East. It appears that all of the ingredients that fit the predictions made by Nostrodamus are currently present. What do you think, Ray," asked the Rabbi.

"I'd say that you're right on target! I think that we ignore the signs because we'd rather explain them away with scientific reasoning. However, they certainly are present. How about the sighting of Halley's Comet? Now, that's weird!" commented Ray.

"Do you believe that it was really Halley's Comet? It's not supposed to appear until the mid 1980's, isn't that right, Dad?" asked Alex as he poured another brandy.

"Yes, son, but it was really Halley's Comet. The astronomers and the NASA scientists confirmed that fact. I heard it on the news this morning, but according to the report, there are no explanations. According to the prophecies that I've read in ancient Hebrew, the astrological signs that happen out of sequence announce the coming of a very great event. It could be the birth of a special child, or it could be a sign that world peace is finally going to be a reality."

"You don't really believe that stuff, do you, Dad?" asked Alex.

"Alex, you should know by now, that men in our branch of science, we find out new and sometimes, strange things every time a new artifact surfaces. And, being in the religious end of this work, I've learned that nothing is truly concrete. There are too many things that cannot be explained away as far as I'm concerned. You'd be wise to open yourself up to the mystical and the miraculous. Who knows, you may find some answers. I often think of my old friend from Jordan, Giryes Nijmeh," remarked Doug.

"How's is he, Dad? I haven't seen him in awhile, of course, I haven't had the time to visit Jordan lately. But what made you think of him?"

"He's fine, Alex and he asks about you every time we talk. He's waiting for you to visit. I mentioned him because he's studied astrology and ancient religions and is an ardent follower of Nostrodamus. He has great insight into current events and how they relate to ancient prophecies. Giryes often speaks in riddles about the future and there are times when he really scares me. There are times when I really believe that he's a prophet because many of his predictions have proven themselves over the years. If you have any doubts, you should go and talk to him," urged Doug.

"Maybe I'll get a chance to pay him a visit as soon as I get back to the Middle East, but now, I think it's time to clear the table. I'll wash the dishes, who wants to dry?" asked Alex trying to change the subject.

I'll be glad to help, Alex, but I'd like to hear about what transpired in Rome. In my opinion, all this talk about mysticism and mystery seems to fit right in with the conception of my grandson," commented David.

"I know I did promise to talk to you, David, but I don't want to say too much in front of Miriam. How about if you, my dad and I take some time and check out the major fishing holes in the area tomorrow? We'll treat you to lunch at the Gravestone and we'll be able to discuss this in peace there," suggested Alex.

"I'd say that peace is an excellent choice of words for that place. Beware, David, this place is named the Gravestone because it's right next to a cemetery! Although, I must admit, it is an experience you'll long remember," laughed Ray.

"Oh, Lord, now I've heard everything! Does that mean if you eat there, you land in the cemetery?" questioned the Rabbi. "I guess it's pretty convenient!"

"Actually, the food is great and wait until you experience the ambiance and the decor. You'll love it! Sherman, you've got to come up here and visit with me so I can take you fishing and buy you a Gravestone dinner. What do you say?" asked Ray.

"Sounds like an adventure that I shouldn't miss! I'll try to get up here before Alex and Miriam leave for Qumran."

"I'll help with the dishes," offered Doug when he saw Alex carrying the dishes to the kitchen.

"No, Dad, you sit and talk with Sherman and David, Ray and I will handle the dishes. Besides, Miriam will have a fit if you break anything else!" chuckled Alex.

"Come on, Ray, looks like we're on K.P. duty! You can dry and I'll wash."

As the two men stacked the dishes in the sink, the lights dimmed and lightning flashed. Zak's ears perked up and he growled. He quickly got up and ran into the bedroom to find Miriam and the baby.

"I wonder if Zak ran in there to protect Miriam and Nathan, or to be protected?" laughed David as he watched the dog run out of the living room.

ALL THAT IS NECESSARY FOR THE FORCES OF EVIL TO WIN IN THE WORLD IS FOR ENOUGH GOOD MEN TO DO NOTHING.
                                    Edmund Burke

CHAPTER XXVI

THE VATICAN, DECEMBER 24, 1967

Cardinal DeGroot continued with his confession as he recalled in detail the events that took place thirty years before...

"My brothers in Christ, I am happy that we are all here today. Coincidentally, tomorrow we celebrate the anniversary of the birth of Our Lord, Jesus Christ. Today, on Christmas eve, I have the honor of making this most important announcement. The child has been born! What we have been waiting for and planning for all these long years has finally come to pass. It is a time for great celebration, my brothers," announced Cardinal Brazini to his six fellow conspirators as they sat around the conference table in the Vatican Library.

"How can you be so sure?" inquired Cardinal Milos Kowalsky, who was beginning to show his age.

"I have seen the sign. A few days ago, I could not sleep and as I sat on my terrace, I saw the comet. I knew in my heart that it was the sign that was to announce the birth of the child, Milos. You remember the prophecy, don't you?" questioned Brazini as he looked at his old friend.

"I'm sure he remembers, Antonio. But, I must admit that I was skeptical at first until I heard that the comet was indeed identified as Halley's Comet by the leading astronomers. They agree that Halley's Comet was not to appear until 1986 and the fact that it has appeared nineteen years earlier than it should have carries a very special meaning. This phenomena was predicted in the Fatima letter according to what Michael revealed to us," remarked Cardinal LeBlanc.

Cardinal Chinua Belawa was visibly upset, "This is a very significant time for me and for my people. The Congo is now under the rule of a new dictator, Mobutu, and my people are not happy. There are reports of many horrible changes taking place in my country. I can only hope and pray that our efforts will not only help my people but all who are suffering from any type of injustice in the world.

"Yes, my brother, we must continue to hope and pray that our plan will have a world-wide effect and bring peace and justice to all mankind," agreed Cardinal Jorge Aceituno. "My people are also suffering from the evils of Communism under the powerful dictatorship of Castro and my own family has suffered greatly because of my position in the Church. May God grant success to our project so that it will bring peace to all."

"I, for one, believe that the child must be found soon, so that all our plans can come to pass. We must not waste any time. We must find him that we can prove to the world that goodness, peace and justice can become a reality," exclaimed Cardinal Brazini. "Michael, how can we find the child?"

"When Brazini asked this question, I remember how Michael stared directly at Brazini and I knew then that Michael was no longer intimidated by Brazini's power. Michael had a slight smile as he continued to look at Antonio and told us that he knew and would always know the exact location of the child," disclosed DeGroot.

"Remember, Antonio, I am always at least one step ahead of you. I have an excellent informant, a person who is very close to Alex and Miriam."

"Brazini's eyes flashed with fury and he confronted Michael with a series of angry questions," related Cardinal DeGroot.

"Why weren't we informed of this? Who is this informant of yours? And, where is the child, now?"

"I will tell you only what I choose to tell you, Brazini. Do not question me or my methods. The child is safe and that is all you need to know right now. As for the identity of my informant, it is of no concern to you. I will continue to keep this information to myself. I cannot and will not risk the success of the project just to satisfy your womanly curiosity," retorted Michael with a sneer. "I am also afraid that divulging this information now will tempt others to use it for personal gain rather than the good of our plan."

Cardinal DeGroot continued his fascinating account, "When Brazini lunged at Michael, I had to intercede once again, Holy Father, because I was sure that Antonio would murder him. Antonio was in such a rage that it took us twenty minutes to calm him down. Within a half hour, we were able to continue our meeting. As Antonio sipped a glass of wine, he appeared to become more relaxed and began to quiz Michael again."

"Well, Michael, I do not think that it is wise that you, alone, are privileged with this information and I also believe that it is time that you reveal the rest of the Fatima Prophecy. We are all curious to know what to expect in the future. I do not believe that any of us here would use the child for our own personal gain since we are all fully aware that we are all in this together. Besides, Michael, what if something were to happen to you? The rest of us should know what is predicted to happen so that we can be prepared, responded Brazini coolly and calmly.

"And, what do you think is going to happen to me? Surely, you are not threatening me, Brazini?" laughed Michael as he looked at Antonio. "I hope that you are not harboring evil thoughts, Antonio! And, if you are, just remember that I can out think any one of you, so don't even attempt to formulate any type of threat against my wellbeing. In fact, if you are wise, my friend, you will continue to pray for my good health!"

"Please, Michael, let's not continue to argue. In the beginning, we all agreed that this project would come first. We must remember that and focus all of our thought and efforts on what we believe will change the world forever. Our constant battling will only ruin whatever good can and will come out of our work. Antonio and Michael, I beg you to reconcile your differences and let us continue to work together on our plan," pleaded Cardinal LeBlanc. "We all have a personal stake in the success of our work. Don't you agree, my brothers?"

"I remember that Michael looked at Rene LeBlanc for a few seconds in silence. Then, he smiled at him and his whole demeanor changed. He agreed with Rene and patted his shoulder" reminisced DeGroot.

"Thank you, my friend, for bringing us back to the reality of our situation. You are correct. We must stay calm and continue to work for the good of Holy Mother Church and for the good of mankind. Antonio, are you willing to forget our differences?" asked Michael as he approached Brazini.

"Yes, if you promise to take us into your confidence and reveal more of the Fatima Prophecy. I think we must be aware of what is about to happen. Don't you agree, my brothers," responded Brazini as he looked to the rest of us for support.

"We all agreed with Antonio because we were very anxious to know about what was ahead of us. So far, Holy Father, we knew that the Fatima Prophecy proved to be correct, that is, the part that Michael chose to reveal to us," continued Cardinal DeGroot. "After Michael sat and pondered for a few moments, he agreed to share more of the prophecy with us."

"My brothers, be prepared for many natural disasters and many other atrocities that will happen throughout the world. Your native countries and your people will suffer. Wars, famine, disease, horrible and unusually weather, and lack of faith and belief in God will continue for many years. Only when all seems lost, will we be saved. This is another part of the prophecy," explained Michael.

"But, Michael, many of those things are occurring throughout the world as we speak. How can we be sure that these are the events mentioned in the Fatima prophecy?" questioned Milos Kowalsky wearily.

"Because the child has now arrived!" explained Michael.

"But, when will we be told of the child's whereabouts? We are all anxious to know!" remarked Chinua Belawa.

"All in good time. He must live in obscurity for awhile and nothing must interfere with the prophetic words that must be fulfilled," answered Michael in a stubborn tone.

"Without any further explanation, Michael bid the rest of us good-night and left us to ponder his words," relayed DeGroot. "We remained in the room and for several minutes, no one spoke. It was evident that we were all thinking the same thoughts, but not one of us were brave enough to confront Michael. We were aware of what Michael had become and the six of us lived in fear of making him angry."

"Michael was in total control and none of us could do much to stop him as we were all aware of his power. We finally discussed this among ourselves and we ended our meeting by praying that God would inspire Michael with the ability to trust us and work with us for the good of the plan. However, Holy Father, this same awful feeling of dread flooded my entire body and soul. I felt sure that Michael's plan was more extensive than any of us realized, but none us did anything to stop him. Little did I or the others guess at the extent of the evil he had planned for the world at that time, but we were to find out the horrible truth much later," confessed DeGroot in a tired tone. "Within the next several years, we were to discover that Michael was once again to trying to control the destiny of the world!"

COMING EVENTS CAST THEIR SHADOWS BEFORE.   Thomas Campbell

CHAPTER XXVII

QUMRAN - 2 YEARS LATER, 1969

"Alex, I don't understand what's wrong with me. Why can't I get pregnant again? I really think that Nathan needs a brother or sister. I know how lonely it is to be an only child and you do, too. Maybe it's time I see a doctor and have some tests done. I'm really starting to get concerned," Miriam whispered to Alex as they tried to fall asleep in the extreme heat.

"Miriam, why are you so worried about having another baby right now? Why don't you just enjoy Nathan?" Alex asked rubbing her back. "I agree that it's lonely growing up alone, but I also know a lot of people who really would have preferred to be an only child. All they ever did was fight with their siblings!" laughed Alex, trying to lighten up the conversation.

"Alex, I really don't care what other people feel, I only know what I feel and I thought you liked kids! Don't you want any more?" asked Miriam with tears in her eyes.

"Of course, I do, Honey, but it won't be easy. I guess I knew that I would have to tell you someday, but I thought that once Nathan was born, that you would be content. I suppose I'm just a coward and I want to apologize for not confiding in you sooner," muttered Alex in a low whisper.

"What are you talking about? Confide what? Are you sick, or is something wrong? Tell me what you have to tell me and do it right now, or I'll never be able to get to sleep!" demanded Miriam.

"O.K. I guess I'm a little embarrassed about the whole thing, although it really isn't my fault. When I was in my late teens, I contracted the mumps and as a result, I'm sterile. In other words, Miriam, I can be a father, but I can't father a child," disclosed Alex with sadness.

"Oh my God! Honey, why didn't you tell me this sooner?" asked Miriam with a shocked expression.

"Would it have made a difference?" asked Alex looking at her.

"Of course not! But, is that why you married me because I was already pregnant?" she asked suddenly frightened.

"Miriam, for God's sake, are you crazy? I fell in love with you the first time I saw you! Your pregnancy only helped to quicken our courtship and it was an opportunity for me to become a father to your child, or I should say, our child. I couldn't love Nathan more if he was my own. He's such a great kid. He's a gentle, kind and loving child and I couldn't imagine my life without him or you. I hope that you don't think that I deceived you by not telling you the truth about myself. If you still want to have another baby, I've read that the doctors are working on methods that can make it possible. Maybe we should think about it awhile and do some research. How does that sound to you?" asked Alex as he hugged her close.

"Honey, I love you and I hope I didn't sound like I mistrusted your motives for marrying me. I know that you love me and Nathan. I consider myself to be very fortunate that God sent you into my life. You are not only a 'helper of men,' but you are our protector and my knight in shining armor!" exclaimed Miriam as she smothered his face with kisses.

A few days later, Miriam and Linda Martinelli, Alex's assistant drove into town for supplies and on the way, Miriam began to talk to Linda about her hopes for having another baby.

"Are you sure you want another one so soon? Nathan is just two, in fact he'll be starting into the terrible two's any day now and maybe when he does, you'll change your mind," laughed Linda maneuvered the jeep on the narrow dirt roads.

"I know that kids could be little demons sometimes, but so far, we've been very lucky with Nathan, he's really a good kid, especially considering the kind of lifestyle we lead. I can't stop thinking about having another baby, though. I guess I was so lonely growing up without any brothers or sisters, that I would rather if Nathan didn't have to go through life alone. Even now, aside from you and Alex, of course, I don't have anyone else that I feel I can talk to or confide in. I guess I just want the best for Nathan," explained Miriam. "What about you, Linda, I never heard you talk about any brothers or sisters, are you an only child, too?"

"No, but I am now, my brother is dead. He died several years ago in a fire. I understand your point about being alone because my brother and I were really close when we were growing up. I'll always miss him no matter how much time goes by, revealed Linda with sadness.

"Oh my God! I had no idea!" exclaimed Miriam.
"I'm so sorry, it was really insensitive of me!"
"Don't be silly, how could you have known. Besides, it happened a long time ago. I still miss him,

but I've learned to accept what happened," said Linda as she turned a corner and almost toppled the jeep.

"Linda! Slow down!" yelled Miriam. "Why do you always drive like a lunatic?"

"I don't know, I guess I just like living life in the fast lane. Calm down, I'll get you there safe and sound."

"You like living in the fast lane and you work on dig sites? Now, that's a real paradox," laughed Miriam.

"Yeah, that's me, a real paradox. You know, Miriam, if you are having problems getting pregnant, medical science had come a long way. I know an excellent doctor in Philadelphia, in fact, he's married to a friend of mine. The last time I was home, she told me that he's doing some innovative research on infertility problems. Maybe when you and Alex get back to the States, you can look him up. But, in the meantime, I think you should relax and enjoy Nathan."

"Oh, I do enjoy my son. It's just that I'd still like to pursue the possibility of having a brother or a sister for him. We're planning a visit to the States soon, so maybe I can meet with this doctor. Alex said that it's pointless to continue with the excavation now since the heavy rains have made it almost impossible to dig."

"I'll say! When it rained for a week straight, I thought that we'd have to build an ark!" laughed Linda as she tried to avoid the deep ruts in the road. "The rain hasn't done much for the road either. Hang on!"

"Thank goodness that Nathan is strapped into his seat. I felt like I was going to fly right out of the jeep! Look at him! He's loving every minute of this," exclaimed Miriam looking at her laughing two year old. "Oh, before I forget, what's the doctor's name?"

"I guess my brain got rattled when we hit that rut! It's Dr. Tom Miller. He's at the University of PA hospital and I'm sure that he'll be happy to meet with you and Alex. If you want, I'll give him a call when we get back to the site and tell him that you'll be calling him soon."

"Definitely, just remind me to write down his name and telephone number. Tell him that we'll be Stateside in about two weeks. I'll talk to Alex, but I'm sure he'll think it's a great idea. In fact, he has to go to the University to get some artifacts tested. Their labs have the latest testing methods and Alex is anxious to try them out. While he's getting the artifacts tested, maybe Dr. Miller can run some tests on me! Do you know anything about the procedure?" inquired Miriam.

"Not really, I do know that it's called *in vitro* fertilization, but please don't ask me how it works because I haven't a clue," admitted Linda as she tried to avoid one pothole and landed into another.

"Nathan is starting to fidget, he must be hungry. How much longer before we get into town?"

"About five more minutes. I'm starving, too, let's stop to eat something before we start to shop."

"Yeah, I didn't eat much of a breakfast so I'm hungry, too. By the way, remind me never to let you teach Nathan how to drive," teased Miriam as Linda hit another pothole.

"Hey, I'm not that bad! Anyway, Nathan loves the way I drive, it's like being on a roller coaster!" said Linda laughing as Miriam grabbed the dashboard to keep from flying out.

EVIL KNOWS THE SLEEPING PLACE OF EVIL.
African Proverb

CHAPTER XXVIII

"Michael, they're on their way to the University of PA. I've made all the necessary contacts, I hope you're ready. Miller told me that he's ready on his end."

"You have done a superb job, and I am ready! I am also anxious, however I know that I must remain patient. My first experiment has proven successful and this time, the results should be even better. Miller has assured me that he's been able to eliminate all genetic imperfections. Now, our plans will finally become a reality," responded Bachman.

THE UNIVERSITY OF PA, PHILADELPHIA, PA

"Your appointment with Dr. Miller is for 1:00, isn't it, Honey? Alex asked Miriam as he parked the car. "How long do you think you'll be in there?"

"I'm not sure, Alex, I guess it all depends on the type of exam and the testing he does today. Why, are you in hurry?"

"No, I'm not in a hurry, I just thought that since we're finally alone, we could have a romantic dinner. I'd like to make reservations at Book Binders, but I wanted to make sure that you'll be finished early enough. I know that we've got to get back to Nathan tonight, but I'd like to take advantage of being alone for a few hours, wouldn't you?" he asked as they walked toward the office.

"Yeah, you're right. As much as I miss him, a nice quiet dinner sounds great and it is nice being alone with you, but don't be surprised if I start to feed you at dinner tonight! I can't remember what we did with our free time B.N." laughed Miriam.

"B.N.? What the hell is that? It doesn't stand for anything like a diaper change, does it?" asked Alex wrinkling his nose.

"No, silly, B.N. means "Before Nathan," you, Mr. Archaeologist, should have been able to figure that one out!" teased Miriam as she held onto Alex's arm.

"Ten points for you!" retorted Alex.

Miriam and Alex were laughing as they walked into the waiting room, attracting the attention of the other women seated in the bright waiting room. A very pregnant woman looked up from her magazine and smiled at them.

Alex smiled back at her as he and Miriam sat down. "Don't you remember what it was like B.N.? We were able to stay in bed alone and we even got to sleep until noon if we felt like it! No getting up for feedings, sniffles and dirty diapers! And, now, if this procedure works, we'll be starting all over again!" commented Alex in a wistful tone.

"Alex, you sound as though you're changing your mind about all of this. You do want another baby, don't you?" she asked looking at him anxiously.

"Of course I do, Honey, I guess I'm just feeling a bit nostalgic for the old days and I miss not having you all to myself. That's all. I'm excited about the prospect of being a daddy again. In fact, I'd like to have a little girl, just like you!" commented Alex as he squeezed her hand. "I hope we won't be disappointed."

"I don't think we'll be disappointed, I just know that I'll get pregnant again. I want you to remember, Alex, I'll always love you, even when I'm busy with Nathan and I'll still love you when I'm busy with the new baby. You'll always be my first love," whispered Miriam as she kissed his cheek.

"Mrs. Stewart? Dr. Miller will see you now. Please follow me." said the nurse as she led Miriam and Alex into a typical examination room.

"While you're waiting for the doctor to come in, you'll have to fill out this form and change into a gown," instructed the nurse as she smiled at them. The pleasant middle-aged woman introduced herself as Terry. "Dr. Miller should be in to see you within a few minutes, here are some magazines for you to look through while you wait."

When Miriam stepped behind the curtain to change into the hospital gown, Alex looked around the examining room and his eyes focused on a set of instruments and he immediately got a sick feeling. As he looked at the shiny metal instruments neatly laid out on the surgical table, his mind wandered back about three years. He was back in the Vatican and he remember the information that the old nun had given Ray about the long syringe that Dr. Ansilio and Bachman had with them the night that Miriam was in the Vatican infirmary. He shuddered and without realizing it, he began to sweat. Miriam stepped out of the alcove and asked Alex to tie the gown in the back. But, when she looked over at him, she noticed that something was wrong.

"Honey, are you O.K.? You look very pale, what's wrong with you?" she asked as she went over to him and felt his head. "Alex, you are clammy, are you getting sick?"

"No, Miriam, but you know that I have a weak stomach when it comes to doctor's offices and just looking at all this stuff especially the instruments, has made me a little sick to my stomach."

"Are you sure? Do you want me to call the nurse back in here? Or, better yet, would you rather wait outside for me?"

"Miriam, I'm alright! The feeling has passed and I feel much better, now. I want to stay in here with you, I promise that I'll be O.K. and if I do feel sick again, I'll call Terry. Is it a deal?"

"Well, if you say so. Just take a deep breath and try to relax. I wonder how Nathan's doing? I'm so glad that he's close to all his grandparents. It makes me more relaxed about leaving him," she added trying to get his mind off the present situation.

"Oh, I'm sure that we'll have to un-spoil him for an entire week after being with the three of them all day. We have got to train them not to give him everything he wants. With my dad and your parents doting on Nathan, we may wind up with a little devil on our hands."

"Alex, I don't think Nathan could ever become a little devil, or at least I hope he won't! You have to admit, that even if he gets everything, he's never demanding," answered Miriam smiling.

"Spoken like a true mother. You are right. I guess we really don't have anything to complain about."

A few seconds later, they heard a soft knock on the examining room door and a tall, blond man, about forty-five years old walked in. He introduced himself, "I'm Dr. Miller and I'm sorry if I kept you waiting, but my appointments have been backed up this morning due to an emergency," explained Dr. Miller as he shook hands with the couple. "In this business, we can't count on the timing to be perfect."

"Oh, that's alright, doctor we weren't waiting that long."

"I'm happy to hear that. By the way, Linda Martinelli speaks highly of both of you. I don't know if she mentioned that I am somewhat familiar with where your dig site is situated. My wife is from Jordan and we visit her family often. When we get over there, we try hard to meet up with Linda and do some sight-seeing with her. She's been a terrific friend."

"Linda has been a valuable asset to me and to the rest of my crew. I really don't know what I'd do without her. She did mention that she does get to see you whenever you are in Jordan. It certainly is a beautiful country. By the way, I have some old friends there, maybe it know them, the Nijmeh family. They are good friends of my father and me," commented Alex.

"I don't recall the name, but I'll try to remember to ask my wife if she knows them. Jordan is a beautiful country and since it's small, it seems as though everyone knows one another," he answered with a laugh. "Well, I hope I can be of some help to you today, Mrs. Stewart. I received all of your medical records last week and I've had plenty of time to look them over. Today, I plan to do a physical and internal exam and I will do an endometrial biopsy which will help to determine the condition of you uterus, Mrs. Stewart. Terry will also draw a few vials of blood so that I can check your blood count and hormone levels. If either of you have any questions, please feel free to ask me at anytime," he explained.

"Before we begin, I insist that you call me Miriam, I'm really not used to the formal Mrs. Stewart!

I do have a few questions, but I think my husband would like to ask his questions first."

"Yeah, if you don't mind, Dr. Miller, do you think that you can explain the procedure in laymen's terms. I mean, how does this whole thing work? As you probably saw in my records, I'm sterile from contracting mumps during my late teens. I'm wondering where you get the donor sperm and how it's selected," quizzed Alex.

"Sure, first of all, the procedure is called *in vitro* fertilization which simply means that the egg is fertilized with a donor sperm outside of the womb, in a test tube or in a pertri dish. Many of the newspapers are referring to the end result as a 'test tube baby.' You've probably heard or read about the baby girl that was born to a couple in England. She is the very healthy result of her mother's egg and a donor sperm that were fertilized outside of the womb," explained the doctor patiently. "But why don't I first exam you, Miriam, then I can spend more time explaining the steps involved in the process."

"Should I leave the room," asked Alex hopefully.

"No, Dr. Stewart, you can stay. I prefer that the couples go through the entire procedure as a team, so that both parties understand everything that's involved," stated Dr. Miller.

"Now, Miriam, I'm going to perform a regular physical exam and then I will do the internal. While I'm doing the internal, I will snip a piece of your uterus to test for tissue health and hormone levels. It will feel like menstrual cramping and you will have some bleeding when I'm finished. Are you ready to begin?"

"Yes, doctor, I only hope that Alex is ready. He doesn't have the strongest constitution when it comes to blood!" laughed Miriam looking at Alex's pale face.

"I think I'll be alright as long as I can sit over here and I don't have to look," said Alex is a weak voice.

"Just grab a magazine and read for awhile. It'll be over within a few minutes, just relax," smiled Dr. Miller.

Within forty-five minutes, the exams and biopsy were finished and Miriam was sitting up on the table. Aside from having cramps, she was fine, "That wasn't too bad. Now, what's the next step, doctor?"

"Well, your physical and internal exams look fine and everything appears to be healthy so far. I should have the results of the biopsy and blood work by Friday. As soon as the results are ready, Terry will call you and schedule an appointment for next week. If all the results show that you are fine, we can proceed with the next step."

"Will there be any more cutting?" asked Alex still looking pale and anxious.

"No," laughed Dr. Miller, "Miriam will have to use a basil thermometer and take her temperature every morning when she awakes and before she gets out of bed. I'll give her graphs and she'll have to chart the daily reading. This will determine the exact time of ovulation."

"How will I know when I'm ovulating?" interrupted Miriam.

"Your temperature rises during ovulation. After about two months of keeping a daily chart, I'll look at the reading on the chart and it will help me to see if your cycle is relatively normal. If it is, I'll be able to continue with the next step, which is to schedule you for the extraction of the egg during the time of your ovulation," explained Dr. Miller.

"Do you do that here?" asked Alex.

"Oh, no, but maybe sometime in the near future, we'll be able to do it right in the office. For now, Miriam will be admitted to a short stay unit and she will be sedated as I extract the egg with a syringe. When I complete the procedure, the egg is put into a petri dish and the donor sperm is introduced. We should know within a few hours if fertilization takes place. By the next day, Miriam will be sedated again and the fertilized egg will be inserted within the lining of the uterus and if all goes well, the egg will implant and continue to grow. In about nine months from now, you'll be the proud parents of a healthy baby," said Dr. Miller as he continued to explain the complex procedure. "Do either of you have any questions?"

At the mention of the syringe, Alex turned pale again. He hesitated, but forced himself to ask, "Yes, I have one more question, I still don't understand about the donor sperm. Where do you get it and how do you determine which sperm to use?"

"Oh, yes, I forgot to answer that one," apologized Dr. Miller. "The donors are kept in a secured area where they are frozen until we need them. They are carefully labeled with all the pertinent information that is taken from each donor. The donors are screened for any type of genetic defect before we even consider freezing the sperm. We also try hard to match the hair and eye color with the prospective parents as well as many of the other genetic features, such as race and ethnic background. We try hard, but as a man of science, Dr. Stewart, you must realize that we cannot guarantee an exact match. Don't forget, Miriam, the egg is a genetic make-up of you, so the baby will have half of your genes."

"I hope it works, but doctor, if I do become pregnant, will I be able to return to Qumran with Alex?"

"I'm sorry, Miriam, but since this whole procedure is still considered experimental, I would rather that you remain in the States until after the baby's born. You'll have to be monitored closely so that we can document any and all changes as they occur."

Dr. Miller hesitated when he saw the disappointed expression on her face, "Please try to understand that we are still in the learning stages with this procedure. It's true that it has been successful in a few other women, but that number is very limited. In fact, Miriam, you are considered to be one of the initial subjects for this procedure in the United States. I hope that you realize that the long air flight along with the living conditions in Qumran can be a risk for you if you do become pregnant. Do you think it will be a problem to stay here if the procedure works?" asked Dr. Miller looking directly at her.

"No, Dr. Miller, my wife will be able to stay. Actually, it's probably the best thing for her and Nathan right now. The hospital is a distance away from the excavation site and our infirmary is not equipped to handle any major medical problems. I think that Miriam and Nathan will enjoy spending time in the States with our families. They certainly will be well taken care of and pampered. In fact, I'm hoping to stay Stateside for as long a possible. Eventually, I'll have to go back to check the progress and give new directions, but I don't plan to stay for too long in Qumran until after the baby is born."

"I hope it will not effect the progress of your work, Dr. Stewart," remarked Dr. Miller.

"I'm not worried, fortunately, Linda is there to handle things while I'm gone. She and the crew are more than competent to get along without me for awhile," answered Alex. "Miriam's health and the health and well-being of the baby come first."

"I'm very happy to hear you say that, Dr. Stewart, because if your wife would have to go back to Qumran, I'm afraid that I wouldn't be able to continue with the procedure. I don't want to risk her health or the baby's welfare," stated Dr. Miller. "You know that the fact that you've had a child increases the success rate for this procedure, Miriam. Did you have any problems or complications during your pregnancy or with the delivery with your son?"

"No, doctor, I felt very well throughout the pregnancy except toward the end. I was huge and very tired, but luckily, the delivery went very quickly."

"Wonderful, now do either of you have any other questions?"

"How about the cost?" asked Miriam apprehensively.

"Here's the good news. Since our hospital is federally funded and since this is considered to be experimental research, the only cost that is passed to you is the cost of the lab tests which are minimal. I'm fairly sure that your medical insurance will cover most of the lab costs anyway. Will that be a problem?" questioned the doctor.

"No! Absolutely not!" responded Alex.

"Fine, now, if you have no further questions or problems, I must get to my next patient. She's expecting triplets, so I don't want to keep her waiting too long! I hope to see you sometime next week. Terry will call you to schedule a time. When you return next time, she'll set you up with a thermometer and chart graphs provided that your tests come back normal. It certainly was a pleasure meeting both of you and I hope that everything goes well for you. Until next time, relax and take care of yourselves," said the doctor as he left the room.

Alex, I'm so excited, but I don't like the idea that I can't go back to Qumran with you. Maybe you can stay here until the baby comes. That is if all the tests are normal and the procedure works," she added cautiously.

"Don't worry, Honey, they can manage without me on the site. When I do go back to check on things, I won't be away for long. Now, get changed so we can make reservations for dinner. In the meantime, I'll take you shopping so you can buy something for yourself and for Nathan."

"Sounds great to me," she said kissing him quickly before she went to change into her clothes.

As they walked through the parking lot toward their jeep, Miriam noticed a frown on Alex's face,

"What are you thinking about, Honey, you look worried?"

"Huh? Oh, I'm not really worried, but didn't you think it was strange that Dr. Miller didn't ask how you got pregnant with Nathan since I'm sterile?"

"Well, I'm sure that my records show that I was pregnant before we were married, so he probably assumes that another man fathered the baby. Why are you so worried about the fact that he didn't ask? I'm sure he was just being polite by not bringing up a topic that would hurt or embarrass either of us," rationalized Miriam.

"Yeah, as usual, you're probably right. I guess under normal conditions, it would be a touchy subject, so it makes sense to me. Now, let's go shopping!" laughed Alex as he hugged Miriam.

THREE MONTHS LATER

Both Alex and Miriam sat nervously in Dr. Miller's office. Suddenly, he burst into the room waving a piece of paper, smiling and shouting, "Congratulations! You are going to have a baby!"

"Miriam squealed with joy, "I knew it! At first I thought it was all my imagination, but by last week I knew that something was different. I started to feel nauseous in the morning. How far along am I, doctor?"

"Only about three weeks. I know that it sounds very early to make an announcement, but in this type of procedure, it is a definite accomplishment to be able to say that the egg is in place and growing normally. You are indeed pregnant which means that the procedure was a success. So, feeling different and nauseous certainly makes sense."

"Oh, thank you so much, doctor," said Miriam as she stood up and gave Dr. Miller a big hug. "This is wonderful news, I am so happy! Now, what do I do next?"

"Well, for one thing, go out and celebrate! But, no alcoholic beverages, no smoking, no aspirin, and eat well, get plenty of rest and enjoy the next eight months or so," laughed Dr. Miller as he gave her the usual instructions.

"Thank you, doctor, for everything, we owe you a great deal!" smiled Alex as he shook the doctor's hand.

"Oh, I can't wait until this baby is born!" exclaimed Miriam.

"Neither can I," smiled Dr. Miller and he added, "He will certainly be a special child."

"He? How do you know that it'll be a boy?" asked Alex surprised. "We're hoping for a girl this time."

"I guess it's just an educated guess, after all, it's a fifty-fifty chance!" he laughed. "Remember to call me if there are any problems. Now, I'm going to spread the good news to my colleagues, and I'm sure that you want to get home and share the news with your families. I'll see you in two weeks for a check-up. Terry will make an appointment for you." He hurried out of the room, anxious to share the news about his accomplishments.

"He's seems almost as happy as we are, doesn't he, Alex," remarked Miriam as she checked for her purse.

"Yeah, he does," answered Alex. "I wonder if he really knows that it's going to be another boy," he added thoughtfully. "I'm really counting on a little sister for Nathan. Where do you want to make reservations for dinner?"

"The food at Book Binders was great when we were there last time, can we go there again?"

"That's sounds great to me! You know I love that place. I'll call from here. I'll use the phone in the reception area. I'll make reservations for 7:00," said Alex as he and Miriam walked hand in hand down the hallway.

LATER THAT DAY

"I'm starved and exhausted from all that shopping," exclaimed Miriam as they drove to the restaurant. "I hope Nathan likes the marionette that we bought for him. The woman in the store told me that it was hand made in France. It's gorgeous, isn't it?"

"I can't look right now dear, this traffic is crazy!

I'm so used to driving dirt roads in the desert that I feel like I'm in the Indy 500! You jerk! Stay in your own lane!" shouted Alex to the car in front of him.

"Calm down, Honey. I'm glad that we're going out to dinner alone. I can see that you need to relax, in fact, you seemed pretty tense since we left Dr. Miller's office. Is anything wrong?" asked Miriam with concern.

"No, Honey, it's just this damned traffic. I'll feel relaxed after a glass of wine and a good dinner. We're almost there? Are you hungry for anything special? My mouth is watering for surf and turf! It's was excellent the last time we were there." exclaimed Alex.

"Believe it or not, I'm going to do a repeat. I'm going to order the Beef Wellington, it's one of my favorites! I should try to make it one of these days, now that we have the modern conveniences of a fully equipped kitchen." laughed Miriam.

After a quiet dinner and conversation about the events of the day, Alex and Miriam drove home to share their good news with their family. David, Rebekah and Doug were waiting for them to return.

"Well, what's the news?" quizzed Rebekah as she met her daughter at the door. "Are you pregnant?"

"Yep! I am!" laughed Miriam. "All of about three or four weeks!"

"Congratulations, Honey!" exclaimed her father hugging her close.

"I second that!" exclaimed Doug hugging Miriam and then hugging his son. "I'm so happy for both of you! When's the big day?"

"The doctor figures the due date should be around March 15th," answered Alex.

"Ah, the Eydes of March! A day of remembrance throughout the history of the ancient world! Very appropriate, don't you think son?" laughed Doug as he headed toward the table covered with food. "Is anyone else hungry besides me? Rebekah wouldn't let us eat until you got home!"

"I'm with you, Doug, I'm starving, too. Are you two joining us?" asked David.

"No way! Alex and I had a marvelous dinner at Book Binders again. I'm sorry that you waited for us, though, I guess we should have called, but we got so caught up in the news and the shopping that we forgot!" apologized Miriam breathlessly. "Where's Nathan?"

"He's taking a nap, dear, so don't worry about being late. I'm glad that you ate something. You can see by the size of your father that he certainly is not starving! In fact, I'm putting him on a diet. Since he's been spending time with Doug, he's gained ten pounds!" laughed Rebekah. "Did you buy anything?"

"Yeah, wait until you see this! Hey, here comes our boy!" she exclaimed as Alex carried Nathan into the room. "Come here, Honey, wait until you see what mommy and daddy bought for you!"

Instead of going to Miriam, the baby clung onto Alex's shirt and refused to go to her. When Miriam saw this, she became very upset.

"I can't figure out what's wrong with him lately! He doesn't want me to hold him. Do you thing he doesn't love me anymore?" she asked as tears filled her eyes. "This started about three weeks ago. Whenever I try to hold him on my lap, he screams like he's afraid of me and he reaches out for Alex," explained Miriam sadly.

"Oh, Miriam, you are too over protective and you worry about everything!" scolded her mother. "He's probably going through a goofy phase! Kids do that all the time! When you were a baby, you used to call me into your room and insist that you were afraid. Whenever I asked you what you were afraid of, you'd answer, 'I 'fraid Bambi'" laughed Miriam mimicking a two year old's voice as she tried to reassure her daughter. "Just relax, all kids go through phases like this. Why don't you sit down and relax, you look very tired."

Miriam couldn't help but laugh at her mother's voice, "Thanks, Mom, I guess you're right, Nathan just wants to be Daddy's boy for now. You know, I am tired and I hate to admit it, but very nauseous, in fact, I think I'm going to be sick," she moaned as she ran into the bathroom and vomited her Beef Wellington.

FIVE MONTHS LATER - THANKSGIVING DAY NOVEMBER 25, 1967

"One of my favorite holidays!" proclaimed Doug as he and Nathan sat on the floor making a house out of wooden blocks.

"Dinner's almost ready, everyone. Make sure that you wash your hands before you sit down at the table," directed Rebekah. "David, put Nathan in his high chair near me so that I can help him to eat."

"Yes, boss," chuckled David as he saluted his wife. "She sure is bossy but she can really cook! That's one of the reasons I stayed around so long. She feeds me well and I don't even have to think, she does it for me!" he said to Doug.

"And, those my friend, are excellent reasons!" agreed Doug. "You have to admit David, that along with her culinary talents and her ability to command, Rebekah is a bright and beautiful woman. You are indeed a lucky man! I wish that Marilyn was here with us. I really miss her especially around the holidays!" he added wistfully as he walked to the bathroom to freshen up for dinner.

"David, can you get Nathan, he just ran after Doug and he still won't let Miriam pick him up. I have to pour the wine," asked Alex as he saw his son running toward the bathroom after Doug. "When you catch him, put him in his highchair. Dinner is almost on the table, I just have to go out for more wood for the fireplace."

"Sure, Alex," answered David as he tried to catch the squealing two-year old.

A few minutes later, Doug came out of the bathroom and noticed David struggling with Nathan.,

"Can I help," he offered, as he grabbed Nathan's kicking legs. "Down, bronco, down. The horsey has to sit and eat so he can run and play again," said Doug trying to humor the baby.

"Don't you think it's strange that Nathan won't let Miriam bathe him or carry him?" asked David in a low voice as he strapped Nathan into his high chair. "What really worries me is that she's been having those seizures again. She was doing so well for the last two years that Rebekah and I though that they were gone for good! Alex told us that Dr. Miller thinks that it's the result of her hormones changing because of the pregnancy, what do you think Doug?"

"David, that's out of my field of expertise. Alex and I weren't really close until he got older and had the same interests as me. I was off in different countries working when he was little, so I've got no idea about how normal two-year olds behave. I've heard that kids go through lots of different phases. Hopefully, this one will pass soon. I don't think it's anything to worry about because he seems well adjusted otherwise," remarked Doug.

During the meal, Alex made the announcement that he had to leave for Qumran the following week.

"It's unavoidable, Rebekah, I have to go back because they've uncovered something new. Linda sounded very excited which means it something significant. Since I was commissioned by the Vatican, I must be there to verify the artifacts before it becomes public," defended Alex to his mother-in-law.

"What about Miriam, she's staying here, isn't she? demanded Rebekah in a forceful tone.

"That's what Dr. Miller ordered but we plan to discuss it with him when we see him on Monday," answered Alex avoiding her stare.

"What's to discuss?" questioned Rebekah. "You don't think for a minute that Miriam is in any shape to go back to that desert, do you, Alex?"

"Mother, Alex and I are fully capable of making our own decisions and I feel that my place is with him. I'm very uncomfortable without him. I know that if he goes away for any length of time, I'll just be more upset and feel worse than I do now!" retorted Miriam in tears.

Rebekah looked at her daughter's face and didn't like what she saw. She was worried because Miriam did not gain the same amount of weight as she did at this point of her last pregnancy. Her usual bright blue eyes appeared glazed and were outlined in dark circles. This made her normally fair skin even more pale and somewhat translucent.

"Miriam, I didn't mean to upset you, but I am very worried about you. Alex told me that along with having seizures again, you're nightmares have returned and as a result, you're not sleeping at night! I can see that something is wrong just by looking at you.

Has Dr. Miller noticed your weight is not what it should be? Maybe you should have Dr. Feldman check you out," suggested Rebekah with a worried look.

"Mom, I'll be alright, it's just that this pregnancy is the totally opposite of the way I felt when I was carrying Nathan. I seem to have one constant headache and on top of it, I am always nauseous. Because of that, I can't eat too much. I am taking the vitamins and drinking the protein drink that the doctor prescribed so I know that I'm getting the proper nutrition. Please don't worry so much, Mom, it'll give you wrinkles," Miriam laughed weakly as she attempted to give some humor to the conversation.

"Besides, Rebekah, if the doctor agrees, Miriam can stay with Ben and Rachel. In fact, we called there last week and hinted around at the possibility and they are thrilled. Of course, we told them that we have to have the doctor's approval first," commented Alex.

"Alex, you know that I don't like this one bit. I wish you would consider having Dr. Feldman check her. She really does not look well," said Rebekah in an angry tone when Miriam left for the bathroom.

"I'll ask Miriam to make an appointment, if it'll make you feel better, Rebekah."

"Yes, it will and don't wait too long either!" she retorted.

"Alex, I learned a long time ago, do not argue with this woman, you'll never win!" remarked David laughing.

"Not just this woman, any woman! Geez, son, I thought you would have learned that by now!" added Doug with a chuckle.

Later that night, as Alex and Miriam were alone in their room changing for bed, Miriam began to cry.

"Honey, what's wrong? Don't you feel well? Should I call your mother?" he asked as he held her close.

"No, I guess I'm just tired and worried. I feel rotten most of the time and the worst part is that Nathan doesn't want to come near me. Yesterday, I tried to get him to feel the baby kick and when I put his little hand on my stomach, he looked absolutely terrified and he began to scream, so I let him go. Last night, I had a dream that Nathan and the new baby were constantly fighting. I was so upset that I couldn't get back to sleep. I don't want you to leave me, Alex, I can't explain it, but I have a very strong feeling that I must go back with you. I don't even mind staying with my grandparents as long as I know that you'll be nearby and that'll I get to see you once in awhile. I just can't stand the thought of being here without you. Please, Honey, I'm really scared!" and she began to sob uncontrollably.

"Honey, calm down, I won't ever leave you! No matter what Dr. Miller says on Monday, you are coming with me. I'm sure that there are doctors in Israel that are fully capable of delivering a baby! Just because this baby started out differently, doesn't mean that it won't be born in a normal way. I know that I'll feel much better if you and Nathan are close by. Come on, Honey, dry your eyes and try to get some sleep. You must be exhausted," coaxed Alex as he helped her get into the bed.

Alex tucked the covers around her an continued to console her, "As far as the way Nathan is acting, just try to remember that he's a very precocious child and maybe he senses that the baby will be a rival for your time. He's probably feeling a bit jealous already.

As far as your dreams, don't worry, the kids will fight. All brothers and sisters do! It's normal! Now, close your eyes and try to sleep. I love you more every day, don't ever forget that," said Alex as he kissed her good-night.

"Alex, I love you, too, you always say the right thing to make me feel better. I hope you're right about Nathan and the baby. I wish I knew someone else who has two kids so I could find out if this is normal. Good-night, Honey," said Miriam returning his kiss as she cuddled close to him.

Alex put his arms around her and when he felt her frail body, he knew that Rebekah was right about Miriam's weight and appearance. Even her mental attitude seemed so different with this pregnancy. When she was expecting Nathan, Miriam was always in good spirits, laughing and teasing. Now, she was always worried over the most minute things and at times, seemed really depressed.

He promised himself that whatever the doctor said he would not leave her behind. He stayed awake for a long time and listened to her breathing. Alex wasn't only worried about her physical health but about her emotional health as well. He knew that she had gone through more stress in the last two years than most people experience in a lifetime. As he finally drifted into a dream state, Alex knew that he had not really lived or enjoyed life until he met Miriam. He truly believed that fate had brought them together.

AL BIEN, BUSCARLO Y AL MAL, ESPERARLO.

**FOR THE GOOD, SEARCH, FOR THE BAD,
AWAIT.** **Spanish Proverb**

CHAPTER XXIX

SUNDAY, MARCH 15, 1970 - BEN ZION HOSPITAL IN ISRAEL

"Can't this damned thing go any faster, Linda," shouted Alex as they raced along the dirt roads on the way to the hospital.

"Wow, talk about opposites! Miriam always yells at me for driving like a lunatic and you're yelling because I'm not doing warp speed! Calm down, the baby has already arrived so there's nothing you could do at this point, except get there in one piece. Besides, we should be there in about fifteen minutes, so relax and enjoy the ride," retorted Linda as she swerved to avoid a huge rut in the road.

"As Linda pulled up to the hospital entrance, Alex jumped out and ran to the elevator. At the maternity desk he asked for his wife's room.

"And, what is your wife's name," asked the amused nurse, smiling.

"Oh, I'm sorry, I guess I'm a little excited right now! It's Mrs. Alex Stewart," he answered.

"Mrs. Stewart is in 443, right down the hall and to your left. She's doing just fine and so is the baby." the nurse called to Alex as he ran down the hallway.

As he entered the room, he was greeted by Miriam's smile.

"Alex, you're here!" exclaimed Miriam. "I couldn't wait for you, or should I say, your son couldn't wait. Have you seen him yet? I'm worried because they didn't bring him to be fed. I haven't seen him since shortly after he was born. The nurse keeps assuring me that everything is alright, but I'd like to see for myself. Will you please go and check with Dr. Robinson? He should be around here somewhere. Ask the nurse to page him for you," insisted Miriam.

"Calm down, Honey, I'll go in a minute, Linda should be stopping in soon. She drove me here in record time, although it seemed like we were on the road forever!" he laughed.

"He went over to his wife and kissed her, How are you feeling? Did everything go all right? I'll never forgive myself for not being here with you. It seems as though every other woman in the world takes several hours to give birth except you!" joked Alex. "You know, Honey, you look great, better than you have in a while," remarked Alex as he kissed her again.

"Believe it or not, for just having a baby, I feel great, in fact, I haven't felt this good in the last nine months," she responded as she returned his kisses.

"Another son! I can't wait to see him. At first I really wanted a girl, but now I'm glad that Nathan will have a brother. I always wanted an older brother to talk to and I think Nathan will be a great teacher for his little brother."

"So do I, but we never decided on a boy's name because you were so sure that it was going to be a girl! Maybe you should go and look at him first and then we can decide. You're the name expert in the family, anyway," laughed Miriam. "But, before you come back here, find the doctor and make sure that the baby's healthy. Don't forget," she warned.

"O.K. Boss," smiled Alex as he walked out the door.

Alex walked down the long hospital corridor and kept an eye out for Dr. Robinson, but he was nowhere in sight. As he approached the nursery, Alex was surprised to see Linda coming out of the nursery door with Dr. Miller.

"Dr. Miller," called Alex. "What are you doing over here? I never expected to see you in Israel!"

"Oh, Alex, talk about timing. It's nice to see you again," the doctor answered with a startled look. "My wife and I are here visiting my in-laws in Jordan. When Dr. Robinson called me with the good news, I thought I'd drive over and check on the baby. As I was doing the exam in the nursery, I looked out the viewing window and there was Linda! I'm trying to convince her to take a day or two off from work and come back with me to Jordan. My in-laws are celebrating their fortieth wedding anniversary and they would be honored and delighted if Linda could be there. What do you think? Can you spare her for a few days?" inquired Dr. Miller.

"By all means! Linda do you want to go back with Dr. Miller or do you want to take the jeep? I can stay around here until Miriam is discharged and then I can rent a jeep to get back to Qumran," offered Alex graciously. "You sure could use a few days off to rest."

"Thanks, Alex, but to make things easier, I'll just hitch a ride with Tom. He's leaving in about an hour so you can have the jeep. I am really looking forward to seeing Najia and her parents again. I'm going in to see Miriam now. Tom, when you're finished here, meet me in Miriam's room. Alex, your son is gorgeous, wait until you see him!" remarked Linda as she went down the hall to find Miriam's room.

"Doc, have you checked the baby, Miriam is a worry-wart and is concerned because she hasn't seen him yet," Alex asked Dr. Miller.

"Yes, and he's in excellent health. And, from what I could hear from here, he's got a great set of lungs! It sounds to me like your son is hungry. Maybe he's been content all this time, so that's why Miriam hasn't gotten a chance to see him. Would you like to go inside the nursery and hold him?" asked Dr. Miller.

Alex nodded and the men went inside. Dr. Miller introduced Alex to the OB nurse and she handed Alex a gown and a mask. As he was putting on the protective clothing, Dr. Miller said that he had some other people to see.

"I'll be in to check on Miriam in a few minutes. Enjoy some quiet time with your son, I'll see you in the room."

"O.K., doc, and thanks again. It looks like you did an excellent job. This kid is huge! How much does he weigh," Alex asked the nurse after she put the wrapped bundle in his arms.

He's twenty-three inches long and weighs 10 pounds, seven ounces," read the nurse from the baby's chart.

"Wow! This isn't a baby, he's a linebacker!" laughed Alex as he proudly showed off his son to the other people standing outside of the viewing window.

Dr. Miller laughed and patted him on the shoulder. "I'll see you in about twenty minutes. Enjoy your son!"

Alex looked around at the other babies lying in the bassinets, smiled at his son and said, "You certainly are a big boy and you look like a real tough guy. I think you need a name to fit your size so we'll talk to Mommy about naming you Maximilian. I thing that Max is a perfect name for you, what do you think, big guy?"

The baby opened his eyes for a few minutes, yawned and fell back to sleep. After a few more minutes, the nurse told Alex that it was time for the baby to be changed. He quickly handed him over, took off the mask and gown, and headed down to Miriam's room. When he walked in, he saw Linda sitting on the edge of the bed laughing and talking with his wife. She had stopped and bought a huge bouquet of flowers for Miriam and their fragrance permeated the room. Alex just walked into the room and Dr. Miller was right behind him.

"Well, Pop, have you decided on a name for that son of yours?" asked Dr. Miller.

"Yes, I did!" exclaimed Alex. "I think he's definitely a Maximilian! We can call him Max. In Latin, the name means, 'greatest,' and from what I could see, our son is the biggest and toughest baby in the entire nursery. What do you think, Miriam, do you like the name Max or would you rather Eric?"

"Maximilian and your explanation makes it more personal, just like when we named Nathan. So, Maximilian it will be, do you like it?" asked Miriam looking at Linda and Dr. Miller.

"Well, Alex is right, the name certainly does fit him and it isn't a very common name. I think it's an excellent choice. Miriam, when did Dr. Robinson tell you that you can be released?" asked Dr. Miller as he listened to her heart. "Are you feeling alright?"

"Yes, I feel great. He said that I can leave either Thursday or Friday, and I can't wait!" she answered smiling.

"I hope you have someone to help you when you leave the hospital. Remember that your recovery will take a bit longer since you had a C-section done. Good old Max was too big! Who's watching Nathan?" the doctor asked.

"He's with Miriam's grandparents and her cousin, Sarah, is helping out with him," said Alex.

"That's a great set-up. I've met Sarah and she's great with kids," commented Linda.

Dr. Miller looked at his watch and gasped, "Oh, no, I had no idea how late it got! Linda, come on, Najia will kill the both of us. We have to get back to Jordan by 7:00 for dinner!"

Dr. Miller shook Alex's hand and he and Linda kissed Miriam good-bye. As they headed toward the door, the OB nurse came into the room with a screaming baby.

"Here he is and he's starving!" announced the nurse as she handed the bundle to Miriam.

Miriam turned to Alex and said, "Honey, we must be the luckiest and most blessed couple in the whole world! Max is a beautiful baby and I'm sure that Nathan will love him and be a terrific big brother!"

THE VATICAN - 1997

"Alex and Miriam had no idea that Michael was also in Israel when Miriam gave birth to her second son. Michael knew that the baby would be born somewhere in the Middle East. You know, Holy Father, that there are prophecies that predict that the Anti-Christ was to be born around the same time period in the Middle East. I often wondered if it was just coincidence. Ray told me much later that Miriam was concerned about the child's health because she was so ill during most of her pregnancy and she couldn't eat very well. As it turned out, the baby was very healthy. Michael made sure of that, he had ordered the doctor to prescribe certain vitamins and other supplements for Miriam. Michael also made sure that he was there to check the child himself when Maximilian was born. He must have been thrilled that Miriam carried this baby to term," said Cardinal DeGroot as he continued to reminisce.

"Paul, what was Michael's interest in the second child? I can understand his involvement with the first child, but what was his connection with the Stewarts' second son?" asked the Pope. "Whose sperm did the doctor use to fertilize Miriam's egg?"

"I have my suspicions about the sperm donor but I have no proof. Perhaps in the near future, I will be able to find out."

"I know how difficult this is for you, Paul, but you must tell me everything, not only for your sake, but for mine also. I need to know so that I could prepare myself to deal with the outcome of the cartel's plan," requested the Holy Father.

"Yes, Holy Father, but it is very hard to have to admit my deception to you all of these years. I shall continue, however, I remember that shortly after the birth of the second child, Alex realized that he had to get his family out of the Middle East. Tensions mounted because of the war in Lebanon. Pope Paul called Alex to Rome and the Pope encouraged Alex to abandon the dig site at Masada in Qumran because of the bombings in Beirut. For a variety of reasons, Alex did not return to Masada again but he did what he could for the Vatican from his home in the States. Both he and Miriam were too afraid to take their children back there while the situation was so unsettled.

"While Alex was in Rome, we met and I asked about his family. His answers were guarded and reserved and I could see that the trust that he once had for me was gone. Alex was still angry and suspicious about Miriam's first son and I believe that he knew about Michael's part in it. He told me that he was offered a job teaching archaeology at the Univerisity of PA and that he and his family settled near the school and were very content."

"I was curious as to how they were raising their children since Alex was Catholic and Miriam was a Messianic Jew. Alex said that Nathan was both circumcised by a Rabbi and Baptized by Bishop Pascal, but when they tried to circumcise Maximilian, the baby had other ideas. When the Rabbi began the Hebrew prayers, the baby screamed and carried on so badly that Miriam was afraid that he would become ill. She insisted in postponing the service. Miriam and Alex agreed that they would wait until they returned to the States and just have Pascal perform the Baptism. When the family was settled in the States, Ray did baptize the baby, but a *Bris* was never performed."

"From all other reports, the family led a fairly normal life until 1972 when Alex, his father and a group of professors took a small jet to a seminar in the western part of the State. About thirty minutes after take-off, the jet exploded and the cause of the horrible accident was never resolved. Miriam and the boys were scheduled to go along as they had planned to make a family vacation out of the trip, however, Max had an infection and couldn't travel. Miriam was devastated by the accident, but fortunately, she is a strong woman with a strong faith. Ray mentioned that she told him that the morning of the flight, she begged Alex and Doug to stay home. She told Ray that she had a terrible nightmare about the flight, but when she told Alex, he just laughed at her and told her that she was over-tired from taking care of the sick child. I always felt bad for her because not only did she have to cope with the loss of her husband and father-in-law, but I understand that she had problems with her children. The boys were total opposites in their appearance, personalities and in their dispositions. From what Ray said, Max was very possessive of Miriam and anytime Nathan came near her, he would scream and carry on.

Pascal told me that Miriam was concerned about the baby's personality traits, but she finally attributed it to normal jealousy. She hoped that he would grow out of it in time. However, after Alex's sudden death, Max became worse and it became difficult for Miriam to deal with it. Her life was in turmoil. She and Alex were seldom apart and Pascal said that for a very long time, Miriam refused to socialize with anyone except him and Linda Martinelli, Alex's former assistant. She was the only one that could control Max and she and Miriam remained very close. Over the years, Miriam became very protective of her sons and the jealousy that Max had for Nathan became her constant thorn."

"Ray did all he could to help the family and for some reason, Ray became as close to Nathan as Max was to Linda. He told me that in order to keep the boys from fighting, he would take Nathan fishing or to a baseball or football game while Linda would take Max. It gave Miriam a chance to rest and get some of Alex's papers in order. Over the years, the relationships became solid and to this day, Max will spend as much time as possible with Linda."

"Things began to change when Nathan was thirteen years old and it was time for his *Bar Mitzvah*. Miriam decided to have the ceremony in Israel because her grandparents were not well and couldn't travel. Although the Middle East was still very unstable, no one could convince Miriam not to go. You should remember the news reports that caused so much attention when the incidents occurred in 1980."

"Are you alluding to the incidents that involved Nathan? I recall some of it, Paul, but please refresh my memory," requested the Pope.

VIRTURE DOES NOT ALWAYS DEMAND A HEAVY SACRIFICE, ONLY THE WILLINGNESS TO MAKE IT WHEN NECESSARY.
Frederick Dunn

CHAPTER XXX

"Yes, Holy Father, the incidents did concern Nathan and I will try hard to remember as much as I can. The first incident occurred in the temple. As customary, he went to the synagogue on the day of his *Bar Mitzvah* and began to read from the Torah. A strange thing happened, Holy Father, Nathan did not read the text in the normal Hebrew, but in Aramaic, the ancient language of Christ. This shocked and amazed the Rabbi and the rest of the congregation. After the service, when they questioned the young boy, Nathan could not understand why they were so shocked. Then, the other strange occurrences began to happen..."

"Ah, yes, I seem to recall that the child had some sort of vision," remarked the Pope.

"Yes, but it didn't end with the visions. The young boy appeared to have flashes of memory that no one was able to explain. For instance, while sight seeing in Israel, he and his mother were walking through side alleys in Jerusalem when the boy began to act strangely. He behaved as though he was in a great deal of pain. When Miriam took him to the doctor, he could not find a reason for his pain. Several days later, Miriam read an article in a local newspaper that reported a team of archaeologists had recently discovered the true path that Christ used on his way to Golgotha. The path runs parallel to the popular Way of the Cross used by tourists for centuries. When Miriam recalled where she and Nathan were when he took ill, she realized that they were walking down a narrow alley located in the same area that was mentioned in the news account. Miriam only told Pascal because she was both puzzled and worried about this information and about Nathan's health. She was not sure if there was a connection between the area and Nathan's physical condition."

"Perhaps the most inexplicable event took place in the hospital. A few days later, Rachel, Nathan's great grandmother was stricken with a heart attack. Because of the damage from previous attacks, the doctors told the family that she probably not live through the night. Miriam and Nathan decided to spend the night at her bedside. During the early morning hours, Miriam left to get something to eat and Nathan was left alone with the dying woman. Miriam was half-way to the cafeteria when she realized that she did not have her purse. She went back to the room and as she opened the door to the dark room, she saw a strange light emitting from Nathan's body. She watched as Nathan put his hand on his great grandmother's head and the glowing light flowed from Nathan into her. Miriam said that she heard Nathan say something and within a minute, Rachel was sitting up in bed."

"Miriam told Ray that she was so stunned that she could not move for a few seconds. When she was finally able to call Nathan's name, he turned around and looked at her. Miriam was frightened because when she looked at his face, he appeared to be in a daze and his body appeared to be transparent. She yelled Nathan's name louder and within a short time, he appeared to be normal. Miriam decided not to say anything about the incident because she feared for Nathan. The night nurse, however, also witnessed the incident and reported it to the doctors and the media. When the doctors examined the old woman who was sitting up in bed and talking to them, they were sure that a mistake had been made because they had no explanation for her sudden change. They compared the tests results with her previous tests, and they concluded that she made a complete recovery."

"Did the doctors believe the nurse when she told them what she saw?" inquired the Holy Father.

"Most of them did not know what to believe. When they questioned Nathan, he simply said that all he did was pray for her recovery as he laid his hands on her. The doctors could not explain the woman's complete recovery scientifically and had to admit that there is often a power beyond medical science that cannot be explained," answered Cardinal DeGroot.

"I do remember that the Church spent a great deal of money to suppress the story. But, the other child, what happened to him?" inquired the Holy Father.

"Maximilian is another story. He and Nathan were always different. Ray told me that even from a young child, Max was a problem. He was a trouble-maker in school and fought with the other children. By the time he was eleven, he was in trouble with the law. Miriam tried her best to control him, but he was totally defiant. He refused to go to church and would not go near a synagogue. Since Miriam was always deeply religious, she was heartbroken over his behavior. Ray told us that because of this, he tried to spend as much time as possible with her and the boys. He made a point to spend every holiday with them so that Miriam would not feel alone. Ray said that there were times that Max would be so misbehaved that he was unbearable to be around. Yet, according to Ray, Nathan would always make excuses for his brother," Cardinal DeGroot droned on.

"Who is this child, Paul?" asked the Pope.

"I don't have any proof, Holy Father, but I do have my suspicions. However, I'd prefer to finish my confession before I make any type of conjecture about Max," responded DeGroot.

"I'm becoming curious, but I can wait. Please continue, Paul," commented the Pope.

"Well, over the next few years, things seemed to calm down and we didn't hear too much about the family. Of course, we learned later that Michael had always kept a close watch on the family, especially on both of the children. Shortly after Nathan's great grandmother was healed, Milos Kowalsky died. We were all happy that he died a contented man. He believed that Michael's experiment with the Shroud was a success. He was sure that it would indeed bring peace and justice to the entire world. Milos was a dear friend, a very devoted Cardinal and a good man, Holy Father."

"I agree, Paul, Milos came from a village close to mine in Poland and we were friends for many years. He was very disturbed by the atrocities that the Nazis committed during the war and he became very disappointed after Vatican II and the turmoil it caused in the Church. I honestly believe that the chaos in the Church during those years cost him his health and I remember how quickly he aged because of it. I am happy to know that he died content," commented the Holy Father. "But, Paul, why did you tell me that it was urgent for me to meet with Nathan? Has anything else transpired?"

"He is now thirty years old, Holy Father, and his popularity as a charismatic preacher is growing daily. He has returned to Israel and has gathered quite a large following. You really must meet with him and talk to him," explained Cardinal DeGroot.

"Paul, my friend, you are taking Milos's place. You worry too much. I will meet with him in good time. Please finish your confession and tell me what part Brazini, God rest his soul, and the others played in this plan. They surely must have reacted the same way when they heard the reports about Miriam's son," remarked the Pope.

"Ah, yes, Holy Father, we were all amazed and pleased with the reports we heard about Nathan. Brazini, like the rest of us, was convinced that Nathan was the Christ child, born again to walk the earth. But, true to his nature, Antonio was not content with Nathan's work. Antonio wanted total control of Nathan so that the Church would become even more powerful. He also wanted that total control for his own personal glory. Once our plans were set in motion, Michael and Antonio became locked in battle for total control of the project. In fact, Holy Father, there were many times when the rest of us were convinced that one of them would harm or destroy the other. Much later, this fear became reality and I must confess to you what I know about Antonio's death."

"What do you mean, Paul, I thought that Antonio died as a result of his heart problems. What do you know about his death?"

"Holy Father, I know that everyone believed that Antonio died because his heart had given out and it did. But, it was no ordinary heart attack. Everyone knew that Antonio's heart was bad and Michael took advantage of this knowledge. Michael knew that

Antonio believed that Nathan is the cloned Christ. Michael bated Antonio by insisting that Nathan was not the person he thought him to be. Antonio approached Michael and tried to protest what he was telling him. Michael cruelly pushed Antonio aside and told him that even though Nathan was cloned from the blood on the Shroud, he was only a genetic clone of the man, not the divine. Michael coldly laughed at Antonio's anguished reaction to this revelation."

"Michael continued to berate Antonio by telling him that he only cloned the blood from the Shroud to prove to himself and to the Cardinals that it could be done. Michael further taunted Antonio by telling him that Nathan was only the preliminary experiment and that he had greater plans in mind. He then told Antonio that he alone was in total control of everything that was done and that will be done. When Antonio tried to argue, Michael told him that he and the other Cardinals were only worthless pawns in the entire plan. Antonio became so angry when he heard these words, that he lunged at Michael and when he did, Michael grabbed his arm and violently pushed him. Antonio lost his balance and fell down the chapel steps."

"How do you know all of this, Paul, I can't believe that Michael would admit this to you," asked the Pope.

"No, Michael did not have to tell me, I am confessing this, Holy Father, because I am guilty of remaining silent until now. I was in the chapel when this meeting took place but neither Michael nor Antonio knew I was there. I was shocked at the contents of the conversation, but I did not make my presence known until Antonio fell down the steps and did not get up. I have been haunted since that day, Holy Father, by Michael's maniacal laughter that echoed throughout the chapel. Michael continued to laugh as Antonio struggled for breath and reached toward Michael for help. But he just stood over Antonio's crumbled body and did nothing. Oh, Holy Father, please forgive me. I blame Michael for pushing Antonio and causing his death, but I blame myself for not stopping their quarrel," lamented Cardinal DeGroot.

"Be calm, my friend, you are here to obtain God's forgiveness and His grace to give you strength. Please tell me, what did the others have to gain?"

"Cardinals Acietuno, Belawa, Brazini, Kowalsky, LeBlanc and myself agreed to form the cartel with the hope of bringing Christ back on earth. We believed that His presence and his words would end the horrors and destruction that were taking place throughout the world. Nathan's preaching has generated a lot of publicity and many world leaders have become interested in him."

"Nathan has been healing the sick and working many other wondrous deeds, but they have not been recognized as miracles. We hoped that through his goodness, Nathan would bring peace and justice to the world. We also hoped that he would proclaim Holy Mother Church as the true church."

"Paul, you indicated before that all of you had you own reasons for being a part of this plan, what were they?" questioned the Pope.

"Yes, we did have personal interests in Michael's experiments. For years, Chinua Belawa worried about the conditions in his country. He was extremely distraught when Mobutu took over the Congo as dictator and suppressed the people under severe rules. Mobutu was greedy and wanted to profit from the country's great supply of gold, copper and uranium. Chinua had tried to reason with Mobutu many times for the sake of his people. Recently Nathan met with

Mobutu and a few weeks later, the dictator agreed to step down and let democracy rule. The country has even changed it name back from Zaire to the Congo. Chinua believes that his prayers have been answered and that our project has been a success."

"What about Jorge Acietuno, Rene LeBlanc and you, Paul, who do they believe he is?" inquired the Pope.

"I believe that Nathan is indeed extraordinary. Many of his healings have been tested and medically documented. This is one of the reasons that you must meet with him, Holy Father, you must support his work for the sake of the Church and for the world. Jorge is convinced that if Castro agrees to meet with Nathan, Cuba will be freed from the harsh rule of Communism. Rene has been praying that France will come back to its faith. He truly believes that it will happen soon especially since there have been so many positive changes throughout the world since Nathan begun his work. Think of it, Holy Father, the Cold War is over, Communism has fallen in Russia, and the Iron Curtain no longer exists. The Berlin Wall is gone and there are possibilities for peace treaties in the Middle East and Ireland. Nathan must be the returned Christ!" exclaimed DeGroot breathless both from excitement as well as exhaustion.

"If what you are saying is true, Paul, have you thought of the consequences that are predicted for the Parousia? The wars, the famines, the floods, the pestilence, the droughts, the suffering of mankind?" listed the Pope. "It is true that many of these horrors are happening somewhere in the world right now. How can you be so sure that Nathan is not just a false prophet or worse yet, the anti-Christ predicted in the Book of Revelations? Remember Paul, Nathan was not sent by the Father. He was made by a man. A man, you yourself, proclaim to be evil! Are Nathan's words accepted by all religious denominations like the Hindus, the Moslems and the Jews?" questioned the Pope in a very serious tone.

"No, Holy Father, what you have just said, needs to be considered," responded DeGroot.

"Tell me what it is that he preaches?"

"In truth, Holy Father, his message is a simple one, one that does not promote any organized religion. Nathan preaches that we are all brothers and sisters and all equal in the eyes of God. Nathan has said that institutions only restrict and twist the minds of people. He claims that we should love one another and do our duty to our God by working to making the world a true community of all God's children. Nathan also preaches that religious leaders have corrupted the message that Christ brought two thousand years ago. He stresses that we must return to Christ's pure and basic message. Many church leaders are concerned about the long term results of the this type of preaching especially in respect to organized religions. They are worried because Nathan's following is growing each day, especially among the young people. When you think about it, Holy Father, Nathan is really not preaching anything that is offensive nor does he preach anything that Christ did not. But, at the same time, perhaps you should talk to him and make sure that he is not saying anything that will hurt our Holy Mother Church," advised Cardinal DeGroot.

"As I mentioned before, when the time is right, I will sit down with Nathan and speak with him. From what you have told me and from what I have been told by others, I do not believe that anything he says indicates that he is dangerous. I believe that the best course of action right now, is to do nothing. We will sit back, follow his progress and wait to see what transpires. Is there anything else that you wish to confess, Paul?" asked the Pope in a tired voice.

"No, Holy Father, although my memory is not what it used to be, I believe that I have confessed the most important details. Even though the six of us may have had personal reasons for beginning our project, our main purpose was to clone the blood on the Shroud of Turin so that the Catholic Church could finally prove to the world and to the faltering Catholics that Jesus Christ truly did walk the earth and is the Son of God."

"Holy Father, we never anticipated the astounding effect that Nathan would actually have on the entire world, nor did we expect Nathan to preach against organized religion. I suppose, not unlike Antonio and Michael, the rest of us wanted to control who he would become and what he would preach."

"I am surprised, Paul, that you and the rest of your group, did not realize sooner that you are guilty of the original sins of Adam and Eve, the sins of Pride and Presumption. You were filled with pride by thinking that you could control others and you all presumed, especially Michael, that you had the ability to create a divinity," said the Pope.

"You were filled with such pride and presumption that you believed you could become god-like yourselves. Paul, you never told me what Antonio expected to get out of this plan. I cannot believe that he constructed this plan for the good of Holy Mother Church. I knew Antonio too well to believe that this was his only mission," commented the Pope.

"You are right, we have all committed two very grave sins. Antonio had great ambitions and it was no secret that he eventually planned to become Pope. He enjoyed the fact that he was the mastermind of the plan, that is, until Michael's genius proved too much for him."

"There is one question that remains unanswered, Paul, did Miriam ever find out what happened to her when she was in the Vatican infirmary?" asked the Holy Father. "Does she know who Nathan really is?"

"She did not know for a very long time. From what Bishop Pascal told me, he had to dissuade the Sharones from instigating a lawsuit against the Vatican. After her parents learned that Alex was sterile, they were convinced that their daughter was raped by some Church official. I am sure that the girl believed the same thing, but her faith and Alex's support kept her strong. She and Alex were very much in love and after their marriage, she refused to dwell on Nathan's paternity. It was not until the miracles began to happen that Ray thought it was time to tell her what he suspected even though he had no actual proof," explained DeGroot.

"How did she accept the news that her son was cloned from the blood of the Shroud?" inquired the Pope.

"Pascal told me that she had a very strange reaction. She told Ray that she always knew that Nathan was not an ordinary child even from the early days of her pregnancy. Miriam also told him that her dreams and nightmares make sense to her now and she finally understands why she was referred to as the Chosen One. Miriam is convinced that Nathan is destined to make positive changes in the world, however, she is very worried about her son's safety now that he is in the public eye. She travels with him and refuses to be separated from him for too long," answered DeGroot in a very weak and raspy voice.

"You are tired, Paul and I admit that I am, too. Reliving the past is often worse than living it the first time. We must rest before our Holy Thursday services tonight. I am grateful that you had the courage to confess. Before I administer you penance and your absolution, I must know one more thing. Who is Miriam's second son?" inquired the Pope.

"I do not know for sure, but I have always suspected that he is Michael's son. I believe that Michael impregnated Miriam with his own sperm so that his genius and his plans to control the world would come to pass," replied DeGroot.

"There are still many unanswered questions to this whole situation. May God give us the strength and the courage to withstand the repercussions of what the cartel and Michael have initiated," observed the Pope in an anxious tone. "Now for your penance, you must pray for Nathan, for his mother, and for world peace and for understanding among mankind. You must also reveal what ever you know to Bishop Pascal, so that he will be able to help Miriam in her time of need. Now, my friend, I want you to make a good Act of Contrition."

"Yes, Holy Father, and thank you for you patience, understanding and advice. You are truly a good friend. Oh my God, I am heartily sorry for having offended Thee..." recited Cardinal DeGroot feeling tired but relieved that he had unburdened his soul.

"I absolve of your sins, in the name of the Father, the Son, and the Holy Spirit, Amen," said the Pope as he made the sign of the Cross over Cardinal DeGroot.

**WE ARE READY TO BE SAVAGE IN SOME
CAUSE. THE DIFFERENCE BETWEEN A
GOOD MAN AND A BAD ONE, IS THE CHOICE
OF THE CAUSE.   William James**

CHAPTER XXXI

ISRAEL - EASTER/PASSOVER HOLIDAYS
1998

   Miriam sat alone in the synagogue. She had come
there to pray, to collect her thoughts and most of all, to
seek comfort, especially now that Nathan was
becoming so popular. She was both proud of him and
worried for him. Throughout most of her life, Miriam
was plagued by dreams and nightmares that foretold
what would eventually come to pass and she still
couldn't escape the glimpses into the future. Miriam
appreciated the opportunity to sit alone in the quiet of
the temple. It gave her a chance to relax for awhile and
to reflect on her life. A sad smile crossed her face
when she thought about Alex and how much she missed
him.

   Alex was not only her helper, her protector and
her teacher; he was her one true love. Miriam looked
down at her wedding band that she refused to remove
after all these years. She remembered how pleasantly
surprised she was when Alex put it on her finger during
their wedding ceremony. The gold band was formed
from Hebrew letters that read, "I belong to my beloved

and my beloved belongs to me." Miriam unconsciously fingered the band as she returned to that hot August day in 1972 when she received the horrible news. When the phone call came to inform her of the plane crash, she tried to keep a glimmer of hope alive because she could not imagine living without Alex. But, when Dean Jackson from the university arrived at the door, she already knew what he was going to tell her.

Alex, Doug and several professors had died in a plane crash on their way to a seminar at Mercyhurst University in Erie, PA. Because of the explosion, the bodies were burned beyond recognition and Miriam was robbed of the normal closure of seeing her loved ones for a final time. The day was hot and humid, but when she heard the news, Miriam felt her blood run cold and over the years, she never really felt warm again.

Whenever she thought of Alex, she knew that a part of her life had drained from her body forever, and even now, she felt the chill. Not one morning passes when she is in the twilight state between sleep and consciousness, when she doesn't search Alex's side of the bed, hoping to find him there. Miriam wiped the tears from her cheeks as she thought of him, but even in her sorrow, Miriam was grateful to God that He had brought them together.

Miriam dried her eyes and sighed deeply. She began the prayer for the dead and prayed for Alex, Doug and her grandparents. No matter how hard she tried to concentrate, Miriam's memory flashed back to Alex and she could almost hear the concern and worry in his voice when he told her the truth about Nathan. Alex cried as he held her close and he asked her to forgive him for not revealing his suspicions sooner. Between his sobs, he explained that he only recently pieced the mystery together. Even though he did not have definite proof, he wanted her to know what happened to her that night in the Vatican infirmary.

Miriam closed her eyes and could see the expression on his face when she told him that she had always known that Nathan was not an ordinary child. She told him that she always suspected that the Vatican knew more than they were willing to reveal. But now, it didn't matter what Michael Bachman might have done, Nathan was the joy of her life. Her mind jumped to the day when Ray sat down with her and Nathan and told him the truth about his conception. She and Alex had planned to tell Nathan when they thought he was old enough to fully understand the complex story, but Alex never got the opportunity. After Alex was killed, Ray offered to tell Nathan. Miriam remembered that Nathan wasn't surprised to hear that he didn't belong to either of the people who were his legal parents. She remembered the deep, soul-searching look that Nathan gave her and when he told her that no matter who the world believed him to be, he is and always would be her son. When Miriam relived the incident, her heart was filled with joy, just as it was when she heard Nathan speak the words. Miriam and Ray thought that Nathan would react with anger or bitterness when he found out that he was an extraordinary scientific and religious experiment and they had prepared themselves for a violent reaction. Much to their surprise, none came. Nathan took the news calmly and the many questions that they were prepared to hear, were left unasked.

When she thought of Max, she shivered and shook her head unconsciously. Miriam believed that she was a failure as Max's mother and she was filled with guilt.

She tried every means possible to treat her sons equally, but Max was so demanding and selfish, that it was very difficult for her not to loose her temper with him. Miriam often thought about having Max tested for psychological problems, but Linda would always reassure her that Max's behavior was nothing more than sibling jealousy. Miriam worried when Max didn't change as he grew older. She whispered a prayer for Linda Martinelli and thanked God for her friendship because Linda supported her and was always able to soothe and calm Max when he threw his tantrums. Even now, as an adult, Max goes to Linda when he needs someone to talk to or when he is troubled. At times, Miriam felt a tinge of jealousy herself and she often envied Linda's relationship with Max.

Despite the fact that she sometimes felt left-out, she was grateful for Linda. As hard as it was for her, Miriam realized that even though she is Max's mother, she has no real connection to him. When Max's behavior became worse after Nathan's *Bar Mitzvah,* Miriam could see the chasm develop between the brothers.

Miriam's thoughts turned to Alex and to the years that she had to cope without him. She missed his advice and support the most especially when Max told her and Nathan that he supported Sadam Hussein's cause in the Gulf War. Miriam's chest tightened with a heavy feeling when remembered how betrayed and hurt she was by her own son. From then on, Max seemed hell bent on denying any Semitic group, including Miriam's Jewish background. In the last few years, Miriam desperately tried to pinpoint any time or instance that would have turned him against her and her heritage. She could never remember anything that would make him so bitter, resentful and hateful toward her and Nathan.

Miriam worried about what would become of her sons and wondered if they would ever be on good terms with each other. Lately, it seemed to be getting worse. The more that Nathan grew in popularity, the more Max resented him and tried to belittle him in any way possible. When a popular magazine interviewed Max and referred to him as the "prophet's brother," Max scorned Nathan's preaching and referred to Nathan's healing abilities as the work of a charlatan.

Miriam's reveries were interrupted when she felt a hand on her shoulder. The unexpected touch startled her and made her jump. When she turned around, she was pleasantly surprised to see Ray Pascal's smile.

"Ray! When did you get here? I'm so happy that you arrived in time to begin the holiday celebrations.

"Shh, you're in the house of God, they kick you out! I hope I didn't scare you too much. I tried to let you know that I was here, but you were so deep in prayer that I guess you didn't hear me," laughed the Bishop.

Pascal had aged over the years, but he was still spry and he never lost his sense of humor which made it difficult for Miriam to realize that more than thirty years had passed since their first meeting. She and the boys spent every holiday with him when they were in the United States. This year, she invited him to spend the holiday with her and Nathan in Israel. Her cousin, Sarah and her husband, Matthew, invited them for dinner later in the day.

"Where's our boy?" asked Ray referring to Nathan.

"Where he usually is, preaching in the field. When I see the crowds around him, I have trouble believing that he's my son. I just hope nothing happens to him," commented Miriam with a worried look.

"Stop frowning and worrying, you'll get wrinkles," laughed Pascal.

"Oh Lord, I said the same thing to my mother a long time ago when I was expecting Max. She was dead set against the idea my returning to Qumran with Alex. She didn't think that I should be out in the desert in my condition," laughed Miriam.

"I really miss not seeing my parents over the holidays, but it's hard for them to travel now. Nathan insisted on staying here for the holiday, and I couldn't leave him here alone. It's always a very special time for him," Miriam added sadly.

"Hey, cheer up! I went to visit your parents and had dinner with them before I came here. They're doing fine. Of course, they've slowed down a bit, but Rebekah can still cook up a storm. Come on, let's go and meet Nathan, besides, you look like you're prayed out!"

Ray looked at Miriam and even though she looked a bit drawn, she was still very beautiful at fifty. Her dark hair was laced with gray and she wore it pulled back in a low bun that emphasized her classic features. Her skin remained clear and smooth despite the hardships in her life and her bright blue eyes were still her best feature. Ray always knew that Alex was a lucky man and he was glad that they found each other. He always thought that they were destined to be together. Ray felt twinges of sorrow when he thought about Alex and Doug. He missed the great times they spent fishing. He even missed the harrowing times confronting the Vatican when they were searching for the truth about Nathan. As he and Miriam walked out of the synagogue, Ray hugged her close and told her again how happy he was to see her. When they walked around to the back of the temple, they were surprised to hear police sirens. They turned the corner and looked into the field where Nathan was preaching. The police were breaking up the large crowds that had amassed and Ray had to hold Miriam back from trying to reach Nathan. He quickly grabbed her arm and led her off to her cousin Sarah's house, "He'll be alright, Miriam, I'll go back and check on him if he isn't here within the hour.

Once inside her cousin's house, Miriam called for Sarah, but no one answered, "I guess they must be at my Aunt Amelia's house getting things ready for tonight."

"Well, to be honest, I'm glad we're alone. Come and sit down in the living room. I have something important to tell you," said Ray as he led her to the couch.

Miriam could tell from the expression on his face and from the tone of his voice that the news would not be pleasant.

"Miriam, I just don't know where to begin. You've gone through so much already that I hate to have to be the bearer of more bad news. But, since it's for your own protection, I have no choice, but to tell you," said Ray, hesitating.

"Ray, you know me too well to think I'm going to wilt if I hear bad news. Stop beating around the bush and just say it already," exclaimed Miriam becoming impatient with him.

"O.K. It's just that I feel like a fool because I had the opportunity to find this information sooner, and I didn't. You know that after Alex and Doug were killed, you were too upset to claim Doug's personal belongings so your parents asked me to do it. I complied with their wishes, but things became so hectic for me between my diocese and worrying about you and the boys, that I never got a chance to look through them. Besides, I just thought that they were old notes that Doug took while he worked, so I put everything in an old trunk in my bedroom and I forgot about them." he paused to take a breath.

Miriam gave him an exasperated look and he quickly continued, "About two weeks ago, shortly after you called to invite me here, I had some free time and for some reason, I remembered Doug's papers. I thought that you or Nathan would like to have them as a keepsake. As I was going through the trunk and sorting the papers, I found his diary."

"What, his diary? I didn't know that he kept one," commented Miriam. "But, what about it, what did you find out," she demanded impatiently.

"Well, it was a log of his discoveries with notes about the dig sites along with personal appointments and memos about events in his life, but it contains other information as well. I know that you and Nathan will want to read it privately because it has a lot of personal thoughts about Alex, you and, of course, the boys. But, I'm getting off the issue. Doug kept in contact with his old friends in Germany, especially after we began to piece together the fact that Bertram and Bachman were the same person. Evidently, Doug's friends continued to probe into Cardinal Bachman's true identity and did come up with some valuable, but shocking information."

Ray paused to check Miriam's reaction, but she looked directly into his eyes and said, "I'm waiting!"

"Miriam, Doug found out that Cardinal Bachman is indeed Dr. Rupert Bertram and the woman that we know as Linda Martinelli has a strong connection to him."

"Oh my God! What are you telling me, Ray? Next to you, Linda is the only friend I have. Are you positive?" quizzed Miriam as she got to her feet.

"Just sit down and listen to the rest of this story. While they were in Germany, Bertram and Linda not only worked together on scientific projects, Doug's informants uncovered something much more important. Miriam, Cardinal Michael Bachman and Linda Martinelli are brother and sister!" exclaimed Ray.

"What? Linda is that madman's sister? Are you sure about this, Ray?" Miriam exclaimed in a shocked tone as the color faded from her face.

"Well, I am as sure as Doug's diary indicates. Doug's friends in Germany kept digging and finally hit pay dirt when they found baptismal records in an old metal box. The box was originally in a church basement and when recent renovations began, the workers discovered it underneath some cracked concrete. Apparently the church was partially destroyed during the air attacks and when the repairs were done after the war, there was no time to sift through all of the debris so the workers just poured concrete over the rubble and started to rebuild."

Oh God, Ray, can this be true? I'm not only shocked, I'm confused! Explain something to me, how and when did Linda get into the United States and why does she go by the name, Martinelli, or is it an alias?"

"Miriam, are you sure you're alright? I really hate breaking this to you. But, I thought it was something that you had to know," said Ray with concern in his voice as he put his arm around her shoulder as if he could protect her from the truth.

"Oh, Ray, I don't know if I'll ever be alright again after hearing what you just told me, but you're right, it's something that I had to hear. Please go on, I'll be fine."

"Try to stay calm and hopefully, I can piece the story together for you. Doug's diary traced Linda's background and found out that her real name is Heidi Bachman Mueller. She was married to an Nazi officer, but when Michael realized that Hitler was losing the war, he made sure that his sister got out of the country even before he did. He knew that the Vatican was providing protection for many of the elite Nazis and he secretly made arrangements through Cardinal Brazini for his sister's safe passage as well as his own."

"When she arrived in Italy, Brazini got her a job as a housemaid for a wealthy Italian family. In fact, the family who hired her was one of Brazini's relatives. While she was living in Italy towards the end of the war, she met an American soldier named Joe Martinelli and according to Doug's sources, they were married. Unfortunately, they were married only a short time when Joe was injured and soon after, he died from his injuries. Linda found her way into the United States through Michael's connections."

"But, how did she team up with Alex?" asked Miriam in a daze.

"When Michael wormed his way into the Vatican and later, into Pope Pius's confidence, he arranged to have an interview set up for Linda with Alex in Qumran. You have to remember that Linda is Michael's sister and although she's not the prodigy that Michael is, she is extremely intelligent in her own right. Alex obviously recognized this and realized that she was a well-trained scientist and, naturally, she came highly recommended. Michael made sure of that! As Alex's assistant, Linda proved herself to him and became a valuable asset to his work. And, later, she became a good friend to him and to you, however, during all that time, she continually kept Michael informed about everything you and Alex and the boys did."

"Oh, no!" shouted Miriam. "She was the one who sent us to Dr. Miller. Ray, what else do you have to tell me? Is that why she's so close to Max? Who's child is he, Ray?" pleaded Miriam, beginning to shake.

"Miriam, calm down! I'm going to pour you a glass of wine and I want you to sip it slowly and try to relax. Please forgive me for telling you all of this and drudging up old pain, but I feel that I don't have much choice or much time for that matter. I have to make you aware of how malicious and evil Linda and Michael are. Don't forget, they are both former Nazis who firmly believe in Hitler's plan for the Aryan Race. As far as Max's paternity, I can only guess. But I believe that he is really Michael's son. Perhaps, it was his little joke of finally producing an off-spring that would be his claim to immortality. I can only imagine what evil influence Linda has had on Max."

"Oh God, you may be right, Ray, it makes sense, especially since Max was always so close to her, even as a baby! I used to feel jealous that he could always find comfort with Linda, yet at the same time, I was torn between Nathan and Max and I felt guilty because Max demanded so much of my attention. So, I was very grateful that Linda could control him and comfort him because he was such a difficult child," rambled Miriam in a whisper.

"Miriam, I have something else to tell you. Remember that this is only conjecture on my part and we may never be able to prove it. Doug's diary indicates that after he discovered the truth about Linda's true identity and relationship to Michael, he confronted her. It was about a week before the plane exploded killing Alex, Doug and the others. Doug never got a chance to warn you because Alex wanted to confront Linda and Michael first. Doug's entry states that Alex was determined to find out the true paternity of both Nathan and Max and he wanted to expose the both of them. As you know, that never came to pass."

Miriam stood up and stared at Ray with an incredulous and frightened expression on her face,

"Ray, are you trying to tell me that Linda and Michael had something to do with the plane crash? Are you trying to tell me that the woman I thought was my best friend for thirty years killed my husband and my father-in-law?" gasped Miriam as she fell to the floor in a dead faint.

Ray quickly knelt down next to her and lifted her head onto his lap. He gently patted her cheeks until he heard her moan. A few seconds later, her eyes opened wide and she whispered, "Ray, she has to be the faceless woman in all my nightmares! Please help me to keep her away from my sons!"

FEAR OF ONESELF IS THE GREATEST OF ALL TERRORS, THE DEEPEST OF ALL DREADS, THE COMMONEST OF ALL MISTAKES. FROM IT GROWS FAILURE. BECAUSE OF IT, LIFE IS A MOCKERY. OUT OF IT COMES DESPAIR.
David Seabury

CHAPTER XXXII

THE VATICAN - DECEMBER, 1999

The Vatican was draped in black as the Church hierarchy mourned the loss of their brother in Christ, Cardinal Rene LeBlanc. His close friends said that LeBlanc died a happy man because he lived long enough to see France return to the more conservative ways of the Church. At the death of one of his fellow conspirators, Cardinal DeGroot reminisced about the last fifty years. He thought of the many twists and turns that were caused by the covert group of Cardinals. During the last three years, DeGroot hoped to rectify all the wrongs that he believed he committed through his involvement with their plan. He continued to work hard for world peace and both he and Cardinal Acietuno were elated in the part they played in Cuba's successful liberation from Communism.

DeGroot was lost in thought as the Holy Father sang the *Pater Noster* at the Mass. He looked across the aisle and was surprised to see that Michael had returned from his self-imposed exile in Spain to work on the *Sudarium*. Michael was given the authority to work on Veronica's Veil after insisting that the Holy Father allow him to run DNA tests on the relic. Again, Michael wanted to flaunt his genius and prove to the world that the images on the Veil and the Shroud were made by the same man. When he completed his tests, Michael brought the relic back to St. Peter's in Rome. DeGroot felt sure that if the results prove that both images had the identical DNA, Michael would most likely announce to the world that he was the 'Maker' of Nathan. DeGroot knew that Michael's ego would only be satisfied when the world knew him as the mastermind of the experiment. Michael would revel in the announcement that he, alone, had the power to give life to the Man on the Shroud. As the Mass continued, DeGroot could feel his dormant anger awaken and as soon as the liturgy was over, he approached Michael.

"Well, Michael, it is about time that you returned to the Vatican. Hopefully, you will resume you foremost duties to our Holy Mother Church. As a man of God, you have been remiss in you duties. Your first priority should be your duty to God and to the Vatican. You should have put science after God and the Church years ago," reproached DeGroot. As he looked at the man who for years instilled fear in him, he noticed the familiar cold stare emitting from Michael's eyes.

"Ah, Cardinal DeGroot, it's so nice to see that you haven't changed since our last encounter. Please remember that you may be able to intimidate others in the Vatican with your position and your power, but remember, Paul, you will never intimidate me!" retorted Michael with a sneer.

"Perhaps now is the time for you to be intimidated, Michael. I want you to know that I have confessed everything to the Holy Father. In fact, he has known the truth for the last two years. You must remember that I begged you to bear your secrets and you soul in confession, but you told me then that you had no reason to confess anything. I think now that the Holy Father knows the secrets behind Nathan, you should reconsider, Michael," suggested DeGroot.

"And, Paul, who does the Holy Father think Nathan is, the reincarnation of Jesus Christ?" asked Michael as he looked at DeGroot and laughed.

Cardinal DeGroot was startled at Michael's words but he quickly recovered and asked, "What are you saying, Michael? Of course he is the reincarnation of Jesus Christ. He was given life from the blood on the Shroud of Turin, who else could he be?"

"And, if he is? What do you think is going to happen next?" quizzed Michael chuckling at the old Cardinal.

"Stop your annoying laughter, Michael. I don't find any humor in what is about to happen! When we began the cartel, we did not anticipate that the project would turn out like this. I am afraid that we are going to be responsible for the Apocalypse," answered DeGroot in a very serious manner. "May God forgive us all."

"You fool, it is people like you that make my life so difficult! You cannot keep up with me or follow anything that I have done. This Nathan is not Christ! Can't you understand that? You are all silly old fools who, in your self-righteous way, thought that cloning the blood from the Shroud would replicate an identical being that lived before. Nathan is the clone from the DNA that was on the Shroud, but he is only a man. He is not divine! Christ's divinity was not in his blood! What I have made is a wonderful likeness to Christ the man! This time period, his environment, and the way he was raised also affected his personality and his total being. You can never duplicate what you believed was a God/Man that walked the earth two thousand years ago," sneered Michael disgusted at DeGroot's ignorance of science and genetics.

"Why were you so eager to do the experiment? You seemed thrilled at the possibilities of being able to bring Christ back to life. I don't understand..." mumbled Cardinal DeGroot, confused.

"Because, you insipid fool, it gave me the opportunity to leave Germany and come to Rome before I was killed with Hitler's henchman. More importantly, it was the perfect diversion to my real plan. I had to play along with the six of you, especially that pompous ass, Brazini. I was eager to do the testing and the actual experiment because I had the plans for the human genetic cloning on paper. However, I only had the opportunity to perform the experiment on animals while I was in Germany. Of course, my experiments were successful, I am only sorry that I did not have the time to try it on any of the prisoners in the Camps. They made such convenient subjects for many of my experiments. The six of you gave me the perfect opportunity and the perfect cover for my real mission," replied Michael with an evil smile.

"What are you talking about? What mission?" quizzed DeGroot as he felt a chill throughout his fragile body. "You are truly an evil man, Michael, you must confess and save your soul."

"You think that I am the evil one? Look in the mirror, DeGroot, and see the face of the man who helped to bring about the total destruction of your precious Church! My true mission will be known soon enough. I don't have any more time to waste talking to a simpering old fool like you!" hissed Michael as he turned to leave the room.

"Wait, Michael, I want you to explain the healing power that Nathan has and the miracles he has performed. How can you deny the reports from around the world? As a doctor, how can you deny the medical evidence that has been documented from those he has healed?" questioned DeGroot in a weak voice.

"I'm not really interested in that nonsense. Perhaps it is a coincidence or maybe he is a great charlatan. All I know is that it is scientifically impossible to clone a divinity. You can continue to think whatever you choose, but now, I must get back to my office," Michael answered in a curt tone.

"Have you met him, Michael?" asked Cardinal DeGroot in a quiet subdued tone.

"Met whom? Nathan? No, what reason would I have to meet him?" asked Michael turning back to look at DeGroot.

"Well, after all, Michael, you are his Maker. Don't you think that you should take the time to meet your most famous creation?" DeGroot questioned in a bating tone.

"You may think he is my most famous creation. Be prepared, Paul, the best is yet to come!" Michael warned with a piercing laugh as he left the room.

Cardinal DeGroot felt as if he was rooted to the spot where he stood. When he first met Michael Bachman, DeGroot was fascinated by his superior intellect and later, he learned to fear it. But now, at eighty-five, he knew that his days were numbered and the real fear that he felt was no longer for himself, but for mankind. The feeling of panic was slowly replaced by a sense of courage as the elderly Cardinal DeGroot resolved to take positive action against Michael's diabolical plan. He had suspicions about the second child, but said nothing to the Holy Father two years ago because he couldn't prove anything. Now, Michael openly hinted that he had a second cloning experiment who would be evil incarnate. What could he do to prevent this from going any farther?

He remained in the church for a few more minutes trying to sort out everything that Michael had said. If Nathan really was not divine at all, why did he have the power to heal and the ability to make people listen and heed his words of brotherhood and love? Perhaps if he could arrange a meeting between Michael and Nathan, it would stop Michael's evil plans before it was too late for mankind. A few minutes later, the old Cardinal decided that he must speak with the Pope.

On his way to the Papal Chambers, Cardinal Paul DeGroot decided to collect his thoughts and entered the Sistine Chapel in order to pray in solitude. The Chapel was nearly empty except for three old nuns praying their rosary. He appreciated this place when it was quiet, but tomorrow, this holy place again would be filled with hundreds of tourists. In the darkened Chapel, DeGroot knelt at the altar steps and he began to pray for courage, stamina and strength because he knew that he would need all three to confront the problem. He was determined to convince the Pontiff to meet with Nathan as soon as possible.

Michael's chilling words hinted of the horror that would soon come and when DeGroot thought of Michael's face and his words, he felt weak and helpless. He continued to pray for strength, when he realized that he could no longer kneel on the altar steps yet, he knew that he was not ready to leave. He needed time to rehearse his words to the Pope. As he stood, his eyes were drawn to the *Last Judgement* and he wondered, as he had many years ago, where he would fall after his death - with the damned, or with the saved. DeGroot shivered in the dampness and again, he began to feel desperate and alone.

He knew in his heart that even though the cartel formulated the plan to clone the blood of Christ for the good of the Church and mankind, each of the six men had selfish reasons. DeGroot knew deep within his being that he, like Brazini and Michael, wanted the fame and the credit for being a part of the scientific miracle. He, too, wanted a share in controlling the destiny of the Church and the world.

DeGroot was overcome with a feeling of piercing sorrow as he remembered the Pontiff's words to him during his confession two years before. He, and the others involved, were guilty of the two original sins of Adam and Eve: Pride and Presumption. Even though Michael was the "Maker" of Nathan, he and the cartel played God when they created Michael. They were also guilty of harboring and promoting the evil that lay beneath Michael's surface. DeGroot realized how foolish they were to believe that they could control Michael's superior intelligence, ego, and pride. He was overcome with a sense of hopelessness and he knew that he had to fight these feelings of despair. He quickly recited a prayer to St. Jude and begged the patron of the Hopeless and the Desperate to help him in his greatest time of need.

As he left the Chapel and headed toward the Papal Apartments, he remembered a time when he once had the courage to face evil. Then, he remembered the consequences. As he walked down the long corridor, DeGroot's thoughts briefly wandered back to the 1940's when he requested Pope Pius XII to urge the Dutch Bishops to publicly denounce Nazism. Unfortunately, the Third Reich became infuriated and retaliated by gathering all Jewish converts. They jammed the victims into a box-car and shipped them to Poland where they were murdered in the Auschwitz gas chambers on August 9, 1942. Among the converts was Sister Teresa Benedicta, the former Jewish woman named Edith Stein. The Pope was planning to announce her canonization when he visited Auschwitz during his world tour. DeGroot never shook the guilt he felt over the loss of so many innocent lives and blamed himself because he pushed for the public denouncement of Nazism in his native land.

Pope Pius XII tried to console him by telling him that it was a greater sin to say nothing in the face of evil. Ironically, these very words inspired him to join the others in the cartel so that he could become a part of correcting the wrongs and evils in the world. He realized that he had lost his courage in the last several years and he ignored any opportunity to stop Michael. DeGroot decided that he must speak with the Pope before he retired for the night.

DeGroot stood at the Papal Apartments and quietly knocked. Within a minute, the Pontiff's secretary opened the door. He asked the kindly old priest, Father Campione, if he could speak with the Pontiff. When the priest returned, DeGroot was relieved that he was going to have the chance to speak alone with his old friend. When he entered the Pope's study, he saw the Holy Father sitting at his desk shuffling through some papers.

When he heard the footsteps, the Holy Father looked up from his desk and greeted his old friend,

"Paul, I am happy to see you. I am making plans for my world trip for the spring of next year. Since there is so much to be done, I want to make sure that I get an early start. My doctor is insisting on a complete physical examination and I hope he gives me a good report. However, do not tell this to anyone else, but I am planning to go ahead with the tour whether my doctor approves or not. He is like a mother hen sometimes and he worries too much about me!" the Pontiff admitted with a chuckle.

The Holy Father, one of the most well traveled Pontiffs, was planning a tour which would coincide with the millennium and would celebrate 2,000 years of Christianity. The Pope is scheduled to visit Cuba, the Congo, Holland, Aushwitz in Poland, and the United States. It will be an exhausting trip for the elderly Pontiff, but all who knew him, admired his mental and physical stamina. They also knew that he was determined to go on the tour.

"Holy Father, I think that you already take too many risks. You really should follow Dr. Rosini's advice. Although, I must admit, Your Holiness, I often admire your stamina, and your ability to take risks. I sometimes have a difficult time making that kind of choice," lamented DeGroot.

"Paul, you sound very sad, what is bothering you? Is there anything I can do to help you? I know that you are saddened by Rene's death, but he is happy with God in heaven," consoled the Pontiff full of concern for his friend.

"Yes, Holy Father, I do miss Rene. It will be hard for me to remember that he is gone because we were close friends for many years. However, that is only part of my sadness. I have just had a discussion with Michael. I have not had the opportunity to see him since he returned from Spain, but I did get a chance to speak with him after Rene's funeral service in the church. Michael revealed some very upsetting news, Your Holiness."

"You can confide in me, Paul, you have done so before. Now, tell me what is troubling you about Michael."

"Michael claims that Nathan is not truly Christ, but only a clone of Christ the man. He also lead me to believe that he had quite a bit to do with Nathan's brother, Maximilian. He's intimated that Max is evil incarnate, Holy Father. I had to warn you and ask you for your advice. We must do something to stop Michael, and this creation of his, from destroying all good within the world. I am begging you to meet with Nathan. Perhaps he can do something to save us from Michael's evil plans," pleaded Cardinal DeGroot desperately. "I cannot stand idly by any longer. I must do something positive no matter what the consequences."

"Paul, calm yourself, you will make yourself sick!" scolded the Pope as he offered him a glass of brandy. "Here, drink this and catch your breath. You know that I told you two years ago that I would meet with this prophet, Nathan, when the time is right. I am, again, telling you the same thing. According to the Prophecies of Fatima, we will have our meeting here in Rome soon."

"The Prophecies of Fatima! But, the final letter was destroyed by Michael, Holy Father! How could you possibly know what was in the letter?"

"Paul, before Pius XII died, he called me into his chambers and revealed my destiny. If you remember, Paul, I was the Guardian of the Archives during those years. I knew that Pius had taken the final Letter of Fatima to read and I became worried when it was never returned. After his initial stroke, Pius never fully regained his speech however, those of us who were in daily contact with him had little trouble understanding him. When he regained his strength, I asked him if he wanted me to return the letter to the Archives. It was then, that he realized that the letter was actually missing and he became suspicious. Although he never verbally accused him, Pius suspected that Brazini took the prophetic letter to use for his personal gain. Ironically, Pius never suspected Michael and remained very close and loyal to him until his death. From what Pius told me, he had great plans for Michael's future."

"Holy Father, are you telling me that you knew what was happening all along?"

"Well, Paul, I was never totally sure of everything. I did suspect that you had become heavily involved with Brazini, Michael, and the others, and I knew that the seven of you met in secret. You must know by now that there are very few secrets in the Vatican," chuckled the old Pontiff.

"As men of God, Paul, we believe in many things that are not easily understood or explained, but over the years, all that Pius revealed to me, has come to pass. When I make my final stop in the United States, I would like to meet with Miriam Stewart, Nathan's mother. I must apologize to her for the many things that have transpired over the years. I want her to know and understand that she was chosen to carry Nathan, but I would like to speak to her about both of her sons. Perhaps you can contact Bishop Pascal and he can arrange for us to meet."

"That would be wonderful, Holy Father, I will contact Pascal as soon as possible. You know that he has remained very close to Miriam and her sons since Alex was killed. But, Holy Father, I must know something. Why didn't you approach me, or any of the others, especially if you suspected Brazini of taking the Fatima Letter?"

"Because, Paul, the prophecy had to played out and most of the events were out of my hands. I could not control you, Brazini, Michael or the others, just as you cannot and never will be able to control Nathan. Paul, you know that Catholicism is based on free will and even Judas, who truly loved Christ, made a choice to hand Him over to the High Priests. Luke's Gospel tells us that Judas was possessed by Satan when he betrayed Christ, but history tells us that Judas believed that he was helping Christ and the Jewish nation. Remember Paul, Michael also has the free will to do what is right."

"I understand, but I honestly wonder if Michael can distinguish what is right and what is wrong. I realize that Nathan is part of the Fatima Letter, but what about you, Holy Father, how did you fit into the prophecy?"

"My friend, I am the present Pope, aren't I?" The elderly pope looked at his old friend and smiled.

"Pius XII told me that I would one day become Pope. He informed me that my reign as Pope would be faced with many difficulties, but also that there would be many miraculous occurrences. You see, Paul, that was one of the reasons that Pius felt that I should know the entire contents of the Letter. I know that you are surprised to hear this news, my friend, but I am sure there are many important details that Michael withheld from you and the others. Many of them will be known before long!"

"Now I understand why you did not stop our cartel or Michael. The prophetic letter must come to pass."

A LITTLE EVIL IS OFTEN NECESSARY FOR OBTAINING A GREAT GOOD. Voltaire

CHAPTER XXXIII

FEBRUARY, 2000

After a grueling pace, the Pope's world tour commemorating 2000 years of Christianity, was finally coming to a close. As the Holy Father's motorcade sped toward JFK airport, the elderly Pontiff leaned over to his personal secretary, Father Campione. He wanted to remind him that he had scheduled a stop in Scranton so that he could meet with Miriam as he had planned. Father Campione assured the Pontiff that he had made all the arrangements with Bishop Pascal. The Bishop would be waiting with Miriam at the Scranton Chancellory for the Pope's arrival. Father Campione praised the success of the Pontiff's trip and although he was drawn and tired, the priest knew that the Holy Father was content with the tremendous reception he received on the tour. The Pope smiled as he recalled the large crowds that welcomed him at each stop and the elderly Pope knew that many of the people were curious and afraid about the millennium. The predictions in the Fatima Letter were foremost on their minds. The Pope asked Father Campione to remind him to speak to the Cardinals and Bishops about the concerns expressed by the crowds. The Pope wanted to ease the anxieties and quell the fears of the faithful about the "end of the world" predictions.

Father Campione agreed and the two men continued to discuss the tour. A short time later, the chauffeur pulled in front of the Scranton Chancellory. He had radioed ahead and Bishop Pascal was waiting at the side door to greet the Pope. When the Holy Father walked into the large Chancellory living room, he greeted Pascal and quickly inquired about Miriam. When Ray led him into a room where Miriam sat waiting for him, the Holy Father asked if he and Miriam could spend a few minutes alone. Ray immediately directed them to his private study and as soon as Ray closed the door, the old Pope grasped Miriam's shoulders, hugged her and kissed both her cheeks. Miriam was overcome with emotion at the elderly man's greeting and knelt before him and kissed his Fisherman's Ring.

"Please, my dear, get up from your knees. I feel as though I should kneel before you and beg your forgiveness for all that has been done to you these last 33 years. I hope that you hold no bitterness in your heart toward the Church," said the kindly old Pope as he helped Miriam to stand. "I am sure, though, that if I did kneel before you, I would need a few strong people to help me back to my feet," he laughed.

"Holy Father, you have no need to apologize to me. I hold no bitterness toward the Church or toward anyone for that matter. I'll admit that I was very bewildered in the beginning when I realized that I was pregnant because it truly was a mystery. I couldn't understand how it could be possible. For a short time, I, like Alex and my parents, believed that I must have been raped."

"You were very brave, especially not knowing whose child you were carrying," remarked the Pontiff.

"Deep within my heart, I knew that I was carrying a special child, Holy Father. My dreams made me realize that I was chosen for a reason and a purpose and as strange as it sounds, for the nine months that Nathan was inside of me, I knew that he was no ordinary child. I also knew that one day, he would be instrumental in changing the world. So, you see, Holy Father, I have no remorse or regrets about the events that have taken place in my life."

"You are, indeed, a special woman, Miriam. You have survived many difficult trials in spite of what was done to you in the Vatican by men of God. I hope you understand that the prophecy had to be fulfilled. Nathan is truly God's messenger and he has done miraculous deeds in proving that he is an extra ordinary man. But, the prophecy also foretells of Anti-Christ who is now among us. I must do what I can to stop him. I must meet with Nathan as soon as possible, but the meeting must be kept secret. He has already attracted so much public attention with his preaching and his healing that many people believe that he is the returned Christ. Others fear that he is the predicted Anti-Christ. Both groups are sure that the end of the world is near because of the symbolic predictions in the Book of Revelations. Since these predictions are capable of causing panic, I am very worried for Nathan's safety," explained the Pontiff.

"I agree with you, Holy Father, I am also very afraid for my son. I'll speak with him about the meeting, but I think that he should wait until things become quieted down. It would be very nice to visit Rome again and in spite of what had happened, I've always had some wonderful memories of my visit there with Alex."

When Miriam heard the soft knock on the door, she quickly got up, "Thank you, Holy Father, for coming to see me and apologizing to me. Your kindness and honesty has deeply touched me and I want to wish you a safe and comfortable trip back to the Vatican. I am looking forward to seeing you again soon as I usually travel with Nathan," Miriam took the old man's hand and kissed his ring, again. She looked into his eyes and asked, "Before you leave me, I must ask one question, Holy Father, who do you believe my son really is?"

"Miriam, I believe that Nathan is a prophet or a messenger from God and I believe that Nathan is very special because he was given life from the blood on the Shroud, but remember, Miriam, that no man can make a God," answered the Pontiff in a gentle tone.

"Do you believe that it is just coincidence that I was chosen to carry him within my body? Your Holiness, Nathan is special, even more special than you choose to believe," remarked Miriam as she watched the Pope walk toward the study door.

When the Pope turned to bid Miriam good-bye, his face wore a puzzled expression but he said nothing, as he turned and walked slowly through the doorway, leaving Miriam alone to wait for Ray.

When the Chancellory was quiet again, Ray handed Miriam a glass of wine and led her into his study so that they could discuss the Pope's visit. Ray was impressed when Miriam recounted what had transpired especially concerning the fact that the Pontiff had apologized to her. Ray stared at her and shook his head in surprise when Miriam told him that she never needed an apology from the Vatican or anyone else.

When Miriam saw Ray's surprised expression, she explained that she never regretted anything that happened in her life because she believed from the start, that Nathan was special.   She continued to tell Ray that God not only blessed her with Nathan, but he gave her Alex, her family and friends, especially him.   Ray was touched by her kind and gentle words and by the fact that this woman, who had lived through so much uncertainty and turmoil, could remain so strong and be so positive.   Ray was very much aware of the fact that she did not mention Max.

Before Miriam left Ray, they discussed the possibility of meeting with Nathan so that they could formulate a trip to the Vatican.

APRIL, 2000

Nathan adjusted his pillow and tried to relax.   He closed his eyes and within seconds, he began to drift back to his childhood.   The pleasant memories were soon tarnished when Max entered his thoughts. Throughout their lives together, neither of the brothers ever agreed on anything.   Nathan knew how much this disturbed Miriam.   Nathan, unconsciously, frowned as he recalled their last meeting and how ugly it became.

Miriam was visiting her parents and Nathan took advantage of that quiet time to organize his trip to Rome.   He remembered being startled when Max came into the den.

"Hey brother, what are you doing?   Writing your next sermon?"   Max asked sarcastically as he sat down across from Nathan.

"Max, I didn't hear you come in.   No, no sermon writing today, I'm leaving for Rome next week and I wanted to get some things together. You know, Max, it's been awhile since you were here?   How have you been?"   inquired Nathan.

"Yeah, well, I couldn't be better, but I'm only here because of Miriam's urgent message's. I guess this Rome trip is what all the urgency is about! So, you're finally going to meet with your 'main man,' or should I say, the white-robed pompous ass in the Vatican? I never understood why either of you waste your time traveling around the world collecting a flock of sheep who believe in something that doesn't exist. While you're pissing your time away on preaching, I've been securing my future by cultivating the 'real people' - the makers and the shakers - the ones who are actually engineering the future of the world."

Max paused for a minute and hoped that Nathan would have some sort of rebuttal, but he continued to sit calmly and quietly.

Max continued, "As a matter of fact, I'm glad that I did come here, because it's time that I make myself clear. Tell that whore bitch to stop trying to get in touch with me because I never want to see her again. As far as I'm concerned, she served her purpose as my incubator, but now I'm embarrassed to admit that she carried me in her tainted womb. The same goes for you, Nathan, we've never had anything in common and I certainly don't need either of you for any reason, so just write me out of your lives. Actually, if it were up to me, I'd have you eliminated, Just like Alex and Doug were disposed of when they tried to interfere with Michael's plans," threatened Max.

When he saw the pained expression on Nathan's face, his deranged laughter filled the room.

"Max, stop and listen to me! I just don't understand you! We've had no idea where you've been for the past two years. You haven't made any attempt to call or get in touch with us and now you barge in here to verbally abuse our mother and to talk nonsense. What's wrong with you?"

"Nonsense! You really think that what I've been doing is nonsense! You stupid son-of-a-bitch! Let me fill you in on some details of an exciting life, big brother! I've been instrumental in cleansing the world of its scum, but maybe I should've started here with you and Miriam first, instead in Bosnia. We'll see if you still think I'm talking nonsense when you hear and see what I do in the Middle East. In fact, I'm leaving for Iran tomorrow, so pay attention to the news, big brother, and maybe then, you'll realize that what I've been telling you is the truth!" shouted Max viciously.

Nathan already knew what Max did, but hearing him say the words and seeing the crazed look on his face made the horror so much more real.

Nathan tried hard to calm Max, "Max, you can't really believe that genocide is morally just! No matter what their ethnic, religious, or cultural background, every person has a God-given right to be on this earth."

"Shut up!" screamed Max jumping out of his chair. "Don't you dare preach to me, you stupid bastard! I don't want to hear your shit about God and doing good. There is no God and you, Nathan, are a god-damned cheap imitation of a fraud, which makes you less than nothing! You are nothing and you have no power! You go around preaching and pretending to heal, but you're no better than the phonies on T.V. who sham fools out of their life-savings! Can't you accept that *I'm* Bachman's real masterpiece? You were nothing but a preliminary experiment that helped him to perfect the process for me!"

Max stopped to catch his breath and started laughing at Nathan's blank expression. Max mistakenly took Nathan's silent, calm demeanor as a sign of weakness as he continued his tirade of abuse.

When Nathan looked at his brother, he could see that Max's face was full of loathing and suddenly something inside of Nathan snapped. He couldn't stand to hear the blistering attack, especially against their mother any longer. He quickly stood and as he backed Max into a corner, he grabbed his arm. When he did, Nathan looked directly into Max's hate-filled blue eyes, but Max quickly turned his head away screaming to let him go. Before Max averted his eyes, Nathan noticed a trace of fear, but at the same time, he could feel that Max's evil was gaining strength.

Max continued to squirm and scream at Nathan to let go of his arm or that he would kill him.

"I'll release my grip after you listen to me! I want you to remember, Max, that God gives each one of us free will that let's us choose between doing the right thing or the wrong thing according to His law."

Max went berserk and a piercing scream came from deep inside him as he finally found the strength to push Nathan away.

"I told you, don't ever touch me again, you bastard, and don't ever mention God to me! I hope I never see you again," Max hissed as he rubbed his arm where Nathan held him. He turned away from his brother and rushed out the door.

Nathan sighed deeply as he envisioned Max's hateful expression and heard the demented laughter as it echoed in his mind. When he opened his eyes and saw his mother talking to Ray, Nathan knew that he could never give up on his brother. He became determined to save Max from himself. He prayed for Max's troubled soul and knew that he would continue to pray for him no matter what happened.

When he heard the captain announce that they were approaching the airport, Nathan turned to wake his close friend and advisor, John Carpenter, who was snoring lightly, "John, wake up, the plane is about to land," he said as he gently shook his friend.

"Huh? What time is it?" asked John still groggy from his nap. "You mean we're in Rome already?" John sat up and fastened his seat belt as the plane began to descend.

In the Rome terminal, Ray spotted Pietro Carzana waiting for them. The four quickly passed through customs, and Pietro greeted them and relieved Miriam and Ray of their carry on bags.

"*Buon giorno*, I've been instructed by the Vatican to take you to my home tonight. The house is not very large, but it is comfortable and very close to the main palace. I hope that you find it satisfactory. The Holy Father thought it best that you stay with me as the Vatican Palace is filled with visitors because of the Holy Week celebrations. His Holiness wants to avoid publicity and most of all, he is worried for your safety, explained the Italian chauffeur to Nathan in his broken English.

"I think it's an excellent idea," answered Ray. "The Pope has thought of everything. But, how have you been? It's been a long time since I've seen you."

"I've been well, Your Excellency, but as you can see, I'm getting old. Soon, I will be retiring from my job."

"Ah, yes, I remember that you were just a young boy when you began working for the Vatican. But, you're not alone, Pietro, we're all getting old!" laughed Ray as they waited for their luggage.

"Yes, I was very young and my uncle, Antonio, took good care of me. It has been a good life, but I still miss my uncle very much. Come now, I will take you to my home so that you can rest."

The large black limousine weaved in and out of traffic as Pietro expertly dodged irate motorists in the crowded streets of Rome. A few drivers who noticed the impressive Papal Seal, were courteous and gave Pietro the right of way. Within an hour, they were in front of a large stone building inside the Vatican gates. Pietro pulled the limo into the driveway, opened the doors for his passengers, and carried their luggage inside.

The visitors stopped to admire the beautiful buildings that surrounded them and told Pietro that he was too modest about his home. He explained that the building was formerly used as a carriage house but was renovated into his residence years ago. Pietro led them into the parlor area. The house was warm and cozy and he invited them to sit down and relax after their flight. He walked into the kitchen to tell his cook, that the guests would soon be ready to eat. Pietro went back into the parlor, but excused himself when he heard the telephone ring. Luisa, a short attractive Italian woman, came into the parlor and pointed to the direction of the bathroom so that they could freshen up before dinner.

Luisa spoke no English, but she conveyed her message in Italian and with hand motions. Smiling, Nathan thanked her, but asked her not to set a place at the table for him. He explained that he was not staying for dinner. Luisa smiled back and complimented him on his excellent Italian.

When Pietro hung up the phone, he went back into the dining room and noticed that there were only four place settings instead of five at the table. He hurried into the kitchen and spoke sharply and rapidly in Italian to Luisa. But, before she could respond,

Nathan came in and informed Pietro that he would not eat dinner with them tonight because he needed time to be alone. He asked Pietro to direct him to a side entrance to the Vatican, so that he could go and pray in one of the chapels. Pietro began to shake his head violently and then in a stream of Italian told Nathan that he had strict orders from the Holy Father to stay with him at all times. Pietro vehemently insisted that he intended to follow the Pope's orders. Then he told Nathan that he would never get past the Swiss Guard at any entrance without him. Pietro agreed to take Nathan there, wait until he was finished and bring him back to his home for the night. Nathan felt badly for the old chauffeur and he thanked him and said that he didn't want to inconvenience him. Pietro convinced him that it was his job and not an inconvenience.

In the meantime, Luisa began to bring the wine and bread to the table and when Pietro told her that he would eat something in the Vatican kitchen, she shook her head and mumbled in Italian about cooking all day. Pietro raised his voice and told her to stop complaining and to serve his other guests as he reached for his chauffeur's hat and coat. He called to Nathan and led him out to the limousine.

THE VATICAN, HOLY THURSDAY EVENING

The Vatican Palace was a short distance from Pietro's carriage house and Nathan suggested that since the night was clear and warm, they should walk to the Palace. Pietro was adamant about driving him there for safety reasons. Nathan agreed and sat in the front with Pietro. Pietro appeared surprised and a bit nervous, but he didn't ask Nathan to move to the back seat. Within a few minutes, the two men were standing at a side entrance. After a brief exchange with a tall and stately Swiss Guard, Pietro and Nathan were allowed into the building.

Once inside, Pietro took Nathan down a series of corridors, pointing out the different works of art in rooms and in the halls as they passed. He asked Nathan where he wanted to pray and whether or not he had a preference of chapels. Nathan said that he didn't really care, so Pietro led him into the closest one.

When they opened the chapel door, Nathan told Pietro that he was free to leave, but Pietro insisted on doing his job. He said that he would stay with him to watch and protect him as he had promised the Holy Father. Nathan realized that nothing would change the old man's mind, so he walked over to a *priedieu*, knelt down and began to pray. Pietro walked to the rear of the large chapel and sat in one of the pews. He looked around and silently hoped that the time would quickly pass.

The old man remembered how hungry he was and when he heard his stomach groan from emptiness, he wished that he had grabbed some of Luisa's homemade bread from the table. Pietro yawned from boredom and exhaustion and he couldn't decided if he was more tired or more hungry. He checked his watch and realized that they were in the quiet chapel for more than an hour and he wondered how much longer he could last. He glanced over at Nathan and he could see that he was still deep in prayer because his position had not changed.

The old chauffeur's eye lids became heavy with sleep and he wondered how anyone had so much stamina to pray for so long. He fought hard to stay awake, but the silence and the boredom overcame his resolve. He closed his eyes and began to doze when he heard the chapel door squeak. His eyes snapped open and he automatically looked toward the door. Pietro could see the outline of a man wearing a cardinal's biretta.

His senses were instantly revived and his eyes quickly scanned his charge and he was relieved to see that Nathan was still in the same position. When the intruded moved into the candle light, Pietro recognized Cardinal Bachman. Bachman saw Pietro's shadow move and called to him. Pietro stepped out of the pew into the light and identified himself. He saw Michael's cold stare so he curtly explained that he was waiting for Nathan at the request of the Holy Father. Michael continued to glare at Carzana for a few seconds recalling that Pietro was Antonio Brazini's nephew.

The recollection of his long-time adversary twisted Michael's face into a sneer as he off-handed told Pietro that it was not necessary for him to remain in the chapel. Michael could read the distrust in Pietro's eyes and voice as the old man quickly and stubbornly insisted that he was to remain with Nathan on orders from the Pope. Michael told Pietro that Luigi was waiting for him in the kitchen and tried to assure him that Nathan would be safe in the chapel.

Michael persuasively told Pietro that the Holy Father would not want him to go hungry. Pietro hesitated, not only because of his orders from the Pope, but because he shared his uncle's hatred of Bachman. He started to protest, but Michael cut him short and told him to go to the kitchen because the cook had been waiting for him for over an hour. When Michael told him this, Pietro assumed that Luisa had phoned the Vatican kitchen and told the cranky old cook to hold a plate for him. His hunger and fear of not eating at all, outweighed his loyalty to the Holy Father's orders. He gave Michael an angry look, glanced over to check on Nathan and then left the two men alone in the holy place as he headed for the kitchen.

On his way to the kitchen, Pietro was disturbed by Michael's eagerness to be alone with the Prophet. Pietro's mind raced and he became convinced that Bachman and the Prophet, Nathan, were plotting something against the Church. Ever since his uncle, Antonio, died after being in a room alone with Bachman, Pietro was filled with hatred and suspicion for Michael. And, although he didn't know the full story about Michael and Nathan, he remembered from his uncle's innuendoes, that there was a close attachment between them and he didn't trust either one. Carzana's suspicious mind recalled the newspaper headlines that referred to Nathan as the Anti-Christ and he knew what he had to do.

The banging of the chapel door pulled Nathan out of his trance-like state. When he lifted his head he found himself face to face with his 'Maker,' Michael Bachman.

"I was told that you would be here. But, please don't flatter yourself by thinking that I'm here to meet the great prophet. I'm only here to satisfy my curiosity. I'd like to know if you believe that you are the remarkable person that they claim you are?" asked Michael looking toward Nathan.

"And who do you believe I am?"

For a few moments, there was total silence in the chapel, then Michael laughed and answered,

"I don't believe in too much, I do know, however, that I created you so I definitely know who you are."

"Are you so sure that I am your creation? Remember, Michael, that you could never have accomplished what you did if you weren't given the knowledge and ability by a greater power and intellect than yours. You must realize by now that the hand of God guided the Cardinals over the years and the hand of God guided you and opened the door to your destiny," responded Nathan in a quiet voice.

"How dare you insinuate that you know what my destiny is?" raged Michael as he sneered at Nathan. "I've created my own destiny, neither you nor your God has had anything to do with my destiny. You, Nathan, are nothing but the clone of the Man on the Shroud! You are not a divinity! You are nothing but a mere man who has fooled everyone into thinking that you are special! And, as for my destiny, it will by fulfilled by Max, not by you."

Michael sneered at him in disgust as he turned toward the doorway to leave. Nathan called to him and when he turned, Nathan grabbed his arm and held onto him. Michael was caught off guard and found himself looking directly into the eyes of the man he created. Within seconds, he felt an inexplicable surge of energy, power and heat emitting from Nathan's touch. The heat grew in intensity and began to burn his arm, he tried to turn away, but he could not.

Nathan's eyes locked him into a hypnotic state and Michael felt as though he was in a dream-state where time stood completely still. He became totally helpless and could not pull away from Nathan's grasp, nor could he avert his eyes. Michael was forced to stare into those deep pools that seemed to draw him deeper and deeper into Nathan's being. Something inside him, made Michael realize that he was bonded with this being and now he could feel whatever Nathan felt, including his joy and his pain.

He was suddenly confronted with a true self-image and Michael, who never knew what it was to feel fear or panic, now experienced these alien emotions as they enveloped his entire being. Michael was forced to relive the terror, dread, pain, and suffering of each one of his many victims in the Nazi death camps. He felt suffocated by fear as the horrific visions raced through his mind.

Within seconds, he saw himself as he really was from the depths of his very soul. He could see the evil that his soul had nurtured and harbored and Michael became truly afraid to die in sin. In an instant, he saw himself as others saw him and he felt the heat from Nathan's hand move from his arm and surge through his body gaining in intensity until it seared him to the very quick of his being.

As he became aware of the intense burning sensation, Michael noticed the glowing light that surrounded both Nathan and him, Another new experience rushed through his mind and purged his heart and soul. Michael became overpowered with remorse and now, for the first time, he understood what he had done. Just at that moment, Nathan released his grip and Michael was abruptly returned to the present.

"It's time for me to go. The Mass will be starting shortly. Michael, I hope that you have the opportunity to make peace with yourself and with God," advised Nathan as he walked out the chapel door, leaving Michael alone and confused. Michael could not respond or move and he remained in the chapel trying to sort out what had just occurred.

When the Holy Thursday liturgy had ended, Pietro Carzana drove Nathan back to the house in silence. As they arrived at the door, Pietro mustered the courage to ask Nathan about his meeting with Bachman. But, Nathan, exhausted and drained with his experience with Michael, told Pietro that he was too tired to talk. He excused himself and went into the guest room that Luisa had prepared for him.

GOOD FRIDAY MORNING

Nathan was awake by 6:00 AM and could hear someone moving about in the kitchen of the sunny carriage house. His meeting with the Pope was scheduled for 8:30 AM so he got up and knelt down next to the bed and began his morning prayers. When he finished, he showered, quickly dressed and entered the warm kitchen. Luisa greeted him with a warm smile and asked him what he would like for breakfast. He told her that since it was Good Friday, he would fast and only take fluids. In the middle of their conversation, Pietro stepped into the kitchen and heard what Nathan had just told Luisa. He offered him some grape juice that was made from his own vines.

"You need something besides water to sustain you throughout the day. Here, have a glass of this, it is juice made from my grape vines and it is all natural and pure. When you are ready, I will take you to the Vatican Palace, but we must be on our way soon because I am scheduled to go to the airport to pick up many of the clergy."

Nathan took the glass that Pietro offered and gave him a long sad look before he drank it down. He thanked Pietro and commented that he, too, had to attend to his business. He said that he would be ready as soon as he said good-bye to his mother and to his friends. He thanked Pietro again for his help and told him that he didn't want to be late for his meeting with the Holy Father.

The men were inside the Vatican by 7:30 AM. Since there was plenty of time before his meeting with the Pope. Nathan decided to finish his morning prayers in St. Peter's. Once inside, he marveled at the beauty of the huge edifice and began praying the Stations of the Cross. As he stood before the Sixth Station, Nathan became dizzy and weak and found himself losing his balance. He felt the sweat run down into his eyes and again, he tried to grab onto the pew in order to keep from falling.

He took a deep breath, wiped his forehead and gasped. He saw that his hand was covered in blood. At first, Nathan felt a sense of panic as he searched a pocket for a handkerchief and dabbed at his forehead and face. At that moment, he heard footsteps and Nathan looked up in to the kind face of the old Pontiff.

"My God, you're bleeding! Are you hurt? What happened?" questioned the Pope as he held his hand out to Nathan for support. "Please come, sit down and rest. Can I do something to help you?" he asked anxiously.

"No, no, Holy Father, I think I'm alright now, but I suddenly became dizzy and I must have passed out. When I fell, my head must have hit the pew."

In concern, the Pontiff immediately pulled his handkerchief from his cassock and wiped Nathan's brow and continued checking for the source of the blood, "My God, you're also bleeding from you're wrist."

"Nathan abruptly sat up and saw the puddles of blood that came from his wrists. Seized with terror, Nathan lifted his head and tried to focus his dilated eyes on the Holy Father. As the Pope's eyes met Nathan's, he realized the source of the blood.

"Nathan, you truly are a prophet!"

"I am only what I was made to be, but no matter how I tried to rationalize the possibilities, the truth of my existence is finally becoming clear," gasped Nathan in a weak voice.

"What is the truth, Nathan? Please tell me who you really are!" pleaded the Pope.

"Holy Father, I know in my heart that I must deliver the message, a message I believe is true. You were chosen long ago, Holy Father to relay my message to the world. I know that time is running out and I must fulfill my reason for being. You know that many believe that I am the Anti-Christ. Yet, many others have put their faith in me and believe that I will save the world. But, I can do neither. I cannot die to save the world again, but I am here to warn you that the Anti-Christ is here. Holy Father, please listen carefully, for I know how to stop him."

"Two thousand years ago, mankind was given these truths, but they were ignored. The prophecies that predicted the Parousia and the coming of the Anti-Christ have been fulfilled. The time has come for you to tell the world that the sins of men have unleashed the Anti-Christ. The solution to stop him is simple. God's message is one of love, understanding and brotherhood.

In the past 2000 years, the world has grown in knowledge and has made many advances and I am living proof of this. It is important for you to tell the world that all things are possible with God. Man has the choice and the free will to use this gift of knowledge for the good of the world rather than for its destruction," whispered Nathan as he became visibly weaker.

"Please let me call someone to help you!" pleaded the Pope.

"No, there is no time, my friend, you must warn the world for I shall never come again as a man to walk the earth. The Parousia has happened and unless the world listens and believes, God will send the reaper and the destroyer. My message is one of love, but the warning is one of destruction. Please believe me when I tell you that the evil one has been unleashed. You must stop him!" Nathan tried to steady himself as he grabbed for the end of the pew. He lost his balance and fell to the floor gasping that he had been poisoned and that he could not breathe.

The old Pope became frantic as he knelt next to the man he came to meet. He lifted his head and cradled it on his lap. Nathan's wounds continued to bleed, and the Holy Father watched his white robe become stained in scarlet. The Pontiff knew as soon as he touched the dying man that this man was indeed extraordinary, more so than he previously believed. Even now, he could feel the energy and heat emitting from him just as he could hear the life ebbing from his body. He tried to lift Nathan's head to make it easier for him to breathe, but as he looked into the man's eyes, he could see that there was no hope.

The old man was filled with anguish as he sobbed and rocked back and forth asking God to bring him back, "Who has done this to you?"

As he knelt on the cold marble floor, he was suddenly aware of a shadow that had cast across Nathan's body. The Pope looked up and saw Michael Bachman. At first, the Pope was shocked by Michael's change of appearance as he looked very different.

Michael's face had a serene appearance and the familiar sneer was gone.

"Michael, help me, he's dying! Please do whatever you can to save him! You must do something!" the pope shouted sobbing. "We cannot let him die again."

Michael quickly bent over Nathan and felt his neck and then his wrist for a pulse. He looked directly at the Pope and shook his head, "He's gone, Holy Father."

Michael lifted Nathan's head from the old man's lap and gently laid his head on the cold marble floor. Michael knew that the old Pope was emotionally and physically shaken and he became afraid for his health. He quickly reached up and stripped the long cloth from the altar and gently draped it over Nathan's body.

The Pope struggled to his feet and Michael could not help but notice that his white robe was now stained dark red with Nathan's blood. He looked at the old man and saw that his face was frozen in a stoic gaze. As the Pope stood motionless in front of the ornate altar, Michael was overcome with the need to purge his soul to this old man. He knelt down in front of him and began to ramble his confession.

"Bless me, Holy Father, for I am the Maker of destruction..."

The familiar words snapped the old Pontiff back into reality and he looked at Michael and said in a subdued, far-off voice,

"Not now, Michael." He slowly turned and walked out of the church.

Left alone, Michael stood over Nathan's covered body and began to weep. He wept for Nathan and he wept in sorrow for all he had done. He looked down at his first creation and could not fight the urge to see his face one last time.

Michael knelt beside Nathan's body and openly expressed his feelings of regret and remorse aloud,

"My son, I denied the fact that I could possibly create something so pure and good, and now, I am sorry that I couldn't accept you in to my life when I had the opportunity."

When Michael slowly and gently folded back the altar cloth from Nathan's body, a mournful wail filled the edifice and his blood became frozen in the veins as he pulled the rest of the altar cloth from the body.

His gaze became transfixed on the cloth as he saw the exact image of the Man on the Shroud.

Within seconds, his mind registered the truth and he began to sob uncontrollably as he threw himself across Nathan's body and cried out,

"Father, forgive me for what I have done!"

IT IS FINISHED, OR HAS IT JUST BEGUN...?